Critical Acclaim for
MAXIMUM SECURITY and Rose Connors'
Marty Nickerson crime novels

"It's always a pleasure to head back into the courtroom with Cape Cod attorney Marty Nickerson. . . . This immensely enjoyable series excels in dynamic courtroom scenes. . . . *MAXIMUM SECURITY* consistently entertains."

—*Pages*

"Rose Connors can hold her own with such heavyweights as John Grisham, Scott Turow, and Nancy Taylor Rosenberg."

—*Midwest Book Review*

"Sparkling dry wit fills the pages [and] the mystery provides intense intrigue."

—*Romantic Times*, Top Pick

TEMPORARY SANITY

"Characters are well defined, and the courtroom scenes are both exciting and realistic. [A] suspenseful legal thriller with a strong female protagonist."

—*Booklist*

"Excellent . . . smart, sassy, and exciting. . . . Connors is so good at creating believable characters that even readers with little interest in courtroom shenanigans should find in favor of her humanity."

—*Publishers Weekly*

"Similar in style to novels by Lisa Scottoline and Perri O'Shaughnessy, this work features strong, likable characters and clean writing."

—*Library Journal*

"This courtroom sequel to *Absolute Certainty* moves [Connors] up to the big time. . . . For fans of legal intrigue . . . it doesn't get any better than this."

—*Kirkus Reviews* (starred review)

ABSOLUTE CERTAINTY
Winner of the Mary Higgins Clark Award

"What brings *Absolute Certainty* into tight focus is Marty herself, an earnest single mom who's not immune to the charms of her rumpled courtroom adversary turned unlikely ally, Harry Madigan."

—*Los Angeles Times*

"Connors' strong sense of pace and skeptical reflections about the morality of the legal system could help her ride . . . into Scott Turow territory."

—*Kirkus Reviews*

"[A] wonderful protagonist—smart, funny, and compassionate."

—*Cape Women* magazine

"Connors is a wonderful new voice—strong and smart, passionate about the law, and as comfortable on the pages of this frightening tale of murder and betrayal as she is in her closing arguments to the jury. . . ."

—Linda Fairstein, *New York Times* bestselling author of *Entombed*

ROSE CONNORS

MAXIMUM SECURITY

POCKET BOOKS

New York   London   Toronto   Sydney

This book is a work of fiction. Names, characters, places and incidents are products of the author's imagination or are used fictitiously. Any resemblance to actual events or locales or persons, living or dead, is entirely coincidental.

 POCKET BOOKS, a division of Simon & Schuster, Inc.
1230 Avenue of the Americas, New York, NY 10020

Copyright © 2004 by Rose Connors

Originally published in hardcover in 2004 by Scribner

ISBN: 0-7434-9269-2

First Pocket Books printing June 2005

10 9 8 7 6 5 4 3 2 1

POCKET and colophon are registered trademarks of Simon & Schuster, Inc.

Cover design by Jae Song

Manufactured in the United States of America

For information regarding special discounts for bulk purchases, please contact Simon & Schuster Special Sales at 1-800-456-6798 or business@simonandschuster.com

For Sam, my sun

ACKNOWLEDGMENTS

My hat's off!

—To the EZ Writers, for uproarious laughter and painstaking critiques. You made this a better book.

—To the Barnstable Law Library team—Martha Elkins, Janet Banks, and Mareda Flood—for unfailing support and meticulous research. You made it fun.

—To Rosemarie and Bob Denn of Cape Fishermen's Supply, for endless nautical know-how. You made a sea dog out of a Philly girl.

—To my agent, Nancy Yost, and my editor, Susanne Kirk, for doing what you do so well. You made it possible.

MAXIMUM SECURITY

CHAPTER 1

Thursday, October 12

An old friend. That's what Harry called her when he broached the subject just moments ago. Would I agree to represent an old friend of his who's in a bit of a jam?

"Of course I would," I told him. "But why don't you represent your old friend yourself?"

I knew his answer before I finished my question. Harry Madigan is uncommonly good at many things, but he'd die of starvation if he had to earn his living playing poker.

He leans forward in his chair by my desk and laughs, knowing I know. "All right," he says, raising his hands in mock surrender. "She's an old girlfriend. And I don't think I should represent her. Not in this case."

"You want me to represent your girlfriend?" I laugh too, fully expecting him to deliver a punch line.

He frowns. "As you happen to know," he says, "she's not my girlfriend. But she was twenty-five years ago. We were law school classmates."

He must be joking. Just in case, though, I turn to the bookshelf behind my desk and tap a pen against the red spine of the *Massachusetts Lawyers Directory*. "What? Is there a sudden shortage of attorneys in the Commonwealth, Harry?"

"Come on, Marty, we're not sixteen. We both have pasts. And we've both had other relationships."

I take off my frameless glasses, drop them on top of a file on the cluttered desk, then rub my tired eyes and roll them at him.

Harry gets to his feet, feigns deep concentration, and starts pacing around my small office. He's six feet tall and built like a linebacker; the room always seems crowded when he stands. His shoulders are broad, his arms muscular, and his hands enormous. His charcoal hair, thick, unruly, and always too long, has gone a paler gray at the temples. Harry can pace all night as far as I'm concerned; I'll watch.

He stops abruptly, glances sideways at me, and taps an index finger against his forehead, as if coaxing a memory to the surface. "Speaking of relationships," he says, "if I recall correctly, Attorney

Nickerson, you even managed to squeeze in a husband."

"True. And if Ralph ever needs a lawyer, I'll be sure to send him straight to you."

My ex-husband is Ralph Ellis, a nationally acclaimed forensic psychiatrist. He tends to show up in high-profile trials and Harry has seen him many times on TV. The two have never actually met, though. And it's no secret between Harry and me that he's not looking forward to the occasion.

He walks to the darkened window, leans against the sill and sighs. "Please," he says. "She needs a good lawyer. She's in trouble."

"You're serious."

He bites his lower lip and nods. "I am."

"What's her name?"

"Louisa Rawlings."

Of course it is. Harry's old girlfriend wouldn't be a Mary or a Peggy or a Sally. She'd be a Louisa. I'm sorry I asked.

"Rawlings is her married name," he adds. "She was Coleman when I knew her."

"How long were you and Louisa Coleman an item?"

"Through law school," he says.

"All of it?"

"Yep."

"What happened?"

Harry leaves the windowsill, drops back into the chair by my desk, and falls quiet, drumming his fin-

3

gers on the armrests. It's pretty clear that whatever happened wasn't his idea. "The public defender thing," he says at last. "It didn't appeal to her."

"She didn't want you doing the dirty work of a public defender?"

He laughs. "It wasn't the dirty work that bothered her. It was the puny paycheck."

"But didn't she know all along that you planned to become a public defender?" It's always seemed obvious to me that Harry was born with that plan.

"She did," he says. "But I think she assumed I'd change my mind—come to my senses—by the time we finished law school." He shrugs. "I didn't."

"So she dumped you and married Mr. Rawlings?"

"Nope. She dumped me and married Mr. Powers. She dumped *him* and married Mr. Rawlings."

"Oh."

"And I'm the one who introduced her to Glen Powers." Harry looks away from me and winces, the memory apparently still chafing. "He was a friend of mine; graduated a class ahead of Louisa and me."

"But your friend had the good sense to pursue a more lucrative career?"

"Bingo," Harry says. "Trusts and estates."

"And Mr. Rawlings?"

"*Cha-ching*. Corporate mergers and acquisitions."

I try to stifle my laughter, but I can't. "All lawyers? All three of you?"

"What do you mean, all three of us? We weren't a men's club, for God's sake. She married the two of them. She wouldn't marry me."

I'm silent for a few seconds, while the implication of his words sinks in. "You asked."

Harry looks down at his hands and then back at me. "Yeah," he says, "I did."

I take the red directory from the bookcase and push it across the desk to him.

"Come on, Marty. That was another lifetime. And she needs help."

"She's a lawyer, Harry. Surely someone from her own firm can hook her up with whatever help she needs."

"She's never practiced."

"Never practiced? The woman graduated from Yale Law School and she's never practiced? What does she do?"

He looks up at the ceiling, as if searching for words. "She marries well," he says.

Well, of course she does. Why didn't I think of that?

"Harry, I'm sorry your old flame is in trouble. Really I am. But I've been in court all day. It's late and I'm starving. Are we going to dinner?"

He jumps up from his chair, hustles to the back of mine, and makes a production of holding my suit coat for me. *"Mais oui, madame."* His French accent is tortured, reminiscent of Pepé le Pew. "Name zee establishment of your choice."

I look over my shoulder and roll my eyes at him again. We both know we'll end up at Vinnie's. The booths are private, the lights are dim, and the food's the best Italian on Cape Cod. Most important, though, the portions are big enough to keep even Harry happy.

"I'll tell you more about it while we eat," he says, pausing to massage my neck and shoulders through my jacket. I close my eyes and lean backward into his big hands. I'd have fallen for Harry even if he weren't a compulsive masseur. But I'll never tell him that.

"Why is this your project, Harry? You just said she marries well. Let her husband find her a good lawyer."

"He can't."

"Of course he can. If he's with a firm large enough to do mergers and acquisitions, he's well connected."

Harry turns me around to face him, still holding on to my shoulders. "Herb Rawlings is dead, Marty. He's somewhere on the ocean floor."

"Oh."

"And Louisa's in a bit of a jam."

CHAPTER 2

"A jam? The woman's husband sleeps with the fishes, his life insurance company smells a rat, the police think she's involved somehow, and you tell me she's in a bit of a *jam*?"

Harry leans back on his side of the booth, drains his glass of Chianti, and pours another. "Poor word choice?" he asks. "A pickle? Would that be better?"

"Harry, this is serious."

He sets the glass down, leans across the table, and holds my eyes with his. "I know it is, Marty. If it weren't, I wouldn't ask you to get involved."

"How did *you* get involved? Where did this thing come from?"

"Louisa called the office this morning," he says. "The cops want her to come in for questioning. She told them she'll cooperate, but not without a lawyer. They agreed to give her a few days to find one."

"She's not in custody?"

"Nope." Harry's been attacking his chicken Parmesan as if the restaurant manager allotted him only five minutes to finish. "Right now they've got nothing on her," he says. "Just a mountain of suspicion."

"And the goal is to keep it that way."

He points his fork at me. "Bingo."

One of the many things I love about eating at Vinnie's with Harry is that I can order a whole cheese pizza—undercooked, the cheese barely melted, the way I like it—knowing not a morsel will go to waste. I slide a steaming slice onto my plate from the platter at the end of our table and wait until he looks up from his food. "Have you two been in touch all this time?"

Harry shakes his head. "I hear about Louisa every once in a while from mutual friends. But I haven't spoken to her in twenty-five years. Until this morning."

"How did she find you?"

He laughs and puts his fork down, and I brace myself. When Harry stops eating to tell me something, it's almost always a bombshell. He plants an elbow on the table, chin on his hand. "You're not going to believe this," he says, "but she lives in Chatham."

"Your ex-fiancée lives in Chatham?"

"She's not my ex-fiancée."

"No thanks to you."

Harry sighs and closes his eyes. I know what he's doing; he's counting to ten. When he's done, he retrieves his fork and digs in again. "She and her husband have only lived here about a month. They've been vacationing on the Cape each summer, though, since they got married twenty years ago."

He pauses, his knife and fork still for a moment, a thought apparently dawning. "She didn't keep Glen Powers around for long," he says. "I remember talking with him in my office shortly after their divorce. He said Louisa had been up front with him about it. Herb Rawlings could offer her more, she'd told Glen. A bigger house, a more lavish lifestyle, and an even more secure future. Glen was appalled that Louisa would actually admit those were her reasons."

Harry looks up from his empty fork and arches his bushy eyebrows at me. "He didn't get a hell of a lot of sympathy from me."

I return Harry's stare and, I hope, his sentiment.

He laughs and goes back to his meal. "Herb Rawlings was older than Louisa, by fifteen years or so. When he retired from New York City practice, they sold their house in Greenwich and bought a place on Pleasant Bay. Louisa noticed our sign the day they moved in."

9

"So she knew you were here a month ago, but you didn't know she was in town until this morning?"

He shrugs and mops up his red sauce with the last of the garlic bread. "She changed her name," he says. "I didn't."

"But Chatham isn't exactly a sprawling metropolis. You never ran into her around town?"

He shakes his head again. "I don't think Louisa and I travel in the same circles."

"Seems like that's about to change."

He takes a slice of pizza from the platter and drops it onto his otherwise clean plate, then leans back against the booth and sighs. "Marty, Louisa is someone I once cared about—a lot. She's in trouble. And she's scared; I heard it in her voice. When I told her I'd have to refer her case to another lawyer, she begged me to find the best one I could. That's why I came to you."

Time to roll my eyes again.

Harry reaches across the table with the wine bottle and tops off my glass. "Tell me the truth," he says, his hazel eyes searching mine. "Does it really bother you that I loved someone twenty-five years ago?"

I lift my glass and shake my head. "Of course not. I'm glad you loved someone twenty-five years ago. Louisa Coleman in the past doesn't trouble me at all. I'm just not sure how I feel about Louisa Rawlings in the present."

Harry pushes the dishes aside, leans across the

table, and takes my hands in his. "You're my present," he says, his eyes still locked on mine. "You're my present and my future. If you have any doubt about that, tell me now, and we'll drop this whole damned thing. I'll never mention Louisa Coleman Powers Rawlings again."

He laughs when he recites all the names, but we both know his question is serious. And he wants a real answer. Knowing I need to give him one, I lean back against the booth and sip my Chianti. He leans back with his glass too, swirls his wine around a few times, and waits.

Harry and I were cautious when we began spending time together. I bore the scars of a failed marriage and the hard-learned lessons of a few relationships that either went south or went nowhere at all. Harry's heart, too, had been wounded more than once. And both of us knew from the start, I think, that what we had found together was worth protecting.

In the early days, unwilling to acknowledge our feelings too soon, we manufactured reasons to touch each other. When we walked on the beach, Harry always wrapped his sweatshirt around my shoulders and pulled me close, as if I might otherwise get swept away by the ocean wind. We slow-danced a lot, sometimes without music. And then we progressed. We kissed through our dances.

Last winter, the night after Christmas, my son, Luke, went to Boston to spend a few days with his

11

father, and I went to Harry's place for dinner. Harry and I were exhausted, having just finished a particularly difficult murder trial, and after we ate we curled up on the couch to watch *The Big Chill* on video. We argued, later, about who fell asleep first, but we agreed that neither one of us lasted long enough to see Glenn Close give her husband away.

When I awoke, the first hint of a gray dawn semilit the windows of Harry's second-floor apartment and large snowflakes drifted down in slow motion outside. The TV screen was black and the logs in the fireplace had burned to embers. I was as warm as I'd ever been, though, tucked between Harry and the soft cushions of the couch, my head nestled in the crook of his shoulder. His arms enclosed me, one hand cradling my hip, the other resting on my waist.

Without thinking, I reached up and ran my fingertips along his jawline and down his neck. I leaned over him, spread the open collar of his flannel shirt, and undid a few more buttons so I could breathe in his scent and press my hand and face against the warmth of his broad chest. He tightened his grip on me then and when I looked up, his eyes were open.

"I'm sorry," I whispered, "I didn't mean to wake you."

Harry fished my hand out from under his shirt, brought it to his mouth, and kissed each finger before he looked at me. "Yes, you did," he said.

His answer caught me off guard. I propped myself up on one elbow so I could see into his eyes. And in that moment I knew one thing for sure. He was right.

Harry introduced me to his brand of passion then, a passion so tender it melted my heart. I realized, that morning, what it takes to open up again after love gone wrong has done its damage and left its wreckage behind. It takes a tender passion. And a heart willing to break one more time.

Harry covers my hand with one of his when I set my wineglass down. He reaches across the table with the other, brushes the bangs from my eyes, and then cups the side of my face in his palm the way he always does now. "Well," he says, half smiling in the candlelight, "any doubts about me?"

I shake my head against his warm hand. "None."

"You'll meet with Louisa?"

"Okay," I tell him. "I will."

"You know," he says, his expression thoughtful, "you might find that you like her."

I lean back against the booth again and retrieve my wineglass. "I'll meet with her, Harry. But don't push it."

CHAPTER 3

Friday, October 13

Louisa Rawlings and I will meet today, Friday the thirteenth. When I looked at the calendar earlier this morning, I assured myself there was no significance to the date. Now that I'm in our office driveway, I realize I've reassured myself twenty-five times. But I still don't believe me.

Harry and I have only one associate in our office and we call him "the Kydd." Kydd is his last name. His first is Kevin, but I can't recall the last time anyone used it. Even he doesn't mention it anymore.

The Kydd hails from Atlanta, Georgia, and he's probably the hardest-working young lawyer on the East Coast. He always beats me into the South Chatham farmhouse that serves as our office building, and today is no exception. His nearly new, red pickup truck is parked in the driveway when I arrive, the passenger side of the cab's bench cluttered with casebooks and files he apparently took home last night.

Like Harry, the Kydd stands about six feet tall, but unlike Harry, he looks as if his last decent meal is a distant memory. He's slouched in a chair in the front office when I come through the door, lanky legs stretched out in front of him. His chair is one of two facing an antique pine table, and Harry's seated on the other side of it. He's just hanging up the phone.

"That was Louisa," he says. "I told her you'd be over there shortly."

"Over where?"

"Her house."

"We're meeting at her house?"

Harry shrugs. "Meet where you want," he says, "but I thought her house would make sense. You'll have to get the layout at some point. Things happened there."

"Things?"

He shrugs again. "Herb left from their dock the day he disappeared. And he wrote the note there—or he left it there anyhow."

"Note? What note?"

"The suicide note."

For a split second I freeze, staring at Harry, my jacket halfway off. "There's a suicide note?"

16

He nods.

"The missing husband left a suicide note and you didn't bother to mention it?"

"There's a lot I didn't mention, Marty. It's complicated. I want Louisa to tell you herself."

"*Whoa,* Kimosabe," the Kydd says.

He's been watching late-night *Lone Ranger* reruns again. He has the Tonto impersonation nailed.

"Time-out." The Kydd apparently thinks Harry and I need the word *whoa* translated. He sits up straight and pounds his hands together in an emphatic T. "What the hell are you two talking about?"

When the Kydd says *hell* it always sounds like *hail.* I constantly marvel at the fact that two and a half years on Cape Cod hasn't put so much as a dent in his Southern drawl. I drape my jacket over the chair next to his and take a seat, holding my hands out toward Harry, giving him the floor. This is his story to tell, after all.

"New client," Harry says to the Kydd. "Dead husband, missing body. Cheap insurance company, suspicious cops. Marty's representing the bereaved widow."

"I said I'd meet with her, Harry. I didn't say I'd represent her."

He bites his lower lip.

"Did you tell her I'd represent her?"

He looks up at the ceiling, as if trying to remember. "I may have," he says.

The Kydd shakes his head at Harry. "I don't get it. If Marty's representing this woman, why is it that you know the facts and Marty doesn't?"

Not much slips by the Kydd.

Harry looks across the desk at me, as if I might field the question for him. I arch my eyebrows and stare back.

"The client called me," he says to the Kydd, "and told me the story, but I didn't think . . . I thought . . ."

"Attorney Madigan recused himself," I pitch in. "He feels a bit conflicted."

The Kydd glances over at me, then turns his questioning stare back to Harry.

"This woman and I . . ." Harry begins once more. He stops, though, seemingly unable to locate the next word, and runs both hands through his thick, tangled hair.

The Kydd scoots forward in his chair, looks at me again, then leans across the desk toward Harry, curiosity burning in his baby blues.

Still, words seem to elude Harry. He waves one hand in front of his face, suggesting he won't bore us with his long tale. "Years ago," he says.

The Kydd appears confused for a moment, but then his mouth spreads into his signature grin. It's lopsided. "You *dated* her?"

"And then some," I tell him.

He leans back on two legs of the chair and puts

his hands behind his head, elbows akimbo. His grin tilts even farther to one side. "Let me make sure I have this straight," he says, squinting at Harry. "Our new client is a former love interest of yours." He twists in his chair, turns his squint toward me. "And *you're* going to represent her."

"Love interest," I say, watching Harry. "That's nice, Kydd, poetic, even. I like it."

The Kydd sits up straight again, the front legs of his chair hitting the floor hard. He claps his hands together and laughs, then hoots. "We're all okay with this?" His expression suggests we're out of our minds.

More than once I've overheard the Kydd on the phone telling his Southern relatives that the goings-on in our Yankee law office never cease to amaze him. The look on his face at the moment tells me we've outdone ourselves this time. "Yeah," I say. "We're swell."

"Of course we are," Harry adds. "We're adults."

"Sure." The Kydd wipes the grin from his face and lowers his voice to a deep bass. "So am I."

"No, you're not," Harry fires back. "Adulthood begins at forty, not a minute sooner."

"I'd love to stay and debate," I tell them, getting to my feet. "But it seems I have an appointment. Where does she live, Harry?"

He grimaces and looks up at the ceiling again.

I'm tired of this case already. "Harry, you told the woman I'd come to her house. That means you have to tell me where she lives."

He keeps his eyes on the ceiling, as if the information I'm asking for will appear there sooner or later. "On Easy Street," he says. The Kydd hoots again.

"That's cute, Harry. I'm sure she does. But where's her house?"

Finally, he tears his gaze from the ceiling and leans forward. "I'm not kidding," he says, squeezing his eyes shut as if he's in pain. "She lives on Easy Street."

The Kydd stands and opens the pine table's single drawer. He pulls out a street map of Chatham, unfolds it on the tabletop, and runs a finger down the alphabetical list of streets.

I stare at Harry while I put my jacket back on. He opens his eyes and nods up at me, apparently trying to convince me he's serious.

"Harry, I was born and raised in this town. There's no such street."

"Oh yes, there is," the Kydd announces, pounding a pen on the map.

I bend over and follow his gold Parker to a spot in Chathamport, past the country club. It's one of the most exclusive areas in our affluent town. And there it is. Barely long enough to display its short name on the map. Easy Street. I'll be damned.

"What's the address, Harry?"

He doesn't answer. When I look up, he's inspecting the ceiling again.

This is getting old. "The number?" I prompt. "On the house?"

"It's number one," he says.

Well, of course it is.

CHAPTER 4

Fox Hill Road is aptly named. A handful of estates enjoys expansive grounds here, and the fox population thrives on the smaller creatures who share the lush landscape—squirrels and rabbits, mostly, along with the occasional household pet. I hit the brakes to slow my old Thunderbird when a healthy-looking vixen with a thick red coat trots into the road ahead. I hit them harder and come to a complete stop when two kits emerge behind her, their noses to the ground, oblivious to my car's approach.

The mother fox stands still in the middle of the road, like a traffic cop, and stares up at me while her young ones cross in front of her. She seems entirely untroubled by my presence. Once the kits reach the safety of the bushes, she saunters after them, in no hurry whatsoever. She pauses before taking cover, looks back at me, and seems to nod. A thank-you, maybe. In this part of town, even the foxes are well bred.

A mile farther down Fox Hill Road, the rolling green hills of Eastward Edge Country Club come into view. The club's oceanside golf course is touted as one of the most prestigious—and scenic—in the world. In the summertime, well-heeled golfers enjoy exclusive use of these hills, their compact carts rolling along narrow paths like busy ants. But in the winter, when the club is dormant and its members have fled to kinder climates, all that changes.

After winter snowstorms, the locals claim these slopes. They come by the truckload with sleds, toboggans, and cross-country skis, their thermoses filled with coffee, hot chocolate, and brandy. When my son was younger, we'd spend entire days here each winter, surrounded by friends and neighbors, hurtling down white hills toward the icy blue of the winter ocean, then climbing back up to do it all over again. Inevitably, Luke's lips would be near-purple, his fingers and toes on the verge of frostbite, before I could convince him to call it a day. Luke and his friends still make a beeline for Eastward Edge after every winter storm, but in recent years they've traded their toboggans and skis for snowboards. And that makes me a spectator.

Just beyond the golf course, Strong Island Road forks off to the left, leading to one of Chatham's busy town landings, where fishermen of all stripes unload their catches. I bear right instead and stay on Fox Hill as it narrows and snakes along the water's edge. I've never been on this portion of the road before. It's no more than a sandy spit, and just when it seems that land is about to disappear completely, Easy Street opens up on my left. I hesitate for a moment, my stomach still questioning the wisdom of this meeting, and then I turn in.

It's clear at once that precious few of us can aspire to live on Easy Street. The road hosts only a trinity of homes. Number three appears first, on my left, a stately colonial on manicured grounds. It's sealed up for the season, sheets of plywood nailed over its windows and doors to protect them from Cape Cod's fierce winter winds.

I pass number two next, on the right, a pristine, newly shingled saltbox surrounded by dozens of hydrangea bushes, their few remaining blossoms a faded blue. It too stands abandoned, its cobblestone driveway empty, its shutters closed, waiting for the warmth of summer to lure its absentee owners back to Chatham's charms.

Number one is on the left at the end, on the water. It's a gem. A classic Cape with a gambrel roof, a waterside deck, and a floating dock, it's obviously an antique that's been painstakingly restored. I park the Thunderbird in the oyster-shell

25

driveway and head for the side of the house, intending to knock on the kitchen door as Cape Codders always do. The front door opens first, though, just as I reach the steps to the deck, and a woman's voice stops me in my tracks.

"This way," she calls at my back. "Right this way. I am some kind of happy to see you, darlin'."

It's a Lauren Bacall voice: deep, throaty. But that's not what makes me freeze. She sounds like the Kydd. Louisa Rawlings is Southern.

She's cut the distance between us in half by the time I turn around. Long, certain strides carry her toward me, across a brick walkway, her full red lips glistening. She's in tight black slacks and heels, her long-sleeved white silk blouse tucked in at her belted waist. Louisa Rawlings is six feet tall if she's an inch. No, taller; she's even taller than Harry.

And she's stunning. Statuesque.

"You must be Mrs. Nickerson," she says, extending her hand. Her French manicure is perfect. So is her makeup. And her shoulder-length, auburn hair.

I'm not quite sure how to respond. My mother was Mrs. Nickerson. "Marty," I tell her as we shake hands. "Please. Call me Marty."

"Marty it is," she says, latching on to my arm as if we're old sorority sisters reunited at last. "Let me tell you right now how grateful I am for your help, Marty. Harry Madigan says you're the very best."

I feel myself tense when Harry's name rolls so

easily off Louisa Rawlings's tongue, but she doesn't seem to notice. She leads me back across her brick walkway and through the front door. As we enter the foyer, I remember she's only lived on Cape Cod a month. She doesn't know, yet, that we don't use our front doors. We come and go through kitchen doors, always.

I follow her down a short hallway and through the living room. It's sparsely furnished in beiges and ivories, each piece looking as if it were created specifically for the spot it occupies. Huge wood beams and uncomplicated moldings throughout the room have been restored, not replaced. The same is true of the dark wooden mantel above the fireplace, as well as the two ovens built into the hearth beside it. And the soft pine floor, though refurbished, is the original. I can tell by the width of the boards, by the way they dip and slant, and by the square heads of the nails that secure them.

We pass through the kitchen next, where top-of-the-line appliances and granite countertops meet the old-world charms of a butcher block table and an antique built-in hutch. On the other side of the kitchen is an enclosed sunroom, a porch of sorts, with screened windows to filter the ocean breezes on warm summer nights. Louisa stops at the entry and steps aside, waving me in ahead of her, a gracious hostess. She follows and shuts the double doors behind us.

The windows are closed against autumn's chill

and the sun-room is warm, bathed in the golden glow of Cape Cod's singular morning light. The room's oversized, curtainless windows frame an unobstructed portrait of Strong Island and the open ocean beyond. A half dozen white wicker rocking chairs, all with cushions that mirror the vibrant blue of the water, face the glass. If there's a more breathtaking view on the Cape, I haven't seen it.

"Sit down, darlin'. Make yourself at home. What can I pour for you?" Louisa turns her back to me and walks toward a brass tray on the white wicker table by the windows. It holds a thermal coffee pitcher and an electric teapot, along with two cloth napkins that match the cushions. When she faces me again, she's arranging bone china cups and teaspoons on saucers. I sink into one of the rockers and set my briefcase on the slate floor.

"Coffee," I tell her. "Coffee would be great."

Her golden tan defies the calendar. Above her scooped neckline hangs a single strand of cultured pearls and a lustrous matching gem rests on each earlobe. She's perfect. My stomach was right; I shouldn't have come here.

"Cream and sugar?"

"No, thanks. Black is fine."

"That's how you keep your girlish figure," she says, looking up from the table and smiling.

I don't want to have this conversation with Louisa Rawlings.

She hands me a cup of coffee and a napkin, then

eases into the rocker across from mine. "Me, on the other hand," she says, crossing her long legs and working her tea bag, "the only reason I drink tea is so I can have lots of cream and sugar."

She needn't worry; the calories seem to know where to go. I don't say so, though. I don't plan to discuss *live* bodies with Louisa Rawlings. Not mine anyway. And certainly not hers.

Once she's settled in her rocker, I set my cup and saucer on the edge of the side table, pull a legal pad from my briefcase and a pen from my jacket pocket. It's time to get to know a few things about Louisa Coleman Powers Rawlings.

CHAPTER 5

Harry taught me an important lesson when I moved from the prosecutor's office to the defense bar: Keep the initial client interview spare. Get the big picture; reread the pertinent cases; think it through. And then hand-select the follow-up questions. On this side of the bar it's better, sometimes, not to know everything.

"Mrs. Rawlings," I begin, "why don't you summarize the events of the past week for me. We'll go back later and fill in the details."

"First of all," she says, leaning into the space between us, "the only Mrs. Rawlings I know is my mother-in-law, a woman who sobbed through her baby boy's wedding, from beginning to end. And let me assure you, darlin', hers were *not* tears of joy."

I almost laugh, but catch myself. This isn't a social call, after all.

Louisa leans back in her chair, smiling again, and recrosses her long legs. "It gives me an enormous amount of pleasure to report that *Mrs.* Rawlings went to her heavenly reward some years ago."

This time I can't help it. I laugh out loud and Louisa joins me. "So please," she begs, mock dismay in her large, chocolate-brown eyes, "let that woman rest in peace."

"Okay," I tell her. "I will. Now why don't you give me the short version of what happened, Louisa."

She stops laughing but her smile lingers. She stares at me and shakes her head. "I'm afraid that's about all I can give you, darlin'."

I wish she'd stop calling me that. I reach for my coffee and stare back at her. "What do you mean?"

She falls quiet and her gaze moves to the water. Her shoulders are broad—swimmer's shoulders—and the sheer sleeves of her blouse hug well-toned, athletic arms. "I mean the short version is all I know," she says. "Only Herb knows the rest."

I nod.

She sighs, shakes her head, and her eyes return to me. "*Knew* the rest, I suppose I should say." She stares into her lap. "I just can't get used to talking about Herb in the past tense."

I nod again. That's a sentiment I've heard before, more than once.

"Anyhow," she says, "I'll tell you as much as I can."

I set my cup down and reposition my legal pad.

"It happened on Sunday." She pauses and swallows hard. "Five days ago, but it seems like a century. I'd gone to the club. A few of the women members had invited me to play nine holes—make it a foursome—and then have brunch at the grill. When I got home, the house was empty. Herb was gone and so was the boat." She looks up at me and reaches for her teacup.

"Was that unusual?"

She sips and shakes her head. "Not at all. Herb was crazy about that boat. *Carolina Girl,* he named it. That's why we moved here"—she points out at the floating dock—"so he could keep his baby girl at the back door. It didn't surprise me at all that he'd taken her out."

I keep my eyes on her, but say nothing. I want Louisa Rawlings to do the lion's share of the talking. It's her story, after all. And once she tells it to the Chatham cops, she'll be stuck with it.

She takes a deep breath and holds it for a moment, then lets it out slowly and leans toward me once more. "It was close to noon by the time I got home. I went straight in to shower, then put on my robe and came in here with *The New York Times.* That's when I found his note."

She opens a small drawer in the wicker table next to her chair, pulls out a single sheet of plain white paper and hands it to me. Five short lines of boxy handwriting in blue ink are centered on the page:

My dear Louisa,
Sometimes I don't make good decisions.
I realize I've let you down.
Please forgive me.
Always, Herb

I pass it back to her, well aware that neither of us should be handling it. But that's the prosecutor's worry, not mine. And so far at least, there is no prosecutor. She returns it to the drawer and looks over at me, apparently awaiting a question.

"Did you call the police?"

She sighs. "No, I didn't. Not then."

"Why not?"

"It didn't even cross my mind. It never occurred to me that I was looking at a suicide note. I wish to God it had. Maybe someone could have reached Herb in time, talked some sense into him." She sighs again, gazes out at the water, and falls quiet.

"What did you think it was?"

She looks back at me, her eyes the darkest brown I've ever seen. "I knew what it was," she says. "At least I thought I did."

She stops, takes a deep breath, and I wait.

"Herb was having trouble," she says at last.

Now we're getting somewhere. We'll be hard-pressed to explain the man's suicide if he wasn't having trouble of some sort. "What kind of trouble?" I ask.

She's quiet again.

"Financial?"

She shakes her head. "Oh no, darlin'. Money was never a problem."

I do wish she'd stop calling me that. "What, then?"

She folds her arms and looks into her lap. "I'm sorry," she says, "but I find this somewhat difficult."

"Take your time," I tell her.

Finally, Louisa swallows and looks up, but not at me. Her eyes rest instead on some spot over my shoulder. "Herb was a good deal older than I am," she says.

"Harry mentioned that. Fifteen years?"

She nods. "And he was having trouble . . . with his . . ."

Her eyes move to mine. She's apparently hoping I can fill in the blank, but I can't. I shake my head at her.

". . . his function," she says.

"His function?"

"His erectile function." She exhales the words, her eyes still averted.

"Oh."

"I urged him to see his doctor about it, but he kept putting it off."

I nod, hoping she'll keep talking, but she doesn't. She seems to expect a reply. "Maybe he was embarrassed," I venture.

"That was part of it," she says, shaking her head, "but it's not the whole story. Since his retirement, Herb put most things off. When he was working, he was a take-charge, get-things-done kind of man. But once he had time on his hands, he turned into a professional procrastinator. He loved this house—threw his heart and soul into the renovations—and he loved that damned boat. But everything else could wait. And I do mean *everything*."

Louisa pauses and sips her tea, then looks over at me to see if I get the picture. I nod again to tell her I do.

"Anyway, we'd had a little . . . session . . . on Sunday morning," she says, looking away again, "before I left for the club. It didn't go very well."

"So you thought the note was about that? About your failed session?"

"Exactly," she says. "I wasn't worried when I found Herb's note. To tell you the truth, I was glad he'd taken the boat out. I enjoyed the afternoon here alone, even finished the *Times* crossword puzzle. Not something that happens every week." She smiles and sips again.

"But then?"

"But then it started to get dark. And I knew

something was wrong. Herb always brought the boat in well before dark, no matter what water he was on. He was cautious that way. And he had a few lobster pots in the channel. He always checked them on his way in—always—and he needed light to do that. He caught so many I'm sick of eating lobster already. We've started giving them away."

She pauses. I wait.

"When I realized it was starting to get dark, I did call," she says. "I called the police; they alerted the Coast Guard and the harbormaster's office. Of course, sunset isn't the best time to begin a search for a missing vessel. They did what they could, called it off at midnight, and then started all over at daybreak."

Louisa looks out at the water again. "They found the *Carolina Girl* early Monday morning, not long after the search resumed. She was up on the shoals in the Great South Channel with a good deal of hull damage. They also found the half dozen life jackets Herb always kept on board." Her eyes leave the water and meet mine again. "They didn't find Herb, though."

"Harry told me they still haven't recovered his body."

"That's right," she says, staring out at the ocean. "Not yet."

"I'm sorry, Louisa." I mean it. And I wish I'd said it sooner.

She's quiet.

37

"When did the police contact you?"

"Right away," she says. "Two detectives came to the house early Monday morning. There'd been an accident, they said, a boating accident."

"Did you think they were right?"

She faces me again, shakes her head. "Not for a minute. Sunday afternoon was glorious. We had some weather that night, but not until late. During the day, seas were calm, winds light. Herb was at home on the ocean. He'd been boating since he was a boy. And as I said, he was cautious; he respected the water."

"Did you tell the police what you thought?"

She shakes her head again. "No."

"Did you mention the note?" I already know she didn't. If she had, it wouldn't be here.

"I didn't even think of the note until hours after they'd gone. I didn't connect it with Herb's death until later in the day."

"What else did the detectives tell you?"

"Very little," she says. "They asked when I'd last seen Herb, where I'd been when he took the boat out. They also asked questions about Herb—basic information—and wrote my answers on a form. They asked me to sign it when they finished, then offered their condolences and left. I didn't expect to hear from them again."

"But you did."

She nods and sets her cup down. "Yesterday. One of them phoned first thing in the morning. Walker, I think his name was."

"Mitch Walker."

"That's it. Anyway, he said additional facts had surfaced, asked if I'd come to the station, answer a few more questions. He was evasive when I asked what the additional facts might be. He said Herb's insurance company had contacted him, had raised new concerns, but he wouldn't say what they were."

"Life insurance?"

"Yes. New England Patriot."

"How much is there?"

"A million," she says. "At Herb's age, it didn't make sense to carry any more than that."

"You're the sole beneficiary?"

"That's right. And I may as well tell you now, that fact didn't sit well with Herb's daughter."

"His daughter?"

Louisa nods. "Anastasia. A product of his first marriage."

I make the initial entry on my legal pad: *Anastasia Rawlings*.

Louisa flashes a devious grin over her teacup when I look up, as if we share a wicked secret. "I'm the trophy wife," she says.

Well, of course she is. The term was probably coined for Louisa Rawlings. "What about your predecessor?" I ask. "Is she still in the picture?"

"No. She was a good sort, Bess. Never cottoned to me, but I rather liked her. Passed on a few years back. Heart trouble."

"Is Anastasia Herb's only child?"

"Yes, thank the Good Lord. And a *child* she is. Forty-five years old going on seven."

"Is she married?"

Louisa laughs. "Married? Anastasia? Good heavens, no. She's a career woman of sorts. A professional spoiled brat."

Second entry: *Only child. No love lost.*

"But she is joined at the hip to a washed-up beatnik," Louisa continues, "a flower child gone to seed. Lance Phillips. Calls himself a murder mystery writer. A modern-day male incarnation of Agatha Christie. Lance is always one scotch away from a runaway best seller, so he finds Anastasia—not to mention her ready access to her father's wallet—rather attractive."

Third entry: *Beatnik boyfriend Lance Phillips. Aspiring writer.*

"Anyway," Louisa says, "I had already heard that New England Patriot was kicking up a fuss about the claim. Steven Collier—he's my financial advisor—had started the process the day before. He'd contacted the agent, had him surrender the policy. But the agent reported meeting with a good deal of resistance. A claim without a corpse is automatically suspect, I suppose."

It occurs to me that a claim submitted less than forty-eight hours after rescue efforts cease might raise a few eyebrows too. A fourth scribble finds its way to my legal pad: *Steven Collier, financial advisor/Quick-draw McGraw.*

Louisa pauses to set her teacup on the side table. "Speaking of Steven," she says, opening the drawer in the small table again, "he thought you'd want this." She hands me a stapled legal-size document that the cover page identifies as a life insurance policy. Herb's. Quick-draw McGraw is on top of things.

"Anyway," Louisa continues, "I couldn't imagine what issues the insurance people might have raised with Detective Walker. He clearly wasn't going to enlighten me on the telephone. And he was abrupt; his tone made me nervous. So I told him I'd cooperate in any way I could, but not without an attorney. He agreed. That's when I called Harry."

She shrugs and folds her hands in her lap, then lets out a small laugh. "And here we are."

"When does Detective Walker expect to ask you these additional questions?"

"On Monday," she says. "He wants me at the station first thing in the morning."

"Then he's in for a disappointment."

"How's that?" Louisa tilts her head to one side, curious.

"You're not going to the station."

"I'm not?"

"No. I'll call Mitch this afternoon and tell him. He can ask his questions in my office. We're talking to him voluntarily. We'll do it on our turf, not his."

41

Louisa folds her arms, smiling at me. "My, you *are* scrappy," she says.

I bite my tongue. If Harry told his old flame that I'm *scrappy*, he's a dead man.

"Between now and Monday," I tell her as I get to my feet, "we have a fair amount of work to do. Are you free to meet both weekend days?"

Another small laugh escapes her. "I don't have a date, if that's what you're asking."

"I like to work in my office in the mornings." I hand her a business card. "But I think we should meet here again, walk through it all a few times and go into a little more detail. I'll plan to be here at noon both days if that's all right with you."

"It's fine," she says.

"And I'd like to bring my associate along. If this thing heats up at all, or drags on longer than we expect, I might need an extra pair of hands."

"Whatever you think." Louisa stands and walks to the window. "I should tell you," she says, her back to me, "that I was planning to leave Herb."

My stomach tightens and I lower into the chair again. "Did he know?"

She turns and walks back across the room toward me. "I hadn't told him yet," she says, her eyes lowered, "but I think he knew."

"Does anyone else know?"

"Yes," she says, and she sits too. "My lawyer, Fred Watkins."

No problem there; it's privileged. And I know Fred Watkins. He'll take every one of his clients' secrets to his grave.

"And my financial advisor."

Problem. I make a check next to Steven Collier's name on my legal pad.

"I'm glad you told me, Louisa. It may turn out to be important. Let me give it some thought. One more question before I go, though."

She nods.

"Was Herb having any difficulties other than what you've already told me?"

She thinks for a moment, then shakes her head. "No, just his . . ."

"Function," I finish for her. I grab my briefcase and stand yet again.

Louisa stands too. "So how *is* Harry Madigan?"

If there was a segue in her mind, I don't want to know about it. "He's well," I tell her.

"We went to law school together, you know."

"He mentioned that."

"I was quite fond of him."

Not as fond as he'd hoped, though. I bite my tongue.

She laughs. "He used to call me *Mona* Louisa."

Too much information. I head for the double doors. It's time to get out of here.

"You're his law partner?" Louisa follows me.

"That's right."

"Such a dear boy," she says to my back.

Of course. Harry's still twenty-five in her mind's eye. A boy.

"I'll never understand it," she says. "He's brilliant, don't you think?"

"I do."

She falls into step beside me and shakes her head. "Graduated near the top of our class. Could have had any job he wanted. Chose that awful criminal work."

Louisa doesn't seem to remember that just yesterday she asked him to do some of that awful criminal work on her behalf.

"I was so pleased," she continues, "when I saw he'd opened a private office, gotten away from that public defender business. But I understand he's handling the same dreadful cases, just doing it under his own roof."

Perhaps I should mention that one of the dreadful cases under his roof is hers.

"And what about you, darlin'? Where did you go to law school?"

I pause at the front door, but not for long. I've had enough *darlin'*s for one day. "Same as you and Harry," I tell her. "I was two classes behind you."

"Really? You and I were on the same campus for a year and I didn't notice you? I can't imagine that."

I can. "Are you from Georgia, Louisa?" I'm surprised to hear myself ask the question.

"Good heavens, no," she says. "I'm a North Carolina girl, a Tarheel through and through."

Of course. *Carolina Girl.*

Louisa's expression suggests North Carolina and Georgia are in different galaxies. "Why do you ask, darlin'?"

I shrug. I don't know why the hell I asked. So she could call me *darlin'* one more time, maybe. I wanted this conversation over five minutes ago. "Our associate is from Atlanta," I tell her. "I thought your accent sounded a bit like his."

Louisa arches her perfect eyebrows at me. "I can see we're gonna have to teach you a thing or two about the South, honey chil'."

Maybe *darlin'* wasn't so bad.

I turn back toward the front door and notice what looks like the face of a touch-tone telephone on one side of it. "A security system?" I ask.

She nods.

"Was it activated on Sunday?"

She shakes her head. "We had it installed when we renovated," she says, "but neither one of us was very good about making use of it. We were never even good about locking the doors, for that matter. I'm not sure I'd be able to find a key."

I stop on the front step and face her. "I don't lock mine either," I confess. "Most people in this town don't."

She laughs. "It's not as if we live in a high-crime neighborhood."

Her smile fades at once. It's pretty clear she regretted her last sentence before she finished it.

"Herb kept saying we should," she adds. "Especially at night, he said, we should lock the doors and activate the alarm. He kept telling me that he, at least, was going to start."

"But he never got around to it," I finish for her.

"That's right," she says. "He never did."

CHAPTER 6

"You didn't tell me she was Southern."

A dangerousness hearing and a motion to suppress kept me tied up in the courthouse all afternoon. It's after six by the time I get back to the
office, but Harry and the Kydd are still seated on
opposite sides of our conference room table, their
noses buried in casebooks, both of them deep in
thought. They bolt upright—startled—when I appear in the doorway, drop my briefcase, and make
my announcement. It's directed, of course, at Harry.
"She's Southern," I repeat. "You didn't mention
that."

He blinks at me. "Does it matter?"

"Yes. It matters."

Harry stares across the table at the Kydd, as if in need of a translation.

The Kydd shrugs. "Don't look at me, Kimosabe," he says, then buries his nose in his casebook again.

Tonto has good instincts.

Harry sets his own book down, takes his glasses off, and looks back up at me, shaking his head. "Why?"

"Because Southern women are so damned . . . *Southern*."

I wish I hadn't put it quite that way.

"Can't argue with that," he says.

"They are, aren't they?" the Kydd drawls. He looks up from his book and it's his turn to take off his glasses. Everyone in this business has bad eyes. His grow wistful. "They really are."

"Don't get weepy on me, Kydd. I'm going to need some help with this case. And you're it."

He grins. "I love being it," he says. "That's why I work here."

Harry and I both laugh out loud. It's true. Between the two of us, we heap enough work on the Kydd to keep four associates busy. He's always it.

I turn back to Harry and point at the Kydd. "He's mine for the next three days. You got me into this mess; your work can wait."

Harry gives in at once, raising his hands above his head, as if I might shoot him otherwise. He started these melodramatic surrenders back when I was a prosecutor, as soon as he learned that I have a permit to carry and I make use of it. "He's yours," he tells me. "Take him, for God's sake. He's all yours."

The Kydd stretches in his chair and yawns, looking up at me warily. "The next three days," he says. "Would that be Monday, Tuesday, Wednesday?"

"No," I tell him. "I'm sorry, Kydd, but it's Saturday, Sunday, Monday."

"You'll never dance at my wedding." He sighs, then turns in the chair and opens the cabinet behind him, grabs a pen and a legal pad.

"Sure we will," Harry counters, returning to his reading. "Say the word when you're ready, Kydd. We'll find you a good-looking inmate."

The Kydd feigns a *ha-ha* at Harry, then turns to me, pen in hand, awaiting his marching orders.

"Life insurance," I tell him. "You need to become an expert on it by noon tomorrow."

Harry laughs into his book. "Another cushy assignment for the Kydd."

The Kydd isn't laughing, though. He glares at Harry before turning back to me, his expression suggesting I've asked him to master Sanskrit by dawn. "Life insurance? I don't know anything about life insurance. I don't know anything about *any* insurance."

I cross the conference room, select the *I* volume of the *Massachusetts Digest* from the bookcase, and hand it to him. "No one in this room knows anything about insurance," I tell him. "One of us has to learn."

The Kydd takes the powder-blue book reluctantly, as if I might be handing him something contraband, setting him up for a bust. He examines its spine, then looks at me and frowns. "I know," he says. "I'm it. But couldn't you narrow it down a little?"

"I can narrow it down a lot," I tell him. I dig Herb Rawlings's life insurance policy out of my briefcase and hand it to him, then settle into one of two worn, comfortable wing chairs in an alcove by the windows.

He sets the policy down, plants his elbows on the table and waits, pen poised, his expression only slightly relieved.

"Best-case scenario, Kydd, is this: Mitch Walker questions Louisa Rawlings about her husband's demise and he's satisfied with her answers. The official cause of death remains an unfortunate boating accident and the widow collects a cool million from New England Patriot."

Harry laughs into his casebook again. "Finally," he says. "Some money in the poor girl's pocket."

The Kydd looks over at Harry; I ignore him. "Worst-case scenario, of course, is this: Walker's less than satisfied with what Louisa Rawlings has to say. He digs deeper, finds evidence of foul play, and thinks the widow is behind it. She forfeits the insurance proceeds, but that's the least of her problems.

She's looking at a murder charge, probably first-degree."

The Kydd nods.

"What I want you to think about, Kydd, is a scenario that falls in between those two: Walker doesn't like Louisa's answers. He has suspicions, but no evidence. And what we have in our arsenal, thanks to your brilliant legal research, is a weapon that will ease his suspicions, maybe even dissuade him from digging any deeper."

The Kydd looks surprised by the enormity of his research prowess. "We do?"

"We do. What you're going to dig up for us is every restriction on recovery of life insurance proceeds that applies to Louisa Rawlings. And I'll give you the first one: suicide negates coverage."

Harry looks up from his casebook. "How the hell do you know that?"

I laugh. "Everybody knows that, Harry. And I went to law school, remember? I was one of those students who showed up for classes, even the classes that didn't involve murder and mayhem."

Harry frowns across the table at the Kydd. "Did you know that suicide negates coverage?" he asks.

The Kydd nods. "Everybody knows that," he echoes.

Harry looks down at his casebook. "I'm in the midst of nerds," he mutters.

The Kydd looks from Harry to me, shaking his head. "I don't follow, Marty."

51

"Louisa Rawlings doesn't believe her husband's death was accidental. She thinks he killed himself. And she has what may or may not be a note to prove it. But Mitch Walker doesn't know that yet. Neither does the insurance company. If this thing takes a turn in the wrong direction, we produce the note, play the suicide card. We also play up any other fact that precludes coverage."

The Kydd still looks confused. "And?"

"And we eliminate motive," I tell him. "Louisa Rawlings went to law school too. A damned good one. She knows suicide negates coverage. And we'll make sure she knows every other impediment to recovery you dig up too. She doesn't collect the million, but she doesn't spend the rest of her days in a cinder-block cell, either."

Harry laughs again. "Marty," he says, "Louisa went to fewer classes than I did. She doesn't know a damned thing about insurance coverage."

I wait until he looks up at me. "And Mitch Walker doesn't know a damned thing about Louisa."

He nods, conceding the point, and then goes back to his reading.

"Why would the guy kill himself?" the Kydd asks.

I shrug. "Who knows? His wife was planning to leave him and she's pretty sure he knew it. And if that's not bad enough, it sounds like the poor man was impotent."

"Ouch," Harry says to his casebook. "Louisa wouldn't be happy about that."

The Kydd freezes even before I do, his wide eyes sounding silent alarm bells at Harry.

Harry doesn't notice. "No, sir," he laughs, shaking his head at the book as if whatever vivid scene is unfolding in his mind's eye is illustrated there. "She wouldn't like that at all."

The Kydd looks over at me, his eyes panicked now, then back at Harry.

"Not one bit," Harry chuckles.

The Kydd steals another glance at me, then kicks Harry in the shins under the table. Hard.

Now it's Harry's turn to freeze. He gapes at his assailant, indignant for a split second, and then he turns slowly toward me. "I'm sorry," he says, burying his face in both hands and lowering his head to the book. "Dammit, Marty, I'm sorry."

I force myself not to laugh. I don't answer, either. Let him stew in his own juices for a minute.

He lifts his head just a couple of inches, keeps his hands over his face, then parts the fingers at his eyes and looks up at me. "I'm sorry. Dammit. I'm sorry."

I have to laugh now; I can't help it. "Since we're on the topic, Harry, what do you think? Would a man kill himself over impotence?"

He lowers his hands, plainly relieved at the prospect of our discussion moving on. "I would," he says, pointing to the windows behind my chair. "I'd jump."

I shake my head at him and close my eyes. We're on the first floor. "What do you think, Kydd? Suicide over impotence?"

The Kydd waits until I open my eyes again, then puts his pen down and grins at me. "I know almost as much about employment law as I do about life insurance," he says, "but I'm pretty sure you can't ask me that."

We're all laughing now. And I'm starting to feel punchy. It's time to go home. "See you bright and early," I tell the Kydd.

"You'll see me early," he says. "I don't know about bright."

CHAPTER 7

Since Luke left for Boston College six weeks ago, Harry and I have fallen into a Friday-evening routine. I get to my cottage first and feed Danny Boy, our eleven-year-old Irish setter. Then I fill the old claw-footed tub with bubble bath and water as hot as I can stand it, light a few candles, and soak. Harry stops at the fish market, picks up a couple of lobsters, and puts a pot of water on the stove as soon as he comes in. Then he joins me, bringing a Heineken for himself and a glass of sauvignon blanc for me. He sits beside the tub, on an old cedar chest that holds summer beach towels, and we enjoy our own, private version of happy hour.

Tonight I could barely wait to slide under the thick white blanket of almond-scented bubbles. Steaming-hot baths have always been my substitute for therapy. They're cheaper, for one thing, and available on demand. Besides, I was married to a shrink once. I can't bear the thought of being alone in a room with one again.

Harry taps on the door and leans into the bathroom. "You want company?"

This is not a question he normally asks. The candlelight is too dim for me to read his expression, but it's pretty clear he thinks he's still in the doghouse for his conference-room comments. "I want wine," I tell him.

He crosses the room, sets both drinks on the windowsill, out of my reach, and kneels beside the tub. "It's a package deal," he says, leaning over and brushing his lips against mine.

I take hold of the knot in his already-loosened tie and pull him closer, so I can kiss him for real. It's hard to resist Harry.

He smiles at me—that narrow-eyed, tight-lipped smile—then retrieves our drinks and assumes his perch on the cedar chest, a patch of white bubbles dissolving slowly on the front of his open-necked shirt. "So tell me, Attorney Nickerson, what's your take on the Rawlings matter?"

I lean back against the cool porcelain and sip my wine. "I don't have a take. Without the body, it's anyone's guess."

"Bingo," he says. "And as long as it's anyone's guess, nobody goes to jail over it."

He's right, of course. I hadn't thought of it that way, but he's right. It's the cops and prosecutors who need to figure out what actually happened, not the defense attorney. A seasoned defense lawyer would be overjoyed to have every one of his cases remain a mystery. And Harry's a seasoned defense lawyer right down to his soul.

He leans over and clinks his green bottle against my wineglass, then swallows a mouthful of beer. "Here's hoping old Herb never surfaces."

I shake my head and close my eyes.

"What?" he protests. "What'd I say?"

I open my eyes again, to see if he's serious. He is. "The man is dead," I remind him.

"I know that, Marty." He sets his beer down and leans forward, resting both hands on the rim of the tub. "That's the point. If I thought the guy could be rescued, I'd want him to turn up. But since he's dead, he may as well rest in peace in the depths of the Great South Channel. He won't cause any trouble there."

"He won't have a proper burial either."

"Says who? What's wrong with the ocean floor? Beats the hell out of a patch of dirt. Tell you what. When the time comes, you can bury *me* in the Great South Channel too. I'll keep old Herb company."

"Swell, Harry. Maybe you and Herb should invite Glen Powers to join you. A reunion of Louisa alumni."

He laughs and retrieves his beer. "How'd it go today, anyhow? Did you two hit it off?"

I don't think Harry's ever asked me if I hit it off with a client before. "It was fine," I tell him. "But we have a lot more ground to cover before Monday."

He nods, then tilts his head to one side. "Did Louisa ever have any kids?"

I *know* Harry's never asked *that* about a client before. "No," I tell him. "But she does have a wicked stepdaughter. Five years her junior."

"Sweet Jesus," he says, taking another swallow. "That could get ugly."

"Louisa refers to herself as the trophy wife," I tell him. "God only knows what the stepdaughter calls her."

"Trophy wife?" Harry laughs. "She must have mellowed over the years. The Louisa I knew wouldn't have settled for being any old trophy. She'd have called herself the Triple Crown."

Well, of course she would have.

I've had about enough of Louisa Rawlings for one day. And my bathwater has grown tepid. I pull the plug and Harry gets my towel from the hook on the door. He wraps it around me as I step out of the tub, then pulls me close for another kiss. Another real one.

"I'll bet the water's boiling," he says. "Ready for lobster?"

Lobster isn't what I want at the moment, but I

don't say so. "Sounds good," I tell him instead. "I'll make a salad."

He kisses me again—a quick one this time—and then heads for the kitchen.

I wipe the mist from the bathroom mirror, turban a towel around my wet hair, and sit for a moment on the edge of the cedar chest. It's just as well. I *am* sort of hungry. And I'm too damned tired to compete for the Triple Crown.

CHAPTER 8

Saturday, October 14

Even on Saturdays, the Kydd is invariably the first one at work. Today is no exception. He's stationed in the front office when I arrive, his feet propped up on the old pine table. His face is buried in an advance sheet, a paper rendition of the Commonwealth's most recent judicial opinions, the industry's heads-up to practitioners. Advance sheets are published within days of appellate decisions being rendered, long before hardbound casebooks can be produced. The Kydd's focused expression tells me one of the high courts of the Commonwealth has recently waxed eloquent on the topic of life insurance.

Casebooks surround the Kydd in stacks of three and four, pink Post-it notes sticking out from their pages like multiple taunting tongues. My watch says it's not quite eight o'clock, but it's obvious the Kydd's been in here working for a while. He looks up as I enter, dog-ears his spot, and takes his glasses off to clean them on his shirttail. "Marty," he says, examining his lenses under the brass lamp at the edge of the table, "I have to thank you. What a career-enhancing assignment you've given me. I don't know that I've ever been exposed to such intellectually stimulating reading material."

"Sarcasm suits you, Kydd." I sink into the chair across from his, awaiting his list of complaints.

"Jesus," he says. "People spend their lives handling this stuff? Day in, day out?"

It occurs to me that the members of our esteemed insurance defense bar might be at least equally appalled by the daily fare we criminal types handle. I don't mention it, though.

The Kydd puts his glasses back on, pulls our copy of Herb Rawlings's life insurance policy out from under an open casebook, and flips to a section highlighted in yellow. The Kydd intends to enlighten me, it seems, whether I like it or not.

"The party of the first part," he recites, "hereinafter the Company, agrees, subject to the provisions and limitations of this Policy, to immediately pay to the party of the second part, hereinafter the Beneficiary or Beneficiaries . . ."

The Kydd sounds a lot like those guys who spit out too many words in too little time at the end of car commercials. He pauses for an elaborate, drawn-out yawn.

". . . the death benefit, the amount of which is set forth in the Policy Specifications, if and when due proof is furnished to the Company at its Home Office that the Insured, while this Policy is in full force and effect . . ."

He stops again, this time for a dramatic intake of breath. "These sentences don't end," he says, "none of them. Not in this policy . . ."

He holds the document up in front of me, as if I might not otherwise know what he's talking about, then taps on the text in the open casebook between us.

". . . and not in any of the policies discussed in the cases. The sentences never end and no one seems to notice. People must either fall asleep halfway through, or they die of asphyxiation."

The Kydd stares accusingly across the table at me, as if I single-handedly drafted every life insurance policy in the Commonwealth.

I can't help laughing. "Don't worry about the policy language," I tell him. "We can't do anything about that anyhow. We're stuck with whatever it says. Just worry about the law. Find as many reasons as you can for the company to deny coverage. At least find the authority that says there's no recovery if the insured's death is caused by suicide."

The door opens behind me and Harry appears, looking well rested and comfortable in jeans and a light gray hooded sweatshirt. His thick hair is still damp from his morning shower. He's carrying three tall coffees in a cardboard tray and a box that's undoubtedly filled with morning treats from Sticky Buns, Chatham's best-kept little secret of a neighborhood bakery. The Kydd looks up at him for a moment and eyes the goodies, then turns his attention back at me. "No can do," he says.

Harry nudges a couple of casebooks aside, deposits his treasures in the middle of the pine table, and then drops into the old wooden chair next to mine. "Tonto," he pleads, looking stricken, "say it isn't so. Kimosabe believes you can do anything."

The Kydd grins at him and takes a coffee from the cardboard tray, along with three plastic thimbles of cream. "Not this time, Kimosabe," he says. "Turns out suicide negates life insurance coverage only if the death occurs within three years of the date the policy issues."

Harry leans toward me over the arm of his chair, tearing open a half dozen packets of sugar all at once. "Uh-oh," he says, dumping a white avalanche into his coffee. "Maybe you missed a class or two after all."

I frown at him. It's true, though; I didn't remember that part. And Herb Rawlings was well into his sixties; his policy almost certainly issued more than three years ago. Folks in his tax bracket start their estate planning early. I look across the table at the Kydd, silently asking the question I think I've already answered.

"You guessed it," he says, tapping his pen against the issue date stamped on the policy's first page. "Three years and a month."

It's worse than I thought. A groan escapes me.

"Damn," Harry says, sipping his coffee. "I hate it when that happens."

"To the day," the Kydd adds. "And that's not all." He pauses, reaches into the cardboard box and pulls out a square knot, Sticky Buns's nautical version of the universal cinnamon roll. "It gets worse."

"Kydd," I say, taking the last coffee from the tray, "I had precisely one strategy for this case. You just told me not only that it's a failure, but that it actually hurts us, cuts the other way. How much worse can it get?"

I regret the question even before I absorb the expression on his face.

"Worse," he repeats, flipping through Herb's policy to yet another highlighted section. "In addition to the other benefits provided herein . . ."

The Kydd interrupts his recitation, looks up at Harry and me to make sure we're listening. We are.

". . . the Company agrees to pay twice the face amount of this policy if the insured has suffered loss of life as the direct result of bodily injury caused solely by accidental means."

A double-indemnity clause. I'm speechless.

Harry lets out a low whistle.

The Kydd sets the policy down, takes his glasses

off again and tosses them on the desk. He leans back and examines his square knot before taking a huge bite. "The motive . . ." he says, pointing what's left of his pastry at us.

I consider telling him not to talk with his mouth full, but I bite my tongue instead.

". . . just doubled."

The Kydd and I turn onto Easy Street on schedule, at high noon. This morning's fog has burned off and the mid-October sun is bright, but not quite warm. It glitters on the small waves lapping at the Rawlingses' dock and turns the crushed oyster shells in their driveway an impossible, almost blinding white. Even the seagulls, busily dropping quahogs from the sky to the rocks below to crack their shells, look cleaner than usual. Sun-bleached feathered fishermen.

It's obvious Louisa Rawlings is expecting us. Her inside front door is open, the screens in the outer door admitting the autumn chill to her otherwise buttoned-up house. Three ears of Indian corn—one yellow, two rust-colored—hang from the shingles beside the front door. A large pumpkin—uncarved as yet—sits on the top step. These are new additions since yesterday. The grieving widow has done a bit of seasonal decorating.

I cut the Thunderbird's engine and grab my beat-up briefcase from the backseat, but the Kydd doesn't reach for his. He doesn't move at all. He seems frozen in the passenger seat, eyes wide as he takes in the Rawlings estate. "Hot damn," he says, "what a spread."

"We're in the high-rent district now," I tell him. "So behave yourself."

He grins.

"If you don't, you'll be exiled to the slums of South Chatham for life."

He laughs out loud.

South Chatham is a quaint seaside village of antique shingled cottages, small professional offices, and family-run shops. It doesn't feature the lavish landscape of its wealthy sister to the north, and it certainly doesn't host an exclusive country club, but it's not a slum by anyone's standards. The Kydd lives there, in a rented cottage. And Harry does too, in a small apartment on the second floor of our office building. They both tell anyone who'll listen that they're slumming it down south.

Louisa emerges from the house as the Kydd and I extricate ourselves and our briefcases from my old, tired Thunderbird. She strides toward us on the brick walkway, perfect crimson lips smiling, every bit as impeccably turned out as she was yesterday. Today's color scheme is different—slacks and heels dark brown, blouse an opalescent cream. And her hair is restyled, pulled back in a French braid. But the overall effect is exactly the same as yesterday's. Long. Lithe. Lovely.

"Marty," she says, checking her watch as she nears us, "you're right on time."

Had I not spent so much of my life with the Kydd during the past few years, I might have thought Louisa said I was "rat on tam." But I know better; my Southern-speak is well honed now. Besides, I'm so happy to be addressed by my given name—as opposed to *darlin'* or *honey chil'*—I don't much care what she said afterward.

I return her smile, then pivot so I can direct her attention to the Kydd. No need, though. She's way ahead of me, waiting for the introduction.

"Louisa, I'd like you to meet Kevin Kydd, our associate. He's going to be working with us."

She takes another step toward him and extends a manicured hand. "Mr. Kydd," she says, "I am delighted to make your acquaintance. And I am truly grateful for your assistance. I cannot thank you enough."

Mr. Kydd looks like he's in the midst of a beatific vision. His expression is one the shepherds might have worn upon discovering the swaddled babe in the manger.

"Oh, ma'am," he responds, receiving Louisa's hand as if it might shatter at the touch of a mere mortal, "the pleasure is all mine. And please do not thank me yet. I only hope my assistance will prove useful."

Maybe I'm imagining it, but both drawls seem to thicken when Louisa and the Kydd speak to each other. The two of them have developed an acute aversion to contractions too. And the Kydd seems to think Louisa's hand is his to keep.

"Please come in," she says, turning in her high heels to retrace her steps to the front door. "I made tea." She glances back at us over her shoulder and flashes her wide smile again. "Iced tea, y'all say in these parts. Sweet tea, we call it at home. Or unsweet tea, for some."

That's the first *y'all* I've heard from Louisa Rawlings. At least it's a contraction.

She faces forward again and heads for the house. I fall into step behind her, but the Kydd doesn't move. After a few paces I pause to look back at him. "Kydd," I say quietly.

He doesn't seem to hear.

"Kydd," I repeat, a little louder this time.

He blinks and shakes his head, as if he's snapping out of a trance. His expression suggests he's never seen me before.

I hold his gaze and walk back to him, so our client won't hear my words. Even at this distance, I don't dare risk more than a stage whisper. "I don't want to be bossy, Kydd, but I think you ought to close your mouth."

He steals a glance ahead, at Louisa, and swallows hard before he takes my suggestion.

"Now come on," I tell him. "Let's get to work. After all, we're rat on tam."

* * *

My teeth have grown fur. One sip of Louisa's home brew did the trick. I don't dare take a second. Calling it sweet tea is like saying there's a pinch or two of salt in the Atlantic.

The Kydd is already finished his and I wonder for a moment if I can get away with switching our glasses. Too late, though. Our hostess is pouring him another. "You were thirsty," she says.

He shakes his head as he watches her pour. "Not especially, but this is fine tea, Mrs. Rawlings. Mighty fine."

That settles it. The Kydd is definitely speaking a new dialect. He's always had a distinct drawl, but he's never sounded like a Ewing before. I expect he'll swagger any minute now.

"Please," she says to him, "call me Louisa."

Either my eyes deceive me or my associate is blushing, right up to the rims of his sizable ears.

Louisa sees it too. She smiles and hands him the refill. "I'm so glad you like it," she tells him. "Herb always said my sweet tea should be patented."

Plenty of liquids are patented. Chemicals, for instance. Commercial fertilizers. Industrial-strength disinfectants. That doesn't mean they're fit for human consumption. I clear my throat, intending to put an end to this meeting of the Southern Admiration Society, but the doorbell drowns me out.

"Excuse me," Louisa says, wiping her hands on a terry-cloth towel at the sink. She leaves the Kydd and me in the kitchen and heads back through the living room toward the front door. Another non–Cape Codder has come to call, it seems, using the wrong door.

I cross the kitchen and hand Louisa's file to the Kydd. For a split second, he seems not to know why. "We came here to work," I remind him. "Not to attend a tea party."

He drains his glass, sets it on the counter, then stands at attention and salutes. I hand him my glass, still full. "Drink that," I tell him. He does.

Louisa returns with a tall, sharp-featured man in tow. He's dressed in a well-cut navy blue suit, starched white shirt, and maroon tie. He looks as if he might be campaigning for political office, canvassing door-to-door in search of votes. "This is Steven Collier," Louisa says to the Kydd and me. "I believe I mentioned him to you, Marty."

She did. He's the money guy, Quick-draw Mc-Graw. He apparently makes house calls. And on Saturday afternoons, no less.

Quick-draw's slicked-back hair is far too black to have come from Mother Nature. He greets the Kydd with a vigorous handshake and then accepts my outstretched hand more reluctantly, tossing his glossy head back toward the other room. He wants to speak privately, his dark eyes tell me. Maybe he plans to diversify my portfolio. Money guys sometimes assume that I have one.

He cups my elbow in his palm—a gesture I find utterly irritating—and propels me toward the living room. "I need some advice," he says as he closes the heavy doors between us and the kitchen.

Yes, he does. And I should give it to him. *Don't steer women around as if we're on wheels,* I should say. But I don't. No need to alienate a potential witness. "Advice about what?" I ask instead.

"About what I know."

"Pardon?"

"How much do I know?"

"How much do you *know*?" He knows more than I do at the moment. I don't even know what he's asking.

"About Louisa," he says.

Now I'm thoroughly confused. "You want me to tell you how much you know about Louisa?"

He crosses the room and leans over to rest one forearm on the mantel, his back to me. He's quiet for a second, staring down at the few logs crackling in the fireplace. The living room's heavy drapes are closed and the only other light in here is thrown by a floor lamp in the far corner.

"I'm asking you how much I *should* know," he says, turning to face me again.

I shake my head. I don't know what the hell he's driving at.

"About her finances, for example." He puts one hand on his hip and raises the other, along with his eyes, to the ceiling. He's annoyed.

"You're her money manager. You should know everything about her finances, shouldn't you?"

He runs both hands through his inky hair and laughs, staring into the fire and then eyeing me sideways. I'm apparently one of the denser people he's come across in life. "I *do*," he says. "Of course I do. But I don't have to tell them that."

"Them?"

"The cops. If they think Louisa offed her husband to get at the insurance proceeds, they're going to want to talk to me, aren't they?"

"They probably will," I tell him, "if the investigation goes that far."

"Then you need to tell me what to say."

I pause for a moment to look him in the eyes, to make sure he means what I think he means. He does.

"You're mistaken, Mr. Collier. I don't need to do any such thing. In fact, I'm specifically prohibited from doing anything of the sort."

"What do you mean, you're prohibited? You're a lawyer, aren't you?"

Every once in a while I meet someone who seems to feel compelled to inform me that I am a lawyer. Generally speaking, I don't like these people. Implicit in the pronouncement is the arrogant assumption that I'm not acting like one.

"Mr. Collier," I tell him, "if the police question you about this matter, you should tell them nothing but the truth."

"The truth." He half laughs, staring at me, as if he's waiting for my real answer.

I nod. "No need to volunteer anything," I tell him. "Just answer the questions asked. But don't try to hide information either."

"That's the best you can do?"

"Yes, it is. Get cute with them and *you'll* be the target of the next investigation."

He laughs again, a full one this time, and heads back toward the kitchen. Apparently I'm dismissed.

"Mr. Collier," I say as he approaches the doors, "I was wondering . . ."

He hesitates, his hand on the doorknob, as if whatever portion of his day he'd allotted for his discussion with me has been used up. After a moment, he turns to face me, his impatience plain.

I walk closer to him, so I can look him in the eyes when he answers. "I was wondering if you might know anything about the Rawlingses' marriage."

"Their marriage?"

"Yes. I'm curious as to whether they were having problems of any kind, what the prospects might have been for their future."

He plants both hands on his hips, forcing his suit coat open in the process. My eyes rest on a shiny revolver in a shoulder holster at his rib cage.

His gaze follows mine for a moment, and then he looks back up at me, smiling. "Don't worry," he says, "it's legit. I'm licensed."

I consider telling him I'm not as worried as he might assume—I'm packing my own Lady Smith, after all—but decide against it. "I was asking about the Rawlingses' marriage," I remind him.

His return gaze is steady. "Herb and Louisa Rawlings were extremely happy together. They had no problems."

I nod, but say nothing.

Now it's his turn to take a step closer. He seems to want to look me in the eyes too. "Their future," he says, "was secure."

CHAPTER 9

It's after five by the time we wrap up. The Kydd has reassembled Louisa's file, adding the copious notes he took this afternoon to the paltry pages I scratched out yesterday. He amassed a small mountain of legal-size sheets today, writing almost non-stop since we got started, and I'm pretty sure I know why. He's besotted with our damsel in distress. Note-taking kept him from drooling. At least most of the time.

I rest on the edge of a kitchen stool and face Louisa, who's leaning against the stove, arms folded, watching the Kydd position her file in the belly of his briefcase. "About Steven Collier," I begin.

Her gaze shifts to me and she tilts her auburn head to one side. "What about him?"

"Did he handle Herb's money too? Or just yours?"

She laughs. "Only Herb handled Herb's money, darlin'. No one else put a hand in that cookie jar."

I look around the kitchen for a moment, and then into the sunroom, where late-afternoon light reflects off the waves outside and casts intricate designs on the far wall. Of course Herb Rawlings managed his own assets. He must've been damned good at it.

"Herb and Steven talked about money all the time," Louisa continues. "They never tired of it—stocks, bonds, tax shelters, you name it. They were always bandying moneymaking strategies about. Investing was a competitive sport for them. They kept tabs on Wall Street the way other men follow football."

"Did Steven have access to Herb's financial affairs? Copies of documents, for instance?"

Louisa pauses for a moment, considering. "Some," she says. "Herb gave Steven copies of whatever documents he thought would affect my estate planning: the will, the insurance policies, that sort of thing."

I tell myself to quell my uneasiness over Steven Collier. It makes sense that he has those documents. He'd have a tough time doing his job otherwise. And plenty of people carry firearms for legitimate reasons. I'm one of them. Besides, there's no reason to think Herb Rawlings was shot. Guns have nothing to do with this case. Plenty of people lie, too, especially if they think it will help someone they want to protect. Clearly Collier has thought about the damage Louisa's divorce plans might cause under the circumstances.

"And Anastasia's trust documents," Louisa adds. "Herb made a point of giving Steven a copy of those. I remember the two of them coming back here after an afternoon on the *Carolina Girl* to discuss it."

"Anastasia has a trust?"

Louisa unfolds her arms and holds both hands up, palms out. "Don't get me started," she says, but apparently I already did. She barely pauses for breath. "Doting Daddy has the dreadful daughter financed for life. Heaven forbid she lift a finger during her stay on earth."

It occurs to me that Anastasia's earthly existence sounds somewhat comparable to Louisa's, but I don't mention it. "Why would Herb give a copy of Anastasia's trust documents to Steven Collier?" I ask instead.

Louisa leaves her post at the stove and examines the floor as she saunters to a stool across the counter from mine. She smiles when she looks up, her rich brown eyes genuinely amused. "That's a fair question," she says as she sits, "from someone who doesn't know Anastasia."

Something tells me I just might get to know Anastasia before all this is over. There's more bad blood here than I'd realized.

"To those of us who know her," Louisa continues, "the answer is obvious. I knew immediately. Steven did too."

She leaves her perch at the counter, takes a few steps and leans against the refrigerator. I wait.

"Anastasia is specifically excluded from her father's will," Louisa says. "And our Anastasia will be apoplectic when she finds out."

"Why?" I ask. "Why is she excluded?"

"Because she's already taken care of," Louisa answers. "Her trust is well funded. It will support her quite comfortably—her and her beatnik boyfriend, I might add—for life. Herb thought it best to keep Anastasia's financial interests separate from mine."

Herb thought right on that score. Too bad he couldn't find separate planets for them too. "I'm not following you, Louisa. I still don't see why Steven Collier has copies of Anastasia's trust documents."

"We'll need them," she says, "when the poor little rich girl contests her daddy's will."

I should have seen that coming. If Steven Collier were here, he'd undoubtedly ask me if I'm a lawyer.

"And she *will* contest it," Louisa adds. "Make no mistake about that. She'll be in probate court before Herb's attorney finishes breaking the news."

Now it's my turn to leave my perch. It's time to get out of here. I have other questions, including more than a few about Anastasia Rawlings, but I want to sleep on them before I ask. We've covered enough ground for one day. No need to open Pandora's box before we leave.

"I'd like to meet earlier tomorrow," I tell Louisa as I take my jacket from the back of the chair. "How's nine o'clock?"

She shrugs. "It's fine with me," she says. "I'll be here."

The Kydd takes my cue and starts for the kitchen door, but then stops. He turns and heads for the living room instead, apparently remembering Louisa's preference. I grab my briefcase and follow, our hostess right behind me.

I'm eager to get going. I'm meeting Harry at his place so we can go out for a quick bite. And Luke should be home by now too. If he doesn't have a date, and hasn't already made plans with friends, we might be able to talk him into joining us. Harry and I are good company, Luke always says, if no one else is around.

The Kydd bids Louisa good-bye with a nod, looks down at his shoes as if he's embarrassed, and then hurries out the front door and down the steps to the brick walkway. She watches as he crosses the oyster-shell driveway, opens the Thunderbird's back door, and slides his briefcase onto the seat. She leans in the doorway and sips from yet another glass of her terrible tea. I hadn't realized she'd brought it along.

"Is he yours?" she asks.

"Pardon me?"

She points her tall, perspiring glass toward the Kydd. "That delightful young man. Is he yours?"

For reasons I don't understand in the least, I feel a twinge of panic. "Mine? I don't know what you mean."

A satisfied smile crosses Louisa's face. "Well, then, he's not. You've answered my question, darlin'."

I wish to God she'd stop calling me that.

CHAPTER 10

Harry and I pull up to my cottage to find a brand-spanking-new Porsche in the driveway. It's cleaner than my kitchen table and waxed to perfection, shimmering even in the diffused light of dusk. I've never seen this car before, but I've heard about it—and its price tag—from Luke. The sight of it makes my stomach hurt.

Luke's truck is in the shop. He stayed in Boston after classes ended yesterday, went to a Celtics game with a group of buddies last night, and then slept over at his father's harbor-front condo. Ralph drove him home this afternoon.

It wasn't necessary for Ralph to make the

ninety-mile trip down here, of course. Luke could have taken the bus from Boston to Hyannis, as he's done a hundred times before, and either Harry or I would have gladly picked him up at the station. Ralph wouldn't hear of it, though. He insisted on driving. And now he'll tell me a thousand times how terribly inconvenient it was.

Harry lets out a long, low whistle. "Sweet Jesus," he says, parking his old Jeep next to the sleek machine. "A Carrera 911. You must be moonlighting."

I laugh and climb out of the Jeep. My day job barely covers the never-ending repairs to the old Thunderbird. I'd have to be moonlighting as a plastic surgeon to imagine a Porsche on my horizon.

"Where the hell did this come from?" Harry gets out of the Jeep too and stands still in the driveway, staring at the Porsche the way he might gaze at an icy case of Heineken if he'd been stranded in the desert for a week.

"It's Ralph's," I tell him. "He brought Luke home from Boston today."

"Ralph," Harry repeats. "He's still here?"

I feel a little bit like a game show hostess, holding my hands out toward the gleaming status symbol. "Apparently he is."

"You want me to disappear?"

Harry's question almost makes me laugh. Ralph walked out on Luke and me a dozen years ago, and he largely ignored us for the first ten of them. He came out of the woodwork two years back, after remarrying and redivorcing. Luke was a junior in high school then. And his father had decided it was time to get to know him.

"No," I tell Harry, shaking my head. "I don't want you to disappear."

He drapes his arm around my shoulders and pulls me close as we head for the back steps. "Okay," he says, kissing my forehead. "I guess I've got an appointment with the shrink who needs his head examined."

Ralph is on his feet when Harry and I come through the kitchen door, his car keys in hand. My heart sinks for a moment when I realize we could have avoided him if we'd arrived just a few minutes later. The old adage is true: Timing *is* everything.

Danny Boy gallops into the kitchen the instant we're inside. He almost never runs anywhere anymore, but Luke is home, and now we are too, and Danny Boy can barely contain his joy. He yelps and jumps up on me, his big paws landing on my stomach, and I fall backward against Harry. If he hadn't pulled the kitchen door shut behind him, we'd both go over like dominoes onto the back deck.

"Luke," Ralph yells into the living room, "come get the damned dog. He's out of control." Ralph doesn't like Danny Boy, never has. Danny Boy doesn't lose any sleep over it, though. He doesn't think much of Ralph, either. And, as far as Danny Boy is concerned, he's the one with seniority around here. Ralph is the newcomer.

Luke strolls into the kitchen, laughing, but doesn't bother to restrain the dog. There's no reason to, of course, except in Ralph's head. Instead, Luke stoops to give me a kiss. At six feet three, he's got a solid nine inches on me. He gets his height from his father but most of his other traits—fair skin, dark blue eyes, and black hair—from me. He trades arm punches with Harry. Hard ones.

"Who the hell is he?" Ralph points at Harry, but asks me the question, as if he's inquiring about a figure in a wax museum.

"Ralph Ellis," I say, "meet Harry Madigan."

Harry extends a hand, but Ralph hesitates. After a moment, he shakes it gingerly, as if Harry might detonate on contact.

"Ralph," Harry says, "how are you?"

Ralph doesn't answer. Instead he looks Harry up and down, assessing him, and then turns back to me. "What the hell is going on with the truck?"

Here we go. "It needs work," I tell him, hoping to short-circuit this discussion.

"I *know* that." Ralph raises his hands to the heavens, the way he always does when he wants to be sure I know he's at the end of his rope.

"Dad," Luke says, "give it a rest. It's not that big a deal."

But for Ralph, Luke's pickup truck *is* a big deal, even when it's operational. Ralph purchases nothing but the best. He can. He doesn't believe in *used* anything. Why would he? He's been mad at Luke, and ballistic at me, since we bought a used truck last Christmas. Funny, though, he hasn't offered to replace it.

"What's this about Luke working at the god-damned garage?" he demands.

I had been hoping Luke wouldn't mention that particular plan to his father. One look at Luke tells me he's sorry he did. "Rematch?" he asks Harry. Luke is feeling the heat and he wants to get out of the kitchen. I don't blame him. I'd like to get out of here too.

"You're a glutton for punishment, kiddo," Harry says, looking a little relieved himself. The two of them escape into the living room, Danny Boy right behind them, to set up the chessboard.

"He's working at the *garage*?" Ralph repeats the word as if it's profane.

"For a day," I tell him. "He'll help Peter with the truck on Monday and Peter will cut him some slack on the bill."

Peter Schaeffer is our mechanic and he's the only reason my Thunderbird is still on the road. I'm hoping he'll perform similar miracles on Luke's truck. Peter and Luke have always gotten along well—they're both car fanatics. And for some reason, that fact has always irritated Ralph.

"Not just for a day," he says. "They can't get it all done in one day. Luke's working there Tuesday too. Monday and Tuesday. Skipping classes both days."

Now that's a portion of the plan I hadn't heard yet.

"So my son's not a college student," Ralph continues. "He's a grease monkey."

I can see into the living room over Ralph's shoulder. Luke jumps up from the couch when he hears his father's words and dashes to the center of the room. He bends in half and scoots around in circles, alternately scratching his head and armpits, then dragging his knuckles on the floor. Harry falls back against the cushions and stomps his boots on the braided rug. He's having a laughing fit, not making a sound.

It takes every shred of willpower I can muster to keep a straight face. "A grease monkey," I repeat. I look back at Ralph with what I hope is a somber expression. Any trace of amusement would send him into a spin. "I guess that's what he is."

Ralph shakes his head, disgusted, and points at the kitchen door. "Come outside for a minute," he says. "I want to talk to you."

I consider telling him I'm not going anywhere. He can say whatever he has to say right here in the kitchen. But it's not worth the scene it would cause. "Let me grab a sweater," I tell him instead, and I head for the living room closet.

Harry and my son the monkey have moved the coffee table into the center of the room. They're sitting on the floor on opposite sides of it, arranging the chessboard between them. Harry looks up as I pass. "You okay?" he asks in a low voice.

"I'm swell," I tell him. "But if Fay Wray isn't back in ten minutes, send King Kong."

Ralph and I are having the talk I knew we would have—the one about Luke's academic endeavors. Ralph, of course, would characterize the discussion differently. He'd say it's about the lack thereof. We've had this debate before. We'll have it again. And Luke will be ready to retire from the workforce long before we reach an agreement.

Luke has always been a good student—in certain subjects. His grades are consistently strong in English, literature, and philosophy; they're not so hot in math. He has a knack for foreign languages, but his chemistry teacher described him as downright frightening in the lab. Luke has never been troubled by his weak spots, even telling his high school guidance counselor they're blessings in disguise, clear indicators of career paths he shouldn't waste time exploring.

I laughed when the guidance counselor took me aside after a basketball game and shared Luke's philosophical approach to academia. The counselor confirmed what I already knew: Luke is comfortable with his foibles, at ease with having limits. And I am glad about that.

His father didn't see it that way.

When Luke graduated from Chatham High School four months ago, he took the top prize from the English department and was recognized for his magna cum laude performance on the national Latin exam. I was proud of his accomplishments, of course, but I was also proud of what he did next. When the physics instructor walked to the podium to present the award to the student who had excelled in the sciences, Luke twisted in his seat and caught my eye, nearly losing his tasseled cap in the process. "Get ready," he mouthed, pounding his thumb against the dark blue gown at his chest. "This baby's all mine." It was all I could do not to laugh out loud.

His father didn't see it that way.

When Luke enrolled at Boston College, I encouraged him to sign up for the courses he likes, to pursue the subjects that interest him. After all, I reasoned, Luke is training for his future. And he's a naturally energetic, upbeat guy. He ought to fashion a future that suits him.

His father didn't see it that way.

Ralph is a forensic psychiatrist. He's a scientist at heart, a man who reduces all aspects of existence to their component parts. For Ralph, there is no life problem that doesn't have a logical solution. And the solution to Luke's problems, Ralph always tells both of us, is simple: He should work harder. He should be more like Ralph.

Luke doesn't see it that way.

Tonight Ralph is worked up over Luke's first-semester schedule. "There's not a single science course in the lineup," Ralph told me ten minutes ago. He had repeated this shocking tidbit of information three times since then. And I kept forgetting to gasp.

It occurs to me that it's a little late to complain about courses Luke selected four months ago, in June, but I don't mention it. When Ralph's worked up, I clam up. That's a routine we established a long time ago.

"He's taking art history, for Christ's sake," Ralph adds now. Apparently this, too, is a capital offense.

Danny Boy has been panting at the living room window, paws on the sill, keeping a watchful eye on us throughout our driveway debate. He starts barking at Ralph now, moving his big paws up to the windowpane, his nails scratching the glass. I'm not sure what prompted his change in demeanor, but I decide to trust his canine instincts. "I'm going in now," I tell Ralph. "There's nothing more to say. We disagree. That's all there is to it."

He clutches his goateed chin between thumb and index finger and shakes his head. He's angry—again—that I don't see life through his cheerless lenses. He opens his mouth, as if he plans to continue the argument, but then apparently thinks better of it. He presses a button on his key chain and the Porsche lights up and honks as I head for the back steps. "Marty," he calls after me.

He's got one foot in the car when I turn around, his left hand on top of the open driver's-side door, his right one still holding the keys, resting on the roof. He juts his goatee out toward the cottage. "Your friend in there," he says. "Henry."

"Harry," I correct him.

"Whatever." Ralph pauses and shakes his head yet again. He's annoyed with my attention to unimportant detail. "The guy's got an attitude," he says, pointing his keys at the living room window. "I don't like him."

Ah, the considered, objective judgment of the scientist. Where would the rest of us be without it? I turn away from him and climb the back steps without another word.

By the time I get back to the living room, it's obvious that Luke is exasperated. This, in itself, is not surprising. Luke always gets exasperated when he plays chess with Harry, but it usually takes a little longer than the fifteen minutes or so they've been playing. He gets up from the floor and flops onto the living room couch. "Wake me up when you move," he says to Harry, "if I'm still breathing."

Harry sits immobile on the floor, his eyes glued to the chessboard on the coffee table, the only sign of life his occasional ogle of Luke's king. "Sure thing," he answers, motionless.

Luke bounds up again. "I forgot," he says, pounding a palm against his forehead as if he's in a V8 commercial. "You cheat."

"It's not cheating if everyone knows you do it," Harry replies.

Luke calls these pearls of wisdom Harry-isms.

There's no reasoning with the guy, he tells me after every chess match. He turns to me now, his hands in the air, his eyes wide. "Do you *see* what I'm talking about?"

I nod at him and laugh. I do.

"I'm gonna order a pizza," Luke says, heading for the phone in the kitchen. "Watch the board for me, will you, Mom? You can't trust this guy for two seconds."

"Sausage and onions," Harry yells after him. "And anchovies," he adds.

"Not on your life," Luke calls back. "Pepperoni. Nothing else belongs on pizza."

"Order two," I tell him. "And one of them had better be half plain cheese."

Luke pops his head back into the living room to see if I'm serious about this outrageous suggestion. I nod to let him know I am. I'm hungry. And at the rate this chess game is moving, we won't get out to eat until *next* Saturday. Luke's eyes move to Harry, as if he needs a second opinion.

"Your mom's a plain Jane," Harry says, his gaze not leaving the chessboard.

Luke rolls his eyes and goes back into the kitchen. Harry's delivering old news.

Harry looks up when Danny Boy and I settle on the couch to do guard duty. "You okay?" he asks.

"I'm fine," I tell him as Danny Boy nestles his head on my lap. "But you're not. My ex-husband doesn't like you, Henry. You have an attitude."

He falls backward, slapping the back of one hand to his forehead. "I'm shattered," he says. "Roscoe and I could've been close. We have so much in common. We could've had a future."

We're both laughing when he sits up, but Harry leans his elbows on the edge of the coffee table and grows serious. "He wants this back, you know," he says.

"Wants what back?"

"This." He gestures to our surroundings and I wonder for a moment if he thinks Ralph wants my cottage. "He wants this life back," Harry continues. "You. His son. All of it. He's feeling proprietary."

This is even funnier than the Roscoe comments. Ralph couldn't keep his hands off his receptionist when we were married. He didn't seem to remember that Luke and I lived on the same planet. The idea of his feeling *proprietary* makes me laugh out loud.

"Trust me," I tell Harry. "Ralph thrives in the fast lane. This is not the life he wants. And whatever woman he's interested in at the moment is half my age, wearing a skirt the length of my jacket."

Luke rejoins us and settles into his spot on the floor again. This conversation is over—at least for now.

"*You* trust *me*," Harry finishes, nodding over Luke's shoulder. "I've got a handle on old Roscoe."

CHAPTER 11

Sunday, October 15

It's a few minutes past nine when I pull up to Louisa Rawlings's Easy Street antique home. The Kydd's small, red pickup is parked at the far end of the oyster-shell driveway, near the house. True to form, he's the first one at work—no matter where work happens to be. I align the Thunderbird next to his truck and cut the engine.

I grab Louisa's growing file from the passenger seat before slipping from behind the wheel. A manila accordion folder with a six-inch capacity, it was sand dollar–flat on Friday, housing only the sketchy notes from my initial interview. Now it's swollen to about half its potential with the fruits of yesterday's labors: the Kydd's morning of legal research, his afternoon of copious note-taking. Let's hope we close the damned thing tomorrow, before it mushrooms.

I tuck the file under one arm as I slam my car door and head toward the house. Morning dew glistens on the roof and hood of the Kydd's truck, tiny droplets merging and trickling like miniature rivers down the fogged windows. Through a gap in the mist on the passenger's side, I see that the solitary bench inside is empty. He must have returned the files and books that cluttered it yesterday to the office. Good. I'll make a point of telling him to leave them there. I want that busy brain of his focused on only one case for the next couple of days. This one.

Louisa's husky laughter tells me they're on the back deck. I walk east of the house, climb a trio of wooden steps, and pass the seemingly never-used kitchen door on my way to the water side. They're seated in Adirondack chairs facing the ocean, both cradling steaming mugs, their profiles toward me. They make quite a picture in the morning sunshine, both lean and long-limbed, their postures relaxed, carefree even. Gives a whole new meaning to Southern Comfort.

Louisa twists in her chair as I approach, sends a slight wave in my direction, and then turns back to the Kydd to finish whatever she's been telling him. The Kydd's cheeks are flushed and I don't think it's because of the ocean wind. His attention to Louisa's story is absolute, the kind a private first-class might pay if he were included in a meeting of four-star generals on the eve of war. It's pretty clear that my arrival is lost on him.

Leaning over a small table between their chairs without missing a beat in her tale—something about childhood summers spent on Ocracoke, an island off the coast of North Carolina—Louisa fills a mug with black coffee, hands it to me, and points to the empty chair across from hers. I'm grateful for the coffee—it's my first cup of the day—but I decline the offer to sit. She doesn't seem to notice.

"And, of course, *there*," she continues, apparently still referring to the summer island of her youth, "a person can swim once in a while. The water actually warms up for a few months each year." She gestures toward the icy gray waves and shivers, then sets her mug on the table so she can pull her unbuttoned cardigan tight around her.

The Kydd laughs. "I know what you mean," he says. "I haven't been in salt water since I got here." He looks up at me for the first time today and shakes his head.

"Is that true?" I ask. The Kydd's been here for three summers—hot ones.

"Hell, yes, it's true." He plasters an incredulous expression on his face and points his coffee toward the water, as if I might not otherwise catch his drift. "You people are crazy to go swimming in that— even in August. It's too damned cold."

The Kydd looks a little annoyed. Apparently I'm

responsible for Cape Cod's failure to heat the Atlantic. I shift my attention to Louisa. "First of all," I tell her, "I'd like you to walk us through the events of last Sunday."

"But I did that on Friday," she says, wiping lipstick from the rim of her mug with a cloth napkin. "And yesterday, too. I told you everything."

"I know you did." I hand her file to the Kydd. "But today I want you to *walk* us through it—literally. Show us where you were, hour by hour."

"I was here. Aside from my morning at the club, I was home all day. You expect me to walk you from room to room?"

I nod. "That's exactly what I expect."

I also expect her to take us to Eastward Edge at some point, review the early-morning round of golf, the chitchat among the foursome. I don't mention any of that, though. We won't get that far today.

"Let's start in the driveway," I tell them both. "Retrace Louisa's steps from the moment she got home."

They exchange puzzled glances, but leave their chairs like a couple of compliant children.

Louisa looks over at the Kydd as they walk across the wooden deck ahead of me. She arches her perfect eyebrows, apparently wondering if he can shed any light on my peculiar request. He shrugs, pulls a legal pad from the file and a pen from his jacket pocket. The expression on his face says they'll just have to humor me.

And they will. It's not that I give a damn where Louisa took her midday shower or read her Sunday *Times*. But I've learned over the years that memory is a fragile, unpredictable thing. It can be blocked—or triggered—by any of the five senses. We're going to do everything we can to trigger Louisa Rawlings's memories today. Otherwise, it'll happen tomorrow. When Detective Lieutenant Mitch Walker does it for us.

Scarlett O'Hara would pine for nothing in Louisa Rawlings's quarters. Louisa apparently plucked her master suite straight from the blueprints of prewar Tara. Its pale yellow wallpaper is daintily flowered. The matching drapes are heavily ruffled. And the king-size bed is a four-poster, canopied and draped in lace. The bed is unmade, the sheer curtains drawn, the sheets and quilts a sea of tangled lilac.

Each bedside table wears a matching lilac skirt overlaid by a dainty white crocheted doily. Each doily has a cut-crystal vase centered on it. The vases hold dozens of long-stemmed pink roses, most barely open, a few in full bloom. Next to each vase sits an ivory candleholder with a single wick floating in scented oil—lavender, I think. It's an aromatic, pastel world in here.

There's a veranda, of course, facing the water. Louisa moves toward it, like a hummingbird to nectar, as soon as the three of us enter the room.

"Did you go out there when you got home from the club?" I ask.

She stops walking and turns to face me. "I did," she says, smiling. "I almost never come in here without going out there. I never tire of the view."

"Then let's do it now."

She shakes her head. "But I only went out for a couple of minutes last Sunday. I didn't even sit down."

"Then let's go out for a couple of minutes now," I tell her. "And we won't sit down this time, either."

She shrugs, looks over at the Kydd, and gestures toward the French doors. Ever the Southern gentleman, he complies. He fiddles with the locks for a few moments—there are two of them—then swings both doors open wide and moves aside. Louisa steps out first and I follow. Rhett Butler leans in the open doorway, his pen and legal pad at the ready.

Louisa clutches the wrought-iron railing and breathes in the salt air. "That's it," she says, looking back at me. "That's exactly what I did out here on Sunday. That's all of it."

I join her at the railing and point down to the floating dock. "Is this when you realized Herb had taken the *Carolina Girl* out?"

"No," she says. "I knew before I came into the house. I thought he probably had, given the glorious day, so I walked around back and checked."

I nod and make a mental note to repeat that walk with her before we finish. When I lean against the railing beside her, she turns her back to the view she never tires of and stares at me. She seems bored with this drill. And apparently she's done talking about this particular spot.

"I'm sorry," she says as if reading my mind. "But there's nothing more I can tell you."

"What did you do next?" I ask.

Her expression brightens and she stands up straighter. "I went to the Queen's Spa," she announces.

"The Queen's Spa?"

"Yes," she says, slipping past the Kydd and back inside. She directs our attention to a door on the east end of the main room. It's ajar. "This," she says, entering ahead of us, "is the Queen's Spa. I designed it myself."

I don't doubt it for a second. A space this size would house a family of four in more than a handful of countries. And the aggregate value of its contents would exceed the gross national product in a few more. Louisa Rawlings's signature is all over this room.

The ceiling is at least twelve feet high and from its center hangs a fan Louisa might have salvaged from the set of *Casablanca*. It rotates lazily above us, emitting a barely audible hum. Two feet below, a single wooden shelf traverses the perimeter of the room. Lush greenery cascades from it, in stark contrast to the white trim and the beige painted walls. Apparently Louisa Rawlings has a green thumb.

Well, of course she does.

Twin sinks with marble vanities face each other

from opposite ends of the room, each lit by two overhead, tulip-shaped lamps. The sinks host diving brass swans, each one flanked by matching faucets. The swans' beaks are open, apparently prepared to spew water into the basins at the crank of a handle. These are the cygnets, I realize after a moment. Their mother is in between them, along the waterside wall, similarly poised to fill the hot tub.

She's got quite a job. A six-foot oval encased in a massive marble deck, the tub is as effective an invitation to soak as porcelain can be. Candles of varying heights share space around it with dozens of vials of lotions, creams and oils. Just above the marble deck, the far wall showcases five inlaid diamond-shaped tiles, each featuring a delicately carved mollusk: distinct sand dollars at each end; a starfish, scallop, and moon snail nestled between them.

The Kydd brushes past me, crosses the room, and points into the tub as if it might be the Grand Canyon. "Look at this," he says, turning back and gesturing for me to join him. "It's four feet deep."

If our client weren't in the room, I'd break the news to the Kydd that we're working here.

"See these jets?" he continues. "They're all over the place." His grin suggests he thinks Louisa might grant him a lifetime easement on her spa.

Louisa smiles at the Kydd's enthusiasm. "Pity," she says. "I've only used it once."

"Once?" For some reason, this revelation makes me cross the room to join the Kydd, staring into the enormous marble-encased oval with him. When it comes to bathtubs, mine's a Model T, but I drive it every day anyhow. If I owned a Cadillac like this one, I might never get out.

Louisa laughs. "Don't worry," she says. "We've only lived here a month. I'll use it again. But I prefer the shower. So did Herb. He did say he'd like to try the hot tub sometime, though." She pauses and sends a small smile my way. "But he never got around to it."

Morning sunshine streams through the block-glass wall above the tub and shimmers against everything in its path: the brass hardware, the pale pink marble, the multicolored candles and vials. Even the floor, a pale oak, seems to glisten in the filtered light. Louisa crosses the room and leans against one of the vanities, beaming. She's pleased with her creation.

"Speaking of the shower," I say, "you took one when you got home from the club last Sunday?"

"Yes." She shakes her head, as if clearing it, reminding herself why we're all standing in her bathroom, and then she points to a frosted-glass enclosure opposite the tub.

The Kydd walks over and opens its door. I follow and we're both silent for a beat as we look inside. The entire bathroom in my cottage would fit easily into Louisa Rawlings's shower stall. A bench outlines its perimeter, and a panel of switches faces us from the wall below the showerhead.

"Look," the Kydd says, flipping a switch. "It's a steam room."

No sooner does he utter the words than a circular opening near us coughs out a puff of vapor. As if taking a cue, a half dozen other metallic circles cough in unison, again and again, filling the glassed enclosure with cloud after cloud of rising steam. The Kydd grins like a five-year-old at his first amusement park.

Louisa smiles at us, obviously amused by our fascination with her plumbing. "The steam," she says to me. "It does wonderful things for the complexion."

Enough of the Queen's Spa. Better to exit before our client starts sharing beauty tips. "To the sunroom next?" I ask her.

She nods and heads for the door. "With *The New York Times*," she says.

Louisa leaves the Queen's Spa and I start to follow, but I pause in the doorway to check on the Kydd. He's still playing with the steam.

"Shut it off," I tell him.

He actually pouts.

"And make a note," I add, "to pull the latest warrant cases."

The corners of his mouth droop farther and I don't blame him. Warrant cases multiply daily, it seems. No two searches or seizures are alike, and each case offers a new wrinkle on what law enforcement can—and can't—seize without that magic piece of paper. Warrant research needs to be updated constantly.

We're hoping we don't get to the point where we actually need it, of course. We'd like our talks with the Chatham police to remain cordial. We'd like Mitch Walker to perceive us as entirely cooperative, having nothing to hide. But we need to know before we start answering questions where we can legitimately draw the line. Just in case.

"I'm sorry," I tell the Kydd. And I mean it. "I know that kills what little was left of your weekend."

He looks almost grief-stricken for a moment, but then the dutiful associate in him takes over. He shrugs. "Weekend? What weekend? I don't have any plans. Hell, I can't remember the last time I had any plans. But I'm damned sure it was before I set up camp with you and Kimosabe."

The Kydd looks sad as he closes the steam room door, as if he's saying good-bye to an old friend. But then he brightens and points to a door across from it. "Look at this," he says, pushing it open. "A completely separate room for the throne. Can you believe it?"

Again the grin. I turn my back on him to follow Louisa, but then think better of leaving him to his own devices in the Queen's Spa. "Hey, Tonto," I call over my shoulder. "Saddle up and ride."

CHAPTER 12

The crush of tires on oyster shells draws Louisa to the beveled window above her kitchen sink. She lifts the muslin curtain away from the glass and then drops it almost at once. "Must be lunchtime," she says, turning to face the Kydd and me. "Anastasia's here."

Car doors slam and, instantaneously, a high-pitched, eardrum-piercing yelping begins. It takes on a regular rhythm as it nears the house: two short, one long. *Yip-yip-wail; yip-yip-wail.* "Oh good," Louisa adds, the corners of her glossy lips turning downward as her eyes roll up. "She brought the beast."

The front door opens and then slams. Heavy footsteps clomp toward us through the living room, lighter ones following a short distance behind. Louisa doesn't budge. She stays planted in the kitchen with us, leaning against the sink with her eyes raised to the heavens. It seems she's not particularly pleased about her Sunday-afternoon callers. She's in no hurry to greet them.

Anastasia strikes a pose in the kitchen doorway, one arm raised to the full height of the entry, "the beast" poking its diminutive head out from under her flowing black cape. She's a large woman, not as tall as Louisa, but much broader, bigger-boned. Her straight black hair is parted down the middle, early-Cher-style, and it hangs well past her buttocks. Her pallid complexion is unblemished and she likes eyeliner. Lots of it.

"Jeepers, creepers," the Kydd mumbles. I glare at him. He has the good sense not to finish his rhyme.

Louisa laughs. "My sentiments exactly," she says in a low voice. She turns a radiant smile toward the doorway, but her dark eyes don't participate. "Anastasia," she croons, "what a treat."

"Save it," Anastasia bellows in a full baritone, "for someone who gives a damn." She barrels into the kitchen and a slight, denim-clad fellow ambles in behind her. He wears narrow glasses and his wispy gray hair is pulled back into a skinny ponytail that hangs to the center of his shoulder blades. He's the beatnik boyfriend, no doubt; the about-to-be, on-the-verge, any-minute-now, runaway-best-selling-murder-mystery author.

Anastasia sets her pooch free on the kitchen floor. It's a miniature poodle, shaved bald except for black muffs above its paws and a matching pillbox hat. Jackie O would be flattered, no doubt. It scampers around the room, takes in the scent of each of us, and then scurries to the hat rack in the corner and lifts its leg.

"Oh for the love of God," Louisa says, closing her eyes against the sight. "Get that animal out of here."

"I'll take care of it," the beatnik volunteers at once. He rests a hand on Louisa's forearm, as if that might make her feel better. Louisa glares at his hand as if it's a branding iron, but the boyfriend doesn't notice; he's looking at the creature in the corner. "Lucifer," he singsongs, "bad, bad dog."

Bad, bad dog yawns and lies down on his stomach, his front paws stretched out toward us. He plans to stay awhile.

Louisa shuts her eyes again and the ponytailed boyfriend hustles to the opposite side of the kitchen. Without hesitating, he opens an end closet and finds a spray bottle of disinfectant and a roll of paper towels. It seems he's done this before.

Anastasia laughs, unties her long cape with a flourish and tosses it on the counter, next to the toaster, as if it belongs there. She's dressed entirely in black, from the high collar of her calf-length dress to the tips of her thick-soled, ankle-high boots. She settles on the edge of a stool across the counter from mine and begins removing her elbow-length gloves, one finger at a time, all the while examining the Kydd and me as if we're for sale.

"Marty Nickerson and Kevin Kydd," Louisa says. "This is Herb's daughter, Anastasia."

Anastasia has lost interest in our faces by the time the brief introductions are made. She's pulling her long gloves across her palm, looking into our open briefcases instead, as if something of hers might be in one of them.

"And that," Louisa continues, extending a hand toward the hat rack, "is Lance Phillips. Same as the screwdriver," she adds, "but no relation."

Lance waves at us, still on his knees wiping up the mess. "Pleasure," he mumbles.

Not so, apparently, for Anastasia. Her upper lip curls back when she looks at us again. "You're *lawyers*?" she asks. Her tone suggests the word is synonymous with *shysters*.

We both nod, guilty as charged.

She turns accusing eyes on Louisa and drops her gloves into her lap. She's quiet for a moment, pulling her lustrous locks over one shoulder, utter contempt displayed on her face. "My father is dead," she spits, "lost at sea. And his merry widow is talking to lawyers."

"Don't sputter, dear," Louisa answers. "It doesn't become you."

"Why are you talking to lawyers?" Anastasia continues. "Are you worried about *money*? Afraid there won't be enough to keep you in style, *Mrs. Rawlings*?"

"No one's worried about money, dear." Louisa's voice is even, her words measured, as if she's coaxing a toddler out of a tantrum. "There's plenty to go around."

Another set of tires crunches in the driveway and Louisa turns to lift the muslin curtain from the window above the sink once more. She smiles through the glass and then faces us again, but doesn't tell us who's here.

Anastasia gets up to see for herself. "Oh my!" she exclaims, pressing her fingertips to her cheeks in mock shock. She turns toward Louisa and glares. "What a surprise. The indelible husband."

Louisa laughs, seemingly oblivious to her stepdaughter's malignant stare. "Glen Powers is here," she says to the Kydd and me. "He's my ex-husband."

"*Ex*-husband?" Anastasia shouts the word, though she's standing almost on top of Louisa and only a few feet from the Kydd and me. Her hair billows around her like a shroud. "*Ex*-husbands disappear, don't they? Or at least take a little time off?"

Louisa doesn't react, so Anastasia tries her luck with the Kydd and me. "Not this guy," she tells us. "Not for a goddamned minute. She divorced this guy so she could marry my father . . ."

111

Anastasia points at us for emphasis, and I notice for the first time that her fingernails are extraordinarily long, painted the color of bruised plums.

". . . and what does *Powers* do?" she continues. "He takes her out to dinner." She pauses for a moment and leans on the counter, winded. "And we're not talking about a onetime event here," she adds. "He does it every month."

"Anastasia, you mustn't talk out of turn," Louisa says calmly. "It isn't ladylike."

"Every month," Anastasia repeats.

"The third Thursday of each month," Louisa says, dismissing Anastasia with a wave of her hand, "Glen and I get together for a bite to eat. Herb's partners hold a dinner meeting on that night each month, so he never minded. In fact, Herb rather liked Glen. They were both big on the boating scene. They got on quite well." She tosses her head toward Anastasia. "His prim and proper daughter, though, finds the whole thing scandalous."

"It's unnatural," Anastasia says. "It's sick."

"So Glen Powers never remarried?" I ask Louisa. These are the first words I've squeezed in since Anastasia arrived.

"He did," Louisa says, "a year or so after we divorced. But it didn't last."

Anastasia throws her arms in the air. "What a surprise! The pitiful man's still stuck on his first wife, the one who ditched him for the rich guy. The pitiful man takes her out to dinner whenever she'll

112

allow it. And the pitiful man's second marriage didn't last." She sends an exaggerated shrug to the Kydd and me. "Go figure."

The doorbell rings and the sounds of the front door opening and closing tell us the caller is letting himself in. Anastasia shakes her long locks. "Make yourself at home, why don't you?" she yells out.

Louisa closes her eyes and looks like she's praying for patience. She leaves her post at the sink and heads toward the living room, apparently eager to greet this particular guest. Glen Powers reaches the kitchen doorway before she does, though. "Louisa," he says, taking her hands in both of his, "I just heard. Good God, are you all right?"

Anastasia snorts and looks up at the ceiling. "All right?" she repeats, shaking her heavy tresses again. "Look at her. Does she seem broken up to you?"

Glen Powers doesn't let on he hears. Louisa leads him into the kitchen and introduces him to the Kydd and me. He offers each of us a firm handshake and then turns to the surly stepdaughter. "Anastasia," he says, "it's so nice to see you—as always."

She growls at him. It's a real one—guttural, menacing—but Powers seems unfazed; he doesn't even look at her. He scans the room instead, as if he expects to find someone else here. His eyes alight on the boyfriend, who's now holding Lucifer near the scene of the crime. "Lance," he says, giving him a short wave, "I knew you'd be in the neighborhood."

Lance returns the wave by lifting the dainty dog and it emits another *yip-yip-wail*.

Glen Powers turns back to Louisa. He's handsome, fifty-something, blue-eyed and sandy-haired, with a well-toned body that suggests it sees the inside of a gym a few times a week. "Let me help," he says. "I'm here for as long as it takes, staying at the Carriage House."

The Carriage House is an antique bed-and-breakfast near the center of Chatham and it's the ultimate in casual elegance. Even now, in mid-October, Glen Powers is lucky to get a room there. If it were July, he'd have had to book a year in advance.

"Let me help," he repeats. "What arrangements have been made so far?"

"Arrangements?" Louisa looks blank.

Anastasia smacks her maroon lips and steps closer to Glen. He backs up. "Hello-o-o?" she chants, her baritone down to a bass and her face too close to Louisa's. "When people die, it's customary in civilized societies to make *arrangements*. A wake? A memorial service?"

Louisa shakes her head. "But we haven't found Herb yet," she says. "We don't have his body."

"His body?" Anastasia plants her hands on her substantial hips and pivots toward the Kydd and me, her heavily outlined eyes opened unnaturally wide. "My father wanted to be cremated," she tells us. "The whole family knew that." She tosses her hair toward Louisa. "Even *her*."

"That's true," Louisa says, "but still." She shakes her head. "It seems like we should find him first."

"My father's been dead a week," Anastasia snaps at her. "And you haven't even *begun* to make arrangements?"

Louisa looks uncertain, as if she thinks perhaps Anastasia has a valid point, as if the idea of a funeral hasn't occurred to Louisa before now.

"Well, of course you haven't," Anastasia continues. She turns toward the Kydd and me, and a synthetic smile spreads across her face. "You've been *way* too busy commiserating with your *lawyers*."

Glen Powers clears his throat. "Maybe now's not a good time to discuss it," he says to Louisa. "Let's talk over dinner."

Louisa looks at the Kydd for a moment and then back at Glen, shaking her head. "Not tonight," she says. "I'm afraid I'm rather exhausted by all of this."

Anastasia laughs and turns toward Lance. "What did I tell you?" she demands. "It's a good thing we came down here. *We'll* have to take care of my father's arrangements. His waif of a wife is *way* too exhausted."

I can think of a lot of words to describe Louisa Rawlings. *Waif* isn't one of them.

Lance nods a silent agreement toward Anastasia, something I suspect he does often, and the beast yips again.

"Tomorrow, then," Glen says to Louisa. "I'll pick you up at seven."

"We'll see," she answers. "Let's talk in the afternoon." Her glance at me is almost imperceptible. "I have a rather busy morning."

Glen Powers seems eager to take his leave. He bids all of us good-bye, even Lucifer, and then heads out of the room far more quickly than he entered. "I'll see you out," Louisa says.

The Kydd turns to me as soon as they're gone. "I'd better get started on that research," he says. His eyes, though, send a more desperate message. Let's get the hell out of here, they scream. Fast.

I couldn't agree more. I've had about enough of *Family Feud* too. I nod at him and we both stand to repack our briefcases.

Lance and Lucifer remain stationed against the far wall as we pack up, Satan's namesake momentarily soothed by Lance's constant stroking. Anastasia strolls to the kitchen sink, where she yanks the curtain aside to watch Glen Powers and Louisa in the driveway. When a car door slams, she drops the curtain and shakes her shiny hair. "*That* guy," she says to no one in particular, "is a *special* kind of stupid."

CHAPTER 13

Monday, October 16

Harry's old Jeep sits alone in the office driveway when I arrive at eight o'clock. It looks worse than usual, as it often does on Mondays. Whenever he has a free Sunday, Harry four-wheels down Nauset Beach and stakes out a remote spot. He spends the day, the evening, and sometimes the wee hours of the next morning surf casting for stripers, blues, or whatever's biting that week. He went yesterday. The Jeep's mud flaps are sand-caked and the bottom half of its olive green chassis is white with the chalky residue of salt water.

The front office is empty. I leave my briefcase and jacket on one of the chairs and head for the kitchen in search of coffee. Harry's office door is open and he's laughing out loud on the telephone. Harry is one of the only people I know who's immune to Monday-morning malaise. I wave to him as I pass, fill my mug from the pot he's brewed, and return to lean in his doorway. He gestures for me to come in and sit.

That's more easily suggested than done. The two chairs facing his desk are piled high with files, legal pads, and photocopied cases. One is topped off with a crumpled deli bag and an empty chocolate milk carton, litter from a prior day's lunch. We all suffer from a chronic lack of administrative help in this office. Harry's case is critical.

I lean against his wooden bookcase instead. He tells the person on the other end of the line to forget it, he'll take his chances in court. He hangs up and laughs again. "She's a piece of work," he says.

Enough said. The person on the other end of the phone was Geraldine Schilling, Barnstable County's District Attorney. She's a piece of work by anybody's standards; a pain in the ass by Harry's. He must be feeling charitable this morning.

"She wants Rinky to do time," he reports. "Sixty days." He shakes his head at the telephone.

Rinky is Chatham's only homeless person and he's homeless by choice. He's a tortured soul who prefers the streets and the woods to the shelter repeatedly offered by locals. He also prefers the voices in his head to anyone else's conversation. Rinky rarely speaks to anybody the rest of us can see.

Court documents dub him Rinky Snow, but no one seems to know where the surname came from. I secretly harbor the notion that it stems from the stuff he sleeps on half the year.

"He could do worse," I tell Harry.

"Not in October, he couldn't."

Rinky has lived on Chatham's streets since his return from the Vietnam War in the mid-sixties. It didn't take long for the year-rounders to recognize his latent wounds. By unspoken agreement, we look the other way when Rinky spends the night in the woods on town-owned property, and when he drinks from a brown paper bag in public, and when he utters the occasional obscenity to an unsuspecting tourist.

Even the cops are in on the arrangement. They turn blind eyes to Rinky's antics too—unless it's winter. In winter they pick him up whenever they can, haul him in, and hold him as long as his transgression-of-the-moment allows. That way he won't freeze to death during our frigid winter nights. Come spring's thaw, they once again look the other way like the rest of us.

Harry's been representing Rinky for decades. Rinky's never done time as early as October, and Harry doesn't intend to let him start now. Hell, sixty days starting now barely taps into the cold season.

But Rinky's transgression-of-the-moment is more serious than usual. When two vacationing women approached him on Saturday night to ask for directions, he took a knife from under his coat and caressed its six-inch blade. As Harry sees it, Rinky didn't actually threaten the visitors—he simply exercised poor judgment in sharing his prized possession with them. The two women don't see it that way.

Of course, in Rinky Snow's universe he could just as easily have been brandishing a bayonet—or a banana.

Rinky will be arraigned later today, but he's not my concern at the moment. Harry will take good care of him, as usual. "Where the hell is the Kydd?" I ask.

Harry shrugs. "Haven't seen him. I thought maybe you two went straight to the station."

I shake my head. "We're not going to the station. We're meeting Walker here. At ten." I lean forward and look out the window to see if the Kydd's truck has pulled in yet. It hasn't.

"Walker agreed?" Harry asks.

"Agreed to what?"

He smiles up at me. "Agreed to meet here?"

I'm distracted. Harry's amused by that. So now I'm annoyed. "Of course he agreed. Why wouldn't he?"

Harry's smile broadens, but he says nothing. I know what he's thinking. Mitch Walker agreed—at least in part—because he knows Louisa Rawlings is a force to be reckoned with. Walker has met her only once, but with Louisa, once is enough. Besides, he knows where she lives and that means he has a pretty good handle on her net worth. Money matters, especially at the earliest stages of a criminal investigation.

I decide to ignore Harry's apparent amusement. I've no interest in discussing Louisa Rawlings's many assets with him.

"The Kydd picked a hell of a day to sleep in," I say as I head out of his office.

"Don't worry," he answers my back. "He's done your warrant research."

"How do you know that?" I turn and lean in the doorway again.

"He was here yesterday," Harry says. "A man on a mission."

"Yesterday? I thought you went fishing yesterday."

"I did. But not until late afternoon. I stopped in here first for an hour or so to check messages and pick up a little." He sweeps the room with one arm, as if he might have a shot at a job with Merry Maids.

I laugh out loud. I can't help it. It's scary to think this is the *after*-cleanup picture.

He frowns when I look back at him, apparently insulted. "Anyway," he says, "the Kydd was already working when I got here and he was still hard at it when I left. He said he would be tied up last night. Wanted to get the job done by the end of the day."

This information should make me feel better. But for some reason I can't articulate, it doesn't.

"And he looked like the future of civilization depended on the results of his research," Harry continues. "So I think you can relax."

I'm not relaxed. Harry's news unsettles me. The Kydd made a point of telling me he had no plans. But so what? Plans develop sometimes. And why the hell should I care anyhow?

Harry rests his head against the back of his tall leather chair and looks up at the ceiling for a moment. "You know," he says, pointing his pen at me, "I think maybe the Kydd has found himself a woman."

"A what?"

"A woman," he repeats, laughing. "You've heard of the species?"

I stand up straight in the doorway. As usual, my stomach races ahead of my brain.

"Think about it," he continues, smiling and tapping the pen in his palm. "Big plans for last night. Working like hell so he could keep them. Later to the office than usual this morning. I smell a romance brewing."

I'm speechless.

Harry winks at me.

I don't wink back. The Kydd's red pickup—parked in Louisa Rawlings's driveway early yesterday—pops into my head. Morning dew undisturbed.

Harry chuckles. "Maybe my offer to hook him up with a good-looking inmate got to him, scared him into finding a sweetheart on his own."

Now I see different scenes: the Kydd matter-of-factly negotiating the hardware on the double doors of Louisa's veranda; his familiarity with the steam room switches in the Queen's Spa.

I force myself to answer Harry. "Maybe you're right," I tell him. But I hope like hell he's wrong. And it's not because I begrudge the Kydd a love life.

I hurry back to the front office, grab my briefcase and jacket, and head out the door. Harry's wrong, I tell myself. And so am I. It's as simple as that. We're just plain wrong.

The lean red fox in the road ahead hesitates when my Thunderbird speeds toward him and then he darts back into the bushes he came from. He's staring after the car when I check the rearview mirror, his head and neck sticking tentatively into the road. He lifts his aristocratic snout in the air as he reemerges, apparently unhappy about riffraff in the neighborhood. *Slow down,* I tell myself. Even the wildlife deems this errand ridiculous.

And it is. The Kydd knows better than to get involved with a client. And what interest would Louisa Rawlings have in a boy little more than half her age? For God's sake, she's old enough to be his mother. Hell, she's old enough to be his big brother's mother too.

My head hurts.

But my stomach feels worse. It knots when I pull into the Rawlingses' driveway. The Kydd's red pickup is here, right where it was yesterday, roof and hood dew covered. Its windows are fogged, just as they were yesterday, and tiny dew-fed rivers once again trickle down the misty glass.

The front door of Louisa's house is closed, but predictably unlocked, and I barge in as if I'm a one-woman SWAT team. From the foyer, I hear the steady pelting of water in the first-floor shower. I pause for just a second—haste is often an effective substitute for courage—and then crack open the door to the master suite.

Apparently Louisa got first dibs on the Queen's Spa. The Kydd is ensconced in her king-size bed, leaning against a mountain of pillows, the lilac sheets pulled up to his stomach. He's naked above the sheets, one arm draped over Pillow Mountain, his hand pressed against a bedpost, a lit cigarette dangling between his fingers. I didn't know he smoked.

He jumps about a foot and a half when the door squeaks.

"Jesus Christ, Marty. What the hell are you doing here?" He bolts upright in the bed, yanks the sheets up to his chest, and damn near drops his cigarette underneath them in the process.

"What am *I* doing here?" I find it hard to believe we're having this conversation. "What am *I*

124

doing here? That's not *really* the question, is it, Kydd?"

He says nothing for a moment, stares down at the sheets he's clutching as if he's never seen them before, and then returns his gaze to me. His expression suggests he's genuinely surprised to realize he's not wearing a suit. "Please," he says finally, swallowing hard and pointing toward the bathroom door. "Give me a minute. I'll meet you outside."

"You'll meet me *in*side," I tell him. No need to invite the neighbors to this gathering. There aren't any neighbors at the moment, of course. But still. "In the sunroom," I add.

He nods like a bobble-head doll. He'd agree to meet me in Hades right now if it'd get me out of Louisa Rawlings's boudoir. He throws his long legs over the side of the bed farthest from me, careful to keep the sheets pulled up above his hips.

"And Kydd."

"What?" He twists back toward me, then jumps up and does a little dance behind the sheets. He really did drop his cigarette this time. "What?" he repeats.

"Don't forget your goddamned pants."

"Are you out of your mind, Kydd?" I slam the sunroom doors and don't wait for an answer. It's pretty clear that he is. "She's a client, for Christ's sake."

"But she won't be," he says. "Not after today."

"What in God's name are you talking about? You're not making any sense." I don't normally hiss, but it comes naturally at the moment.

The Kydd's wearing faded blue jeans and a short-sleeved undershirt. He's barefoot and beltless. "Marty," he says, his tone suggesting this is nothing more than a minor misunderstanding, "Louisa didn't have anything to do with her husband's death."

"Oh, really?"

"Really."

"This is your professional opinion?"

"It is," he says, his grin not nearly sheepish enough.

I throw my hands in the air.

"Marty," he tries again, "she didn't. And it's obvious she didn't. Mitch Walker will see that as soon as he talks with her this morning. That will be the end of this whole damned thing. She won't be a client anymore."

The sunroom doors open. Enter Louisa, elegant as ever, even with wet hair. She's in a pale blue dressing gown—satin. It hangs to her ankles, clings to each curve along the way. "Marty," she says, sounding genuinely happy to see me. "Good morning."

Good morning? Has the world gone tilt?

"Oh," she says, looking from the unshaven, almost-dressed Kydd to me. She seems to recall—slowly—the connection between the two of us.

126

"Oh, dear," she adds after a pause. "This is awkward."

"No," I tell her. "We passed *awkward* a long time ago, Louisa."

The doorbell. This is swell. With any luck it's a delegation from the Board of Bar Overseers, preferably with a *Cape Cod Times* reporter in tow. A photographer would add a nice touch too. This is a Kodak moment if ever there was one.

Louisa turns to answer the bell, but she hesitates at the sunroom doors. "Perhaps you should wait here, Kevin," she says to the Kydd.

He nods.

"*Kevin?*" I repeat, gaping at him.

"It *is* my name," he says.

I leave him standing shoeless in the sunroom and follow Louisa's blue satin sashay toward the persistent chimes of the doorbell. My stomach is already knotted, but the knots develop knots of their own when I see that she's headed toward the kitchen door. It's a Cape Codder who's come to call, a local, and whoever it is has given up on the doorbell and has started knocking. Hard.

Louisa's kitchen door has a dead bolt at eye level, but apparently it isn't engaged. The persistent knocks of the visitor push the door partially open as we approach. Louisa gets to it ahead of me and pulls it open the rest of the way. Her polite smile suggests it's Avon calling. "Can I help you?" she says.

"Mrs. Rawlings?"

I freeze. I know that voice. It's Tommy Fitz-patrick, Chatham's Chief of Police.

"Yes," Louisa replies. "That's me."

"You're under arrest," he says, "for the murder of your husband, Herbert Andrew Rawlings."

CHAPTER 14

Tommy Fitzpatrick looks only slightly surprised when I step into the doorway beside Louisa. He stands on the deck, warrant in hand, Detective Lieutenant Mitch Walker at his side. They're the same height, and in the glare of the morning sunshine they look like uniformed negatives of each other: the Chief fair-skinned and strawberry blond; Mitch Walker swarthy and dark-haired. The Chief's car sits in the driveway, engine running and lights swirling. Two cruisers idle behind it, a pair of troopers in each.

Mitch Walker recites Miranda warnings at Louisa and the Chief volunteers the warrant to me.

I take it, though I know I needn't bother. Tommy Fitzpatrick does it right—always. He wouldn't have come here this morning unless one of his minions had jumped through all the proper procedural hoops beforehand. And my involvement in the case has nothing to do with it. Tommy would do it right even if the accused were *pro se,* representing herself.

Louisa's smile has vanished. She turns away from Mitch Walker, ignores his monologue. Her dark, moist eyes dart from the Chief to me, panic beginning to set in. "There must be some misunderstanding," she says, leaning into the doorknob with one hand, fingering her slender throat with the other. Her voice is raspy, barely more than a whisper.

No one answers. Instead, Tommy Fitzpatrick faces me. "Taylor Peterson hauled the body in at about four this morning," he says, "with his first codfish catch of the day."

Louisa gasps and I put my hands up, signaling her to be quiet. She covers her mouth with a fist.

"Peterson phoned the station," the Chief continues. "We met him at the Fish Pier a few hours ago."

I nod. Taylor Peterson is an old friend of mine. We went through grade school and high school together. He's a fifth-generation Chathamite, a quiet man whose family has always made its living at sea. I wonder if any of his ancestors ever hauled in a comparable catch.

The Chief takes a deep breath. "We had plenty

of company," he says, "even at that hour. The Coast Guard boarded and a crew from the ME's office was waiting; they did the post right away."

My throat closes. A postmortem posthaste. Only the DA can make that happen. Geraldine Schilling must think she's looking at a real one. And when Geraldine sees a real one, she sinks her teeth in like a pit bull. No doubt the ugly details are spelled out in the warrant I'm holding, but I don't read it. Not yet.

The Chief still faces me, but he tilts his head toward Louisa. "I'm guessing your client would like to get dressed before we go."

I nod again.

The Chief turns and signals to the first cruiser in the driveway and a petite female officer emerges from the passenger side. We stand mute until she joins us—even Mitch Walker has finally fallen silent—and then the Chief arches his pale eyebrows at me. He's asking if I'd like to be the one to tell my client she'll have company while she dresses. If not, he'll do it for me.

"Louisa," I tell her, "Officer . . ."

I know this cop's name but it escapes me at the moment, so I check the narrow silver badge on the pocket of her long-sleeved navy blue shirt. Young. It's hard to believe I forgot that one. She looks like she's about twelve. "Officer Young will go with you and stay in the room while you change. It's standard procedure."

Louisa sizes up the freckle-faced policewoman and then turns her wide eyes back to me. Her expression says I must be joking. Little does she know. In the world of indignities that awaits her, this one is minuscule.

"Just do it," I tell her. "Go get dressed. And keep your mouth shut."

The Chief signals to the idling cruisers once more and, simultaneously, they cut their engines. Officer Young's partner steps out from the driver's side of the first car, two more male uniforms from the second. I check the last page of the warrant as they cross the deck and approach the kitchen door. I find what I knew I would find: they have judicial authority to search the premises.

I step back so they can enter. The Chief and Mitch Walker come inside first, the trio of uniforms in single file behind them. The last one in deposits an evidence crate just inside the door and each officer takes a pair of gloves, a fistful of bags, and a black marker from it. With a silent gesture, the Chief directs each of them to a different section of the house. I check their name tags to refresh my memory as they receive their assignments: Stahley to the second floor; Glover to the foyer and living room; Holt to the sunroom and kitchen.

The sunroom.

Officer Holt's hand is on the doorknob before I can speak. Not that I have a damned thing worth saying anyhow. He opens the door, then stops cold.

He sends a surprised glance over his shoulder to the Chief, the faintest hint of a smile coming to his lips, and then stares into the sunroom again.

"Working," the Kydd mumbles from inside. "I'm, uh, working here."

If the place weren't crawling with cops, I'd strangle the Kydd now instead of later.

Tommy Fitzpatrick crosses the length of the kitchen and stands behind Officer Holt. Mitch Walker follows.

The Kydd clears his throat. "Gentlemen," he says, as if he'd been expecting them.

All three of them nod at him. "Mr. Kydd," they say, almost in unison.

The Kydd emerges from the sunroom, careful not to brush against Officer Holt as he slips past. "I was, uh, working in there," he says again.

All three cops take him in from head to toe: his stubbled chin; his beltless pants; his bare feet.

Now it's my turn to clear my throat. I tap the warrant I'm holding when the Kydd looks my way.

"Ah," he says, as if the universe makes sense to him now. "I can, uh, finish up later." He gestures toward the sunroom as if he's trying to sell the place. "Please," he says to Officer Holt, "go right ahead. I'll just, um . . ."

He looks over at me and I glare back.

"I'll just wait right here. That's what I'll do."

That's what he'll do, all right. I head back toward the kitchen door and out to the deck, leaving the Kydd to deal with law enforcement on his own.

Tommy Fitzpatrick is right behind me. I figure since Officer Holt is searching the sunroom, Mitch Walker must be enjoying a little private time with the Kydd. Mitch probably hasn't had this much fun in years. I remind myself again to strangle the Kydd as soon as time permits.

The Chief leans on the deck railing beside me, both of us looking out at the crashing waves. Winds are brisk today, seas rough. "Have you read it?" he asks.

He's referring to the warrant.

"Not yet," I tell him. "Want to give me a sneak preview?"

He leans down a little farther, clasps his hands together and rests on his forearms. "Your client's story didn't check out," he says. "She lied to us about where she was last Sunday."

I keep my eyes on the waves and wait.

"She did go to her club," the Chief continues, "and she played nine holes, just as she said. But she didn't eat. She never made it to the grill."

I turn from the water and look at him.

"Seems she had something else to do," he adds.

Tommy Fitzpatrick knows me well enough to know I won't react. He looks out at the waves and apparently decides to move on. "Official cause of death is drowning," he says to the pounding surf.

I nod, knowing there's more.

"Secondary to head trauma," he says.

I feel a tiny surge of hope. Head trauma isn't inconsistent with a boating accident. It doesn't necessarily rule out suicide either.

"The body was bound," Tommy adds. "Wrists and ankles."

I'm embarrassed more than anything else. Embarrassed by my millisecond of hope. I should know better by now.

CHAPTER 15

Officer Glover lays a hand on top of Louisa's head as she lowers herself into the backseat of the cruiser. She swats at him. "Don't touch me," she says, enunciating her Southern-speak precisely. "Keep your hands to yourself, young man."

Glover backs away from her, looks first at the Chief and then at Mitch Walker. Mitch pops a stick of gum into his mouth and elbows the Kydd. "She's a feisty one, hey, Counselor?" He grins and holds out the yellow pack, offering the Kydd a stick of Juicy Fruit.

The Kydd shakes his head. He looks pale, a little bit sick.

The troopers finished the evidence search quickly, filling their crate with items of little significance, as far as I could tell. The notable exception, of course, was Herb Rawlings's handwritten apology. Officer Holt brought the solitary page from the sunroom, bagged it, and delivered it to the Chief instead of the evidence crate. Tommy Fitzpatrick scanned it quickly at first, then read it over more carefully, and then stared across the room at me. He asked nothing.

The Commonwealth's lab technicians weren't so speedy. The duo arrived in time to put an end to my oceanside conversation with the Chief and then spent hours dusting, brushing, and photographing. They scrutinized the entire house, even spent a good chunk of time in the basement. Their efforts struck me as overkill, given that Herb Rawlings perished at sea. The two huddled periodically, compared notes, and then continued their work. Unlike the Chatham cops, the state guys were secretive about the items they confiscated, carrying lidded crates out to their van every half hour or so. They didn't wrap it up until more than three hours after they'd arrived. And by then, I was worried.

The Chief starts toward his car and slaps the Kydd on the back as he passes. "The DA wants to arraign this afternoon," he says to me.

The DA seems to be in quite a hurry. The autopsy, the arrest, and the arraignment all in the space of twelve hours. At this rate, I expect she'll schedule the trial to begin next Monday.

"At open session," the Chief continues, "unless an earlier slot opens up."

Open session starts at four o'clock each day in Judge Leon Long's courtroom. No matter what case is in progress before him, Judge Long adjourns at four to tend to what he calls the "untidy" business of the system: matters no one put on the regular docket because no one saw them coming. Matters like Rinky Snow. And Louisa Rawlings.

The two cruisers back out of the driveway, lights active but sirens mute. Louisa stares straight ahead from the backseat of the lead car. She's wearing a calf-length beige trench coat, a matching broad-rimmed hat, nylons, and heels. Teardrop diamonds glisten on her earlobes. Her jaw is rigid, her eyes hidden behind Versace sunglasses.

The Chief backs up next. Mitch Walker is in the passenger seat, still grinning and chewing his gum. He waves to the Kydd. The Kydd stares at him but doesn't wave back.

Just like that, they're gone. We stand silent for a moment in the oyster-shell driveway, the Kydd seemingly oblivious to the fact that I'm still planning to strangle him.

"Now where were we," I ask, "before we were so rudely interrupted?"

He stares at me, blank.

"Oh, I know." I feign a sudden recollection.

"You were offering your opinion—your professional opinion, I believe it was—about the course this case is certain to follow."

His eyes move to his feet—his bare feet.

"Any other opinions you'd like to share?"

He takes a deep breath, looks up at me again, and shakes his head. "What do we do now?" he asks.

I should tell him that *we* don't do anything now, that *we* no longer work on this case, that *we* disqualified ourselves the minute *we* got involved with the client.

But I can't. There's more to be done than one person can do. And most of it should've been done yesterday. I need help and, as always, the Kydd is it.

"First of all," I tell him, "we establish a few ground rules."

He nods emphatically. He knows what's coming.

"*If* she's lucky enough to be back in her own home at the end of the day, you aren't to be anywhere near the place."

"I know," he says, still nodding.

"You don't set foot on this property again unless I'm with you."

"Okay." He stares at his feet.

"And no matter where she is, you act as her lawyer, nothing else."

"I get it."

"Every word that passes between you two had better be about the case. Nothing else."

He looks up at me. "I get it," he says again. "I swear I do."

His eyes tell me he does.

"Marty," he says, "would you do me a favor?"

"A *favor*?" He's out of his mind.

He swallows hard. "Would you not mention this to Harry?"

Harry. Another problem. I'm silent for a few seconds, as if I'm thinking it over, but I'm not. I already know I won't tell Harry. Questions about my motive would plague me if I did.

"If he sees anything between the two of you that makes him ask the question, I won't lie," I tell the Kydd. "But I won't bring it up either."

"Thanks," he says. "So what do we do now?"

"We split up. You head to the courthouse. Get into lockup if you can. Nobody questions her. Nobody talks to her. She doesn't utter a word. Not even to the janitor."

He nods. He knows this drill. He's done it before.

"And call me if it looks like arraignment will happen before four," I add. "I'll keep my cell turned on."

"Where will you be?" he asks.

"At the Fish Pier. I want to have a word with Taylor Peterson and his crew, if I can find them." I fish my keys from my pocket and head for the Thunderbird.

When I back up, the Kydd is planted right where

I left him. He makes me think of Lot's wife, after she looked back at Sodom and turned into a pillar of salt. I stop in front of him and roll down my window. "Before you head to lockup, Kydd, remember the rules."

He squares his shoulders in the morning sunshine, no doubt bracing for a continuing lecture on the Canons of Professional Conduct.

"Lockup's a lot like the corner grocery store," I tell him instead. "No shirt. No shoes. No service."

CHAPTER 16

It's one o'clock by the time I park in the upper lot of
the Chatham Fish Pier. This morning's sunshine has
taken a powder and it seems more like twilight here
than midday. I get out of the Thunderbird and the
sky rumbles, fair warning of what lies not far
ahead. Out over the Atlantic, a single sword of
lightning stabs the horizon, Mother Nature's version of the Nike logo. And as if on cue, large globes
of rainwater land on my face and hands.

Sheets of Chatham fog roll in from the roiling
ocean as I hurry down the steep hill to the lower lot.
Parking here is officially by permit only, unofficially
for trucks only. The lot is packed with pickups, old

and new, pampered and trashed. Their beds are laden with stacks of empty fish totes, mounds of entangled nets, and coils of thick black chain. And, though the National Dairy Association would almost certainly object, more than a few of them sport bumper stickers that ask the all-important question: *Got bait?*

A few large box trucks are down here too, backed up to the dock, their rear double doors wide open. Two belong to wholesale fish buyers, the other to a commercial ice supplier. Guys in heavy hooded sweatshirts under orange oilskin overalls load and unload, using nothing but pure brawn. I recognize a couple of the younger guys from Luke's crowd; they should be hauling textbooks through the hallways of the high school instead.

Taylor Peterson's boat, *Genesis*, is one of a half dozen commercial fishing vessels tied up at the dock. I use the pier's wooden pilings to steady myself as I lower onto its deck. Two bearded crewmen sit on inverted bait buckets, mending nets. They have a six-pack of Coors on the deck between them, an open bottle next to each bucket. They look up when I arrive, but say nothing, as if middle-aged women in suits climb aboard all the time. But then again, I remind myself, these are the guys who hauled in a corpse with this morning's first codfish catch. On the list of the day's surprises, I'm a distant second at best.

"Taylor here?" I ask.

One of them moves his hands, net and all, toward an opening in the center of the deck. "Down below," he says. "Captain's down below."

"You press?" the other one asks. "Captain doesn't talk to press."

Well, that's the first good news I've heard today. "No," I assure him. "I'm not press."

They both lower their long beards to their chests and return to their mending. I have their blessings, I guess. I can go below.

Taylor is seated at a makeshift table, an upside-down brown wooden fish crate stacked on top of a larger upside-down green plastic one. There's an open porthole behind him, salty wet wind gusting through it, but still the odor of codfish guts almost overpowers me as I reach the bottom of the ladder. Taylor looks up as I semi-stand in the cramped hold, a small but genuine smile spreading across his weathered face. "Marty," he says, his dark eyes amused, "something told me I'd run into you today."

I laugh, realizing I've sunk to a lifetime low. Dead bodies now herald my social calls.

"Or your partner," Taylor adds.

"I drew the short straw on this one," I tell him.

"Pull up a bucket," he says, tipping backward on his.

I find an empty white one in the corner, flip it over, and wipe my hand across its bottom, hoping for the best. Gives a whole new meaning to bucket seats. I settle across from Taylor at the makeshift table and realize its surface is covered with nautical charts. But those aren't what he's been studying. On top of them, neatly lined up side by side, are four Polaroids. I scoot my bucket chair closer to Taylor's, so I can look at them right side up. And I don't need to ask what—or who—I'm looking at.

The first photograph is one of Herb Rawlings's body, nude and horribly bloated, surrounded by hundreds of enormous, glistening silver codfish. Their bug-eyed expressions suggest they're somewhat shocked to find Herb in their midst. The second is a snapshot of his corpse too, but in this one he's been moved away from the rest of the catch, quarantined, and the handiwork of the bottom feeders can be seen on his extremities. The third and fourth shots are close-ups: one of Herb's tightly tied wrists, the other of his similarly bound ankles.

Taylor shakes his head and chuckles a little. "Now there's something you don't see every day," he says.

It occurs to me that I'm looking at something else you don't see every day: Taylor Peterson sitting still. Taylor is one of the hardest-working commercial fishermen in town, always has been, even when we were in high school. He's not staring at these pictures because he's got nothing else to do.

"What is it?" I ask him.

"What's what?"

I tap the fish-crate table near the photographs. "What bothers you?"

He lowers the front edge of his bucket chair, stares down at the Polaroids, and then looks back up at me, shaking his head. "I'm not a detective," he says.

"I know that," I tell him. "If you were, you wouldn't be talking to me."

He nods, acknowledging the point, and pulls the two close-up shots to the edge of the fish crate closest to us. "These," he says. "These bother me."

I wait. Taylor Peterson knows me well enough to know I won't leave until he tells me why.

"The rope," he says, pointing to the wrist shot. "It's a six-thread sinking pot warp."

"What's it called in the English-speaking world?"

He laughs. "It's a blend of polypropylene and Dacron," he says, "so it's also known as poly-dac." He takes a knife and a roll of black electrical tape from the pocket of his oilskins, then reaches up to a coil of rope hanging from a nail overhead. He cuts off an eight-inch length and binds one end with the tape. "It's this," he says, handing it to me. "Fishermen's rope. You'll find it on every commercial boat in the harbor."

The rope is a plait of three separate cords, woven together the way some women braid their hair. I unravel it and realize that each cord is actually a collection of dozens of finer strands, all but two of them white. A red and a black stand out in the middle section.

Taylor reaches over and fingers the innermost strands of the center cord. "Feel those," he says, and I do. They're white like most of the others, but the texture is different, coarser.

"That's the polypropylene," he says. "It floats."

"It floats," I repeat.

"Unless," Taylor continues, reaching over to finger the ends of my unraveled rope, "it's embedded in this much Dacron."

"And then it doesn't float," I venture. "It sinks."

He nods. "That's why it's the fishermen's rope. It's got the strength of the poly at its core, the abrasion resistance of the Dacron on its exterior, and the right ratio to allow the Dacron to override the buoyancy of the poly."

"So it sinks," I repeat. "And that's why it's called a sinking . . ."

"Pot warp," he finishes for me.

"Are we talking about lobster pots?"

"Very good," he says, looking every inch the distinguished professor.

"Well, that makes sense," I tell him. "Herb Rawlings—the dead guy—probably had the rope on board. He had a few lobster pots out. Nothing commercial. A family license."

Taylor snaps his fingers. That piece of information seems to be significant. "Okay," he says, pointing at me, "then that explains the rope. And ten bucks says he kept his pots in the channel."

He did. Louisa said so. "How did you know that?" I ask Taylor. Lobster pots are all over Cape Cod waters. Herb Rawlings's pots could have been anywhere.

"This," he says. He puts the other close-up shot, the one of the dead man's ankles, on top of the wrists shot. "Look at the free end of the rope," he tells me.

Herb Rawlings's ankles are bound tightly in this photo with what I now know is poly-dac, just as his wrists were in the last one. The ankle poly-dac, though, has what appears to be a thin cable attached to its end. And something that looks like the eye portion of a hook and eye attached to that.

"What is it?" I ask Taylor.

"You can't really tell from the photograph," he says. "But I got a good look at the whole apparatus before they carted him away. This strip"—Taylor uses a chewed-up pencil to point at the narrow cable in the photo—"is a plastic-jacketed wire. It would have been used to attach the body to something heavy, to weigh it down."

"Like what?"

He shrugs. "Tough to say. This harbor is full of equipment that could weigh a man's body down for the next century. It could've been just about anything. A mushroom, a trawl anchor, hell, even a decent length of sweep chain would do it."

"But I thought it was the Dacron that sank."

He smiles and shakes his head. "The Dacron

makes the rope sink," he says. "It wouldn't hold a body down."

I should've figured that much out for myself, of course. I'm lost, so I decide to move on for a minute. Sometimes that helps. "And what's this?" I ask, pointing to the little eyelet on the end.

"That's a pop-up," he says. "Or part of one anyhow."

I'm in a vocabulary class, it seems. "Help me here," I tell Taylor. "To me, a pop-up is one of the little creatures that jumped off the storybook page when Luke was a toddler."

He laughs. "Well, to us," he says, "us fisher types, a pop-up is a TFR—a timed float release." He smiles at me and tugs at his short, dark beard. He knows I don't know what the hell he's talking about. He also knows I desperately want to.

"Spill," I tell him, "or I'll be unavailable the next time one of your crewmen calls from lockup after the barrooms close."

He laughs again, harder. "Whoa," he says, "take it easy. That's my livelihood you're talking about. Them's fightin' words."

I rest my forearms on the fish tote and wait.

"TFRs," he says, "are underwater timers. They have a lot of uses, but around here they're most often used to hide gear."

"Hide gear?"

"Right," he says. "If you've got traps set in the channel, say, and you're not going to check them for a few days, you can use TFRs to hold the buoys and the lines underwater for that long. From the surface, no one can tell where your traps are."

"So no one can steal your catch?"

He shrugs. "Some guys use them for that reason," he says. "Poaching happens. But the bigger concern—in the channel, anyhow—is traffic. The volume of boat traffic out there is so high that gear gets taken out by accident all the time. And when that happens, you lose more than your catch. You've got to replace the damned gear."

I shake my head. "But if no one else can tell where your traps are, how can you?"

"You can't," he says, "until the TFRs let go and your buoys pop up."

I'm still lost and the look on Taylor's face tells me he knows it. "Stay with me," he says. "I can explain."

He grabs a coffee can from the shelf behind him and roots through it. "This," he says, handing me a small metal gadget, "is a pop-up. Just like the poly-dac, you'll find a bunch of those in a bunch of different sizes on just about every boat in the harbor."

This one is a little bigger than my thumb, a pewter-colored barrel with an eyelet on either end.

"If I'm not going to check my traps for a week," he says, "I can use one of these on each of them. I attach one end of it to the trap, the other to the buoy. The weight of the trap holds the buoy—and the lines—down. My gear sits on the ocean floor, out of traffic, for the week."

"And then?"

"And then the pop-up releases," he says. "It lets go in the middle and my buoy floats to the surface when I want it to."

"It's accurate?"

"You bet it is," he says. "It's a little more complicated than I'm making it sound, though. Water temperature plays a part too—"

"Please," I interrupt. "Keep it simple. Remember your audience."

He smiles at me. "The bottom line is, if I know the size of the TFR that was used and the average water temperature for the time period we're talking about, I can be out there in time to watch the gear float to the surface."

I'm quiet for a minute, still fingering the little metal device.

"They come in different sizes," Taylor says, "for different durations. Two-day, five-day, seven-day, you name it."

I look up at him. I still don't get it.

"That's a seven-day," he says, pointing to my pop-up. "And so is this." He uses the pencil again and taps the photo of Herb Rawlings's ankles. "But this is just one end of it. It would've let go in the middle, remember. The other end is still attached to whatever held the guy down there for a week."

"Taylor, please, I still don't understand. Can you

just tell me what you're thinking and why?" I'm starting to worry about time. My head aches. And I've got to escape these codfish guts.

"I'm just about there," he says. "But I have a question for you first."

"Just one?"

He shrugs. "For now. Do you know anything about where this guy was attacked? Whether he was on land or sea?"

I shake my head. Until this morning, I'd assumed that whatever happened to Herb Rawlings happened at sea. But this morning's discovery changed that, I realize now. "I don't have a clue," I tell Taylor.

"Okay," he says, "then here's what we do know." He points to the little gadget in the photograph, the used version of the one I'm still fingering. "That pop-up did what it was supposed to do," he says.

My pulse quickens a little as the pieces of what Taylor's been telling me start to meld. "Go on," I tell him. "Please."

"So somebody went to great lengths to hide a body," he says, "but secured it to the ocean floor with a device that's specifically designed to let it go after seven days."

"Don't stop," I tell him. "I'm with you."

He leaves his seat and starts pacing, hunched over, tugging at his beard. "There are two possibilities, I guess. But only one makes sense."

"Nothing makes sense to me right now, Taylor, so tell me both."

"Theoretically," he says, "it's possible that someone clobbered the guy on land, loaded him onto the boat, and then motored out to the Great South Channel to dump him."

"Theoretically," I repeat. "Why just theoretically?"

"Because to do that," Taylor answers, "whoever it was would have to know boats. And he'd have to know a hell of a lot about these waters. Because he'd have to be able to negotiate the cut."

The cut is a treacherous stretch off the coast of Chatham that keeps the Coast Guard's helicopter rescue team busy year-round. It's redefined every time a winter storm pummels the coastline; every time the beaches and sandbars get rearranged; every time a waterway opens up where none existed before.

"And anybody who knows how to negotiate the cut," Taylor points at my pop-up again, "would know a TFR when he sees one. He'd sure as hell know better than to try to hide a body with it."

"And the other possibility?" I'm pretty sure I know what's coming.

"Simple," he says. "The now-dead guy was alive and well when he left the dock. He motored out to the Great South Channel himself. And *then* he bought the farm. Whoever did him in was on board. Someone he knew."

"And someone who *didn't* know the nautical

world," I add. "Someone who didn't know a damned thing about pop-ups."

Taylor tilts his head to one side. "Looks that way to me," he says. He stops pacing and eases back onto his bait bucket. "One thing we know for sure," he adds. "The dead guy surfaced on schedule."

CHAPTER 17

Leon Long has been a Barnstable County Superior Court judge for two decades. Other judges of that tenure might claim to have seen it all. Not Leon. He's fond of telling anyone who'll listen that he hasn't seen anything yet, that he's just getting started. He says each day on the bench delivers spanking-new issues to tackle—both legal and moral.

And tackle them he does. A criminal defendant in the Commonwealth of Massachusetts couldn't handpick a better judge than Leon Long. In his courtroom, the Commonwealth's burden of proof is onerous, the presumption of innocence sacrosanct. He is one of a dwindling number of jurists who still believe the Bill of Rights exists for good reason. He has a myriad of fans in the county, many of them courthouse workers and members of the criminal defense bar. Harry and I are among them.

Geraldine Schilling isn't. It's not that Geraldine doesn't like Judge Long. Deep down, she does. But she'd like him a hell of a lot better if he'd get out of her way, if he were as jaded—as uninterested—as most other judges. She'd like him even more if he'd retire.

She doesn't seem to mind being in his courtroom today, though. She's here with her newest sidekick, Clarence Wexler, a nervous young fellow who's been out of law school all of five months. Clarence is busy sorting out documents, arranging them in neat piles on the table for Geraldine's convenience. She ignores him, her nose buried in a police report.

The Kydd and I both used to work for Geraldine. We were ADAs back when she was the First Assistant. I prosecuted cases for more than a decade, until I resigned a little over a year ago. The Kydd worked for her for about eighteen months, until Harry and I stole him last December. Geraldine is still furious with both of us about that. Then again, Geraldine is usually annoyed with me over one thing or another. And she's eternally mad at Harry.

When it comes to the Kydd, though, I can't really blame her. Even now, when he's on my to-strangle list, I have to admit he's a hot commodity.

He's a quick study, a competent litigator, and a damned hard worker. Geraldine hasn't had much luck with ADAs since we snagged him. I don't see a boatload of promise in Clarence Wexler either.

Harry bursts through the double doors just as the bailiff tells us to rise. He hurries down the center aisle and drops his battered schoolbag on the last seat against the bar, two down from me, on the other side of the Kydd. He leans forward and winks, buttoning his suit jacket. "Showtime," he stage-whispers.

Judge Long takes the bench and tells us to sit. There are only about a dozen people scattered around the room: the two prosecutors at their table, a half dozen defense lawyers in the chairs at the bar, a few curiosity seekers in the gallery, and Steven Collier, the money guy, in the front row. Louisa would have been allowed a single phone call when she got to lockup. Apparently she called her financial advisor. It occurs to me that the Kydd might not be the only sailor in this port.

Judge Long turns his radiant smile on each of us in turn, white teeth in dazzling contrast with his ebony skin. He reserves his final beam for Geraldine. She frowns at him.

Wanda Morgan is the courtroom clerk. She recites a docket number and then calls out *Commonwealth versus DeMateo*. One of the lawyers seated near us moves to the defense table and sets his briefcase on it. He's Bert Saunders, an overweight, perpetually tired-looking man who's been around the courthouse for as long as I can remember. "Saunders for the defense," he announces as he takes his place in front of the bench. "Your Honor, we have a problem with this one."

Judge Long chuckles and scans the paperwork the clerk has handed him. "I'm sure we do, Mr. Saunders. We have a problem with most of them, don't we?"

Harry leans forward and whispers to the Kydd and me, "What are you two doing here?"

He hasn't heard.

The Kydd looks at me and shakes his head. He's not willing to be the messenger on this one.

I return Harry's stare but say nothing. That's all it takes.

"Uh-oh," he says. He looks down at his shoes, then back up at me. "Uh-oh," he repeats.

Sometimes Harry is downright eloquent. He stares at me for a moment and then raises one eyebrow. I know what he's asking.

"First degree," I whisper.

He winces.

Geraldine and Bert Saunders are arguing about marital privilege when the side door opens and two shackled arrestees—a man and a woman—shuffle into the courtroom. The DeMateos, I presume. They're wearing street clothes, so they must have been picked up today. And they seem quite upset about it. They're shouting at each other, apparently unaware that there's a case in progress. Their case.

"I told you to shuddup," the man yells over his shoulder at the woman.

"So what else is new?" she fires back. The missus seems to be missing a couple of teeth. Her esses aren't quite right.

One of the court officers—visibly struggling to swallow his laughter—hurries to silence his charges. The DeMateos look surprised when he points to Judge Long. Their baffled expressions ask who the hell invited him to this meeting.

"See what I mean?" Bert Saunders says to the judge. "It can't be done."

"Don't be ridiculous," Geraldine responds.

Geraldine doesn't think much of Bert Saunders and she makes no effort to hide it. She turns away from him and speaks to the judge as if Bert isn't in the room. "It's a rolling domestic," she says. "Nothing more complicated than that."

A rolling domestic is a marital battle that happens to take place in a car—while it's moving.

"Attorney Schilling," Judge Long says, "it *is* more complicated than that. Far more complicated."

Bert Saunders nods up at the judge, vindicated.

"An unlicensed handgun, six thousand dollars in cash, and two kilos of cocaine," the judge continues. "I'd say this one is a little dicier than your average rolling domestic, Attorney Schilling."

Sounds like the DeMateos operate a little mom-and-pop shop.

161

"I'm going to allow the motion to appoint separate counsel for the codefendant."

Geraldine shakes her head at the judge, feigning resignation. Her argument was a loser from the beginning and she knows it. Defendants in joint possession of contraband—whether they're married or not—are always entitled to separate counsel. Add the sticky wicket of marital privilege to the mix, and it's a no-brainer. But Geraldine would argue against the existence of gravity if Bert Saunders were its proponent.

"Now let me see," Judge Long says, looking over the flat rims of his half-glasses at the handful of us seated at the bar. His eyes settle on Harry, then move back to the paperwork on the bench. Harry doesn't notice, though; he's reading Rinky's thick, tattered file. The Kydd elbows him.

It takes a second for Harry to digest what's happening. "Oh no, Your Honor. Please. Don't appoint me."

Judge Long finishes writing, signs off with a flourish, and smiles at Harry. "I just did," he says.

Harry's on his feet. "But, Judge, I'm up to my eyeballs. I'm flat out."

"That's good," Judge Long replies. "You know what they say about idle hands."

Harry looks confused—as if maybe he doesn't know what they say about idle hands—and Judge Long takes advantage of the momentary silence. "Mrs. DeMateo," he says, "this is Mr. Madigan. He's your new attorney."

Mrs. DeMateo is wearing a crushed-velvet baby blue pantsuit with matching eye shadow. She takes a moment to look Harry up and down, then turns to the judge, shaking her head. "He ain't too happy about it," she complains.

The judge hands the file back to Wanda Morgan. "Not to worry," he says. "Mr. Madigan will take good care of you."

Mrs. DeMateo smacks her lips and stares up at Judge Long. She doesn't buy it.

"Mr. Madigan," the judge continues, checking his list, "you're here on . . ."

"Snow," Harry answers, looking like he can't quite believe what just happened. "I'm here for Rinky."

The judge smiles at the mention of Rinky's name. "Call the Snow matter next," he tells Wanda. She leaves her desk and consults with one of the court officers. He hurries through the side door, presumably to retrieve Rinky from the ranks of those waiting to face the music.

The guards herd the not-so-happy couple toward the side door. "Mrs. DeMateo," Judge Long says as she passes, "Mr. Madigan has other business to attend to right now. He'll come see you when he's through, so the two of you can get acquainted."

She pauses in the doorway, looks Harry up and down again, and then smirks at him. Her expression says she ain't too happy about him either.

Rinky Snow stumbles into the courtroom as

Mrs. DeMateo exits, the two of them eyeing each other warily. Rinky's been here since Saturday night, so he's wearing the standard prison-issue orange jumpsuit. He walks freely, no shackles on his ankles, but his wrists are cuffed behind his back. The guards know Rinky well. He wouldn't run, but he'd haul off and deck one of them in a heartbeat.

They deliver Rinky to the defense table, where Harry is waiting. When Rinky sits, Harry rests a hand on his shoulder and whispers in his ear, both gestures no other mortal would get away with.

Geraldine jumps up like she's been waiting all day for this one. And she has. At least since she and Harry had their little phone spat this morning.

"Your Honor," she says, approaching the bench, "Mr. Snow is charged with assault with a dangerous weapon, to wit, a knife, to wit . . ."

Geraldine stands still and glares over her shoulder at Rinky, a practiced dramatic pause.

". . . *this* knife." She passes an evidence bag up to Judge Long.

Rinky is on his feet before Harry can stop him. "Hey," Rinky shouts at the judge, "that's mine."

Everyone freezes. It's unlikely that Harry was planning a mistaken identity defense, but if he was, he isn't anymore.

"That's mine," Rinky shouts again, in case we didn't hear him the first time.

Judge Long sets both the evidence bag and his glasses on the bench. He takes a deep breath, closes his eyes, and massages the bridge of his nose. I know Judge Long; he's battling an urge to laugh out loud. And he's giving Harry a chance to tell his client to shut the hell up.

Rinky isn't taking Harry's advice at the moment, though. "Where'd you get that?" he demands of Geraldine.

She ignores him. "The defendant assaulted two women with that knife in Chatham on Saturday evening."

Now Harry's on his feet. "He didn't *assault* anybody."

Rinky's still standing. "Where'd you get that?" he insists again. "I been looking for that!"

Geraldine continues as if Harry and Rinky don't exist. "The women were on Main Street," she says, "at about six-thirty. They'd just attended a wedding at St. Christopher's Chapel. We have a dozen witnesses—other wedding guests—in addition to the two victims."

"Oh, for God's sake," Harry says, "there weren't any *victims*."

"Where the hell did you get that?" Rinky's shouting louder now and growing more agitated, banging his cuffed wrists together and rattling the chain between them.

Judge Long opens his eyes and pounds his gavel, just once. "I want quiet," he whispers.

He gets it. Everyone in the room shuts up, even Rinky. His cuffs settle down too.

The judge spends a minute reading the police report, then he looks up at Rinky and points at Geraldine. "Mr. Snow," he says, "do you know who this is?"

Rinky has faced Geraldine in this courtroom a hundred times before, but he gapes at her now without a flicker of recognition.

"This is Attorney Schilling," Judge Long says. "Her first name is Geraldine. But do you know what we call her?"

Rinky's eyes are glued to Geraldine. He shakes his head.

"We call her Geraldine the Guillotine."

Geraldine groans. The Kydd stifles a guffaw. Harry doesn't bother; he laughs out loud.

Rinky stares at Geraldine the Guillotine a moment longer, then looks back up at the judge and swallows.

"So I suggest, Mr. Snow, that you sit down now and remain quiet. Mr. Madigan is here to speak for you."

Rinky checks in with Harry. Harry nods. Rinky sits.

"Now," Judge Long says, looking first at Geraldine, then at Harry, "I'll tell you what we're going to do here."

Harry leaves the defense table, walks up to the bench, and stands beside Geraldine. She steps away as if she's certain he has leprosy.

"We're going to continue this matter without a finding," the judge says, "for six months."

Harry nods in agreement.

Geraldine shakes her blond head, annoyed. "Did you *look* at that knife, Judge?"

"I most certainly did, Ms. Schilling. I also looked at the police report. There's no suggestion here that Mr. Snow intended to harm anyone with that knife."

She throws her hands in the air, the way a frustrated parent might when dealing with an impossible teenager.

"Mr. Snow," the judge says.

Rinky stands again. "Do I get my knife back now?"

The Kydd tries to stifle another bout of laughter, but he's only partially successful this time.

"No, you don't, sir." Judge Long leans forward on the bench, rests on his forearms. "You don't get your knife back now and you don't get your knife back later."

Rinky looks perplexed.

"No knives, Mr. Snow. Mr. Madigan will explain what we've done here. But the bottom line is: no knives."

What they've done here is humane. Rinky won't do time on this charge—other than the two nights he's already served—unless he gets in trouble again. And he will. When he does, he'll be sentenced on whatever the new offense is as well as this one. But by then, just maybe, it will be winter. And though the Barnstable County House of Correction offers little in the way of creature comforts, it does have heat.

Of course, Rinky could just as easily land back here tonight.

Harry returns to the defense table and chats with Rinky in low tones while Judge Long finishes the paperwork and Geraldine collects her next stack of documents from Clarence Wexler. Rinky nods at Harry, asks loudly if he can go now, and then feigns attention again as Harry keeps talking. Rinky understands that Judge Long just let him off the proverbial hook. As for the rest of it—the continuance without a finding, the likelihood of doing real time in the future—he doesn't give a damn.

A prison guard shows up at the table and Rinky shoos him away with both hands. The guard looks at Harry and chuckles. Harry tells Rinky he has to return to lockup. He has to change clothes, retrieve noncontraband possessions, and sign off on release forms. Harry points to the guard and tells Rinky to go with him.

Rinky complies, but he's not happy about it. He glares over his shoulder at all of us as he leaves the courtroom. This is a trick, his eyes say, and he knows every last one of us is in on it.

Harry packs up his old schoolbag, then sends a mock salute in Geraldine's direction. "Ms. Guillotine," he says.

She scowls at him. Clarence does too.

Harry laughs and turns to leave. "Wish me

luck," he says, pausing beside the Kydd and me.

Now it's my turn to laugh. "Wish *you* luck? We're the ones staring a first-degree murder charge in the face."

"I know that," he says as he heads for the center aisle. "But *I* have a date with Mrs. DeMateo."

The Kydd laughs, but I don't. I turn in my chair to watch Harry's departure. He looks over his shoulder at me and his worried hazel eyes say it all. He can joke all he wants about Mrs. DeMateo but it's not her case he's preoccupied with at the moment. The case he's concerned about is mine. And he's not just concerned. He's worried sick.

CHAPTER 18

The grieving widow is turned out in yellow. She's shed her hat and trench coat, revealing a long-sleeved, knee-length coat dress, butter yellow with slightly deeper-hued trim. I'm not certain, but I think yellow is one of those colors we're not supposed to wear after Labor Day. Life's rules don't seem to apply to Louisa Rawlings, though. None of them.

A stern-looking matron relieves Louisa of her handcuffs and then delivers her to us. The Kydd stands and pulls the middle chair out from our table as they approach.

"Thank you, Kevin," Louisa says as she sits between us. He nods at her and turns pink, but says nothing.

"How are you doing?" I ask her. She seems calm, composed, as if she consciously collected herself during her hours in lockup.

"I'm ready to go home," she says, rubbing her wrists together. "This place is dreadful."

She's right, of course. Lockup is no picnic. But compared with the female violent offenders' ward of the Barnstable County House of Correction—where Louisa will await trial if this case is bound over—it's a veritable cocktail party. That's a reality I won't mention, at least not at the moment. Louisa will hear a lifetime's worth of awful realities during the next fifteen minutes. No need to start early.

Geraldine leaves her table and saunters toward ours, her three-inch heels sounding like a metronome as they strike evenly against the wooden floor. Without looking at me—her eyes are focused on Louisa—she hands me a stack of documents. She stands still in front of our table, idly fingering a pack of cigarettes in the pocket of her camel-hair suit coat. She plans to stay awhile, it seems.

On top of the stack is a legal memorandum, a thick one, no doubt researched and authored by Clarence. Beneath it are a few preliminary analyses from the state crime lab as well as the Medical Examiner's report, hot off the presses. I wonder if his signature is dry yet. I pass the stack to the Kydd and he digs in at once.

Geraldine is still planted in front of our table, blond head tilted to one side, thin arms now folded against her chest, green eyes boring into Louisa. She's preparing for battle, antagonizing the enemy. Geraldine does this to murder defendants. All of them.

Louisa stares back at her, undaunted. I'm impressed. Murder defendants don't do that to Geraldine. None of them.

Without a word, Geraldine pivots and strides back to her table. She retrieves another package, a duplicate of the one she gave me, no doubt. She walks to the bench and hands it up to Judge Long. He thanks her and dons his half-glasses.

"Who is that woman?" Louisa asks.

"She's the District Attorney," I tell her. "Geraldine Schilling."

"Is she competent?"

I almost laugh out loud. Louisa may as well have asked if Barbra Streisand can carry a tune. "Yes," I answer. "She's quite effective."

"Too bad she couldn't find day care for her little boy." Louisa nods toward the prosecutors' table and I almost laugh out loud again. Our new Assistant DA looks like he just stepped out of an early episode of *The Brady Bunch*.

"Be careful," I tell Louisa. "That's Clarence Wexler. He's older than he looks."

"Perky little thing, isn't he?"

I'd never thought of Clarence as perky before,

but I suppose he is. "He's Geraldine's latest protégé," I tell her.

"He's an attorney?"

I nod.

"He's licensed?"

"As of last month he is. Fresh out of law school. Just passed the bar."

Louisa doesn't seem troubled by the fact that her day-care candidate is just a few years younger than her most recent paramour. She shakes her head as if she knows for sure now that the entire profession has gone to the dogs.

Wanda Morgan reads out a lengthy docket number and then announces *The Commonwealth of Massachusetts versus Louisa Coleman Rawlings*. Louisa jumps a little beside me. She looks somewhat surprised, hurt even, as if it were terribly impertinent of Wanda to mention Louisa's name in open court.

Geraldine is still on her feet, facing the judge. "Your Honor, Mrs. Rawlings stands charged with first-degree murder, based on extreme atrocity or cruelty, in the bludgeoning death of her husband, Herbert Andrew Rawlings."

For a moment the room falls quiet, the only sound a sharp intake of breath from the chair next to mine.

"As you can see from Dr. Ramsey's report, the cause of death is drowning, secondary to head trauma."

Dr. Ramsey took over as Barnstable County's Medical Examiner little more than a year ago. He's already proved, more than once, that he's damned good at his new job. Geraldine isn't taking any chances with the Rawlings case. She went straight to the top gun.

"The victim's injuries are consistent with a single blow from behind with a blunt object," she continues. "Dr. Ramsey concludes that the blow rendered Mr. Rawlings unconscious, after which he was bound with rope at the wrists and ankles, and then dumped into the ocean, still breathing."

Geraldine pauses and turns to fire a theatrical glare at Louisa, but the attempt at drama is wasted. Louisa doesn't notice. She's rigid in her chair, her eyes closed, her left fist pressed against her mouth. Two tears seep out from beneath her long lashes and meander down her right cheek.

"When the Chatham police questioned the defendant as to her whereabouts when her husband disappeared . . ."

Geraldine pauses again and stares at our table until Louisa opens her eyes.

". . . she lied."

Louisa turns to me and shakes her head, but her eyes are worried.

"The defendant stands to inherit a substantial estate as a result of her husband's death," Geraldine continues. "Two million in life insurance proceeds if we'd all been duped into thinking his death was an

accident, but that's just the beginning. Mr. Rawlings's net worth exceeded six million exclusive of
insurance. And his will names the defendant as the
sole beneficiary."

Judge Long takes a minute to scan Geraldine's
paperwork and Louisa leans toward me during the
lull. "That's wrong," she whispers, shaking her
head. "I didn't lie to anybody. And the life insurance part is wrong too. There's only a million."

"Okay," I tell her.

So Louisa Rawlings is unaware of the double in-
demnity clause. My gut tells me to leave her in the
dark on that issue—at least for a while.

"Ms. Nickerson," the judge says without looking up from his papers, "how does your client
plead?"

I stand to address the court but another voice
fills the room first. "Not at all guilty, Your Honor,"
Louisa says from her chair.

"Not at all," she repeats when I look down. For
a moment, she seems to think I'm the one she needs
to convince.

Judge Long stares at her.

Geraldine does too.

"Not the least little bit," Louisa adds. She's
wiped her tears away, but her cheeks are still wet
and her mascara is smudged.

I lean over to silence her, but think better of it
when I take in the judge's expression. He's not reading anymore. He's looking at Louisa, his eyes wide,

his smile quite different from the one he earlier bestowed upon the rest of us. If he were a white man, his cheeks would probably be red right now. I wonder if there's a male on the planet who's immune to Louisa Rawlings's charms.

I clear my throat and Judge Long seems to snap out of his reverie. He smiles at me, still looking a bit bemused. "Should I take that as a garden-variety not-guilty plea, Attorney Nickerson?"

"Yes, Your Honor, you should."

The judge turns his attention back to Geraldine. "Attorney Schilling," he says, taking his half-glasses off and tapping the documents with them, "I'm sure it's all in here, but enlighten me, please. You've mentioned a possible motive—and you seem to have reason to believe this defendant was less than forthcoming with the Chatham police officers. But what have you got in the way of physical evidence that ties this woman to the crime?"

Now we're getting somewhere. Judge Long won't hold any criminal defendant on the basis of motive alone, even a plausible motive. If Louisa Rawlings is telling the truth—and my gut says she is now, even if she didn't come clean with the cops—then the Commonwealth won't have any physical evidence implicating her. That won't get us out of the woods permanently, of course; Geraldine's just begun to sink her teeth into this one. But it will buy us some time.

Geraldine turns away from the bench and sends

an index-finger signal to Clarence Wexler. My stomach somersaults. I know that look on her face. She's got something. Or at least she thinks she does.

Clarence jumps to his feet and rushes forward as if summoned by God Himself. He's holding an evidence bag, a large one. From here, I can't make out what's in it.

I start toward the bench so I can see, but I stop when the Kydd slides two sheets of paper across the table to me. One is a report from the crime lab. The other is Clarence's summary of the lab report's contents. I lean over to read and my eyes absorb the words as Geraldine speaks.

"What we've got," she says, "is this. On it are skin fragments from the victim's skull. And two of his hairs. And traces of his blood."

Geraldine pauses for a moment and I look up. "Also on it," she says, "are Louisa Coleman Rawlings's fingerprints. No one else's."

Judge Long takes the evidence bag and holds it up to the light. "But what *is* it?" he asks.

"It's a decorative plumbing fixture," Geraldine replies. "A brass swan."

CHAPTER 19

Judge Long called a thirty-minute recess to give the defense time to examine the Commonwealth's surprise exhibit, time to digest the contents of the lab report, time to construct our own version of what it all means. Normally, the prosecutor is required to disclose all such evidence before presenting it in court. Trial by ambush went out with the Dark Ages.

The disclosure rule is always malleable at this stage of the game, though. The government's version of probable cause came to light today, not yesterday. And since Geraldine's office received the report from the Commonwealth's crime lab just an hour or so before open session began, Judge Long ruled that the Commonwealth's failure to disclose was harmless.

As a practical matter, of course, the judge is right. This judge usually is.

We'll be given ample opportunity to have an independent lab examine the brass swan before this case gets to trial. We'll hire our own forensic experts to analyze DNA, to determine blood type, and to identify fingerprints. But the answers I want right now can't come from a lab or a physician or a scientist. They have to come from Louisa Rawlings. And so far at least, she doesn't seem to have any.

She's shivering, though it's not the least bit cold in here. We're in the jury deliberation room, across the hall from the main courtroom. Louisa and the Kydd are seated at a long, narrow table; I'm on my feet. The Commonwealth's documents are spread out in front of the Kydd and he's still wading through them. The bagged brass swan is in front of Louisa. She doesn't touch it.

I take it from the table and hold it up to the fluorescent light. It's the mother swan, not one of her two cygnets. Portions of the skin fragments Geraldine referred to would have been scraped off at the crime lab for analysis, but two remain affixed to the brass. Even through the plastic, the fragments are easy to see with the naked eye. And I'll be damned if they were there twenty-four hours ago.

We'll get to the swan in a minute. I have another

issue on my mind. "Louisa," I ask, "did you have brunch at the club last Sunday morning?"

She stares at me for a moment before she answers. "No," she says. "I didn't. Truth is, I found my companions rather dull. And I had a lot on my mind. I bought a coffee and drove to Lighthouse Beach with it."

"But you told Mitch Walker you ate at the club."

"No, I didn't. I told him exactly what I told you—that I'd been *invited* to play nine holes and have brunch. He didn't ask anything else about it."

I shake my head at her.

"What was I supposed to do?" she asks. "Volunteer that I needed time alone to think about my impending divorce? Tell the cop I didn't want to go home until I was pretty sure my husband had gone for the day?"

She can protest all she wants. Her eyes tell me she knows how stupid she was.

"Well, your clever little answer is what landed you here, Louisa. And this"—I hold the swan out toward her—"just might keep you in."

I set the wrapped fixture back on the table, closer to Louisa than it was before, hoping she'll shed some light on its current condition. She recoils from it, shaking her head. "I can't explain this," she says, her voice trembling along with the rest of her. "It makes no sense."

"Hold on," the Kydd says, pulling a page free

from a stapled packet. I walk behind him, so I can look over his shoulder and read. He's holding a sheet divided into three columns. It's the inventory of items confiscated by the two guys from the state crime lab. The swan is near the bottom of the list.

The Kydd runs his finger horizontally across the page on the swan line. The middle column, the widest of the three, gives a brief description of the item identified in column one. The final entry, in the third column, tells where it was found. The brass swan, the state guys claim, was discovered in the Rawlings's basement.

"What was it doing down in the basement?" the Kydd asks Louisa.

She looks blank. She doesn't know what he's talking about. I take the inventory sheet from him and put it in front of her, on top of the bagged exhibit, my index finger directing her attention to the swan line. "Did you remove it from the hot tub for some reason?" Surely Louisa would have noticed if the mother swan had migrated from the Queen's Spa.

She's silent. After a moment, she sits a little straighter, tapping the sheet. "Wait," she says, "that must be the other swan."

"The *other* swan?" I wonder how many brass swans one household can support.

"Yes," she says, more animated now. "When the plumbing fixtures first arrived, just a week or so before we moved in, the plumber called us in Greenwich to say the largest master-bath faucet was defective, stripped threads or some such thing. Anyhow, there was no way he could create a proper seal. It was leaking from the base of the neck."

"So you ordered a replacement?" I ask.

"Herb did," she says. "He called the plumbing supply company—a place in Ohio, I think it was—and they agreed to ship a new one right away. We'd spent a buck or two on them, after all."

"What happened to the first one?"

"The plumber left it on top of one of the bathroom sinks. I found it the day we moved in. Herb was out on the dock, fussing with the boat as usual, and I carried the swan out to the back deck to ask him what I should do with it."

Hence her prints. "And what did he say?"

"He said to just leave it there, on the picnic table; he'd take care of it. He said he'd agreed to ship it back to the company. They thought it could be refurbished. He must have moved it into the basement and then . . ."

"And then he never got around to it," I finish for her.

She nods, her spurt of animation visibly fading.

"Who had access to the basement, Louisa?"

Her eyes grow wider. "Anyone who wanted it, I suppose. Herb always went down through the bulkhead in the yard. He kept his tools and boating equipment down there."

"Is that the only way to get there?"

183

She shakes her head. "No. There's a stairway from the kitchen, but it's steep. Herb never used it, as far as I know. He always used the bulkhead."

A rhythmic series of knocks breaks the silence and then Wanda peeks in. "You folks ready?" she asks. "The judge wants to wrap it up."

"Two minutes," I tell her. She nods and leaves, the wooden door clicking shut behind her, and I turn back to Louisa with Taylor Peterson's theory running through my head. "Shift gears with me for a minute," I tell her.

She nods.

"Who did your husband normally take out on the boat with him?"

She laughs. "It'd be easier to tell you who he didn't take. Herb would have taken the mailman if the mailman would have gone. Herb loved that damned boat, loved showing her off as much as anything."

"Did you go with him?"

"On occasion," she says. "It's not my cup of tea, tossing about on the waves. But I'd go with him once in a while to keep him company."

"What about Glen Powers?" I ask. "You mentioned he and Herb had boating in common."

She shakes her head. "They weren't *that* chummy," she says. "Herb and Glen would *talk* about boats occasionally. But they never went out on one together."

"Steven Collier?" I try next.

"Sometimes," she says. "They'd take the *Carolina Girl* out on a weekend afternoon every now and then. But Steven has his own boat, so it wasn't that often. They spent more time together talking about gear than they did on the water."

I'm not getting much here, but I may as well finish my short list. "Anastasia?" I ask. "Lance Phillips?"

She laughs again. "Herb had Anastasia around boats all the time when she was a child, hoping to get her hooked. But alas, the dear girl grew up to loathe the great outdoors. And Lance gets seasick in the shower."

Well, this discussion has got me nowhere.

"We'd better head across the hall," I tell her. "I think we've used up our two minutes."

I take the inventory sheet from her and hand it back to the Kydd. He restacks his documents and then leads the way out of the jury room. Louisa follows. Mother Swan and I bring up the rear.

"Louisa," I say as we cross the hallway, "when we go back inside, it's probably best if you let me do the talking."

She glances over her shoulder as we enter the courtroom, her perfect eyebrows arched. "All of it?" She's incredulous.

"Yes," I tell her. "All of it."

She looks disappointed, as if I've just taken all the fun out of this for her. She settles into the chair the Kydd offers and then turns to face me. "I went to law school too, you know."

"I'm aware of that," I remind her. "So did Clarence."

She glances over at young Clarence and nods, conceding my point, and her expression grows more somber. The bailiff tells us to rise as Judge Long emerges from chambers, but Louisa leans closer to me before she complies. "Who would do such a thing to Herb?" she asks. Genuine sadness fills her dark brown eyes.

I shake my head as we stand, but say nothing. My question is more basic than that. It makes perfect sense that Louisa's prints are all over the Commonwealth's exhibit. *But where the hell are Herb's?*

CHAPTER 20

Judge Long isn't a particularly tall man, but he reaches the bench with just five energetic strides. He nods a greeting into the gallery as he climbs the few steps and takes his seat. A handful of newcomers has arrived in the courtroom, and a flurry of activity is now audible behind us.

Among the new arrivals is Woody Timmons from the *Cape Cod Times*. He's the reporter regularly assigned to the Barnstable County Complex and it's no surprise that he's here. He seems to be hardwired into these buildings. Rarely does any case of import escape his radar.

Woody has scores of cronies among the staff of

the county complex—intake officers, victim advocates, and docket clerks—many of whom get the earliest glimpses of each new matter as it arrives. Along with most other county staffers, they congregate after work every Friday at the local watering hole, the Jailhouse. They spot one another drinks, shoot darts, and exchange well-informed opinions on the county's latest crises. Woody takes good care of his courthouse contacts; he almost never misses the Friday festivities. Any number of his cohorts would have telephoned his office this afternoon to deliver this week's hottest scoop.

But Woody's not the only late-afternoon arrival. Three still photographers pace the length of the bar, their shutters clicking steadily. Judge Long is one of the only judges in the county who allows flash photographs in his courtroom. "It's all part of the process," he always says. "The citizens deserve accurate information from their courtrooms, and photographs provide part of it." The press, of course, agrees.

The photographers' partners—guys with notebooks open and pens poised—crowd into the front bench with Woody, prompting Woody to move back a few rows. Their press badges identify them as representatives from the *Providence Journal*, the *New Bedford Telegraph*, and *The Boston Globe*. Word is out, it seems. And it's already over the bridge.

I'm taken aback by their appearance here so

soon, but I realize, after a moment, that I shouldn't be. Any woman charged with the murder of her husband ignites a media fire. She's hot news. But adding wealth to the story is like pouring gasoline on the flames. If the accused is a socialite, she's more than news. She's a front-page photograph, a screaming, large-print headline.

Louisa appears oblivious to it all. She seems not to hear her name whispered repeatedly from the other side of the bar, not even to notice the flash-bulbs that explode each time she turns her profile to the gallery. She's leaning sideways, toward the Kydd, scanning the Commonwealth's lengthy documents along with him, pointing to a particular entry now and then to ask him for an explanation. I'm glad she's willing to participate; I want her to be proactive in her own defense. I just hope the Kydd remembers how to comprehend the written word while she's breathing over his shoulder.

Judge Long repositions his half-glasses and signals for the rest of us to sit. With the solitary exception of Geraldine Schilling, we do. Few directives apply to our District Attorney. She wouldn't take a seat at this stage of the proceedings unless a lit cigarette and a dry martini were waiting on the table in front of it.

"Attorney Nickerson," the judge says, "I trust you and your client have had sufficient time to examine the Commonwealth's evidence?"

"We have, Your Honor." I stand and approach

the bench. Geraldine follows, as if the judge and I need a chaperone, and I spin to fire a silent warning in her direction. I imagine Pedro Martinez might get a comparable feeling when he hurls an inside pitch and edges Derek Jeter away from the plate. She stops a few feet behind me and folds her arms, a reluctant concession to the fact that I'm up.

"At this time, Your Honor, we believe the Commonwealth's exhibit is a plumbing fixture Mr. and Mrs. Rawlings purchased when they were renovating their home. It proved to be defective and the retailer replaced it. It was stored in the basement so eventually it could be shipped back to the vendor."

Geraldine moves closer to the bench and turns to face me, her thin eyebrows arched. Her question couldn't be any plainer if she flashed it on a neon billboard. *So what?* she telegraphs. Geraldine is a master of dramatic presentation; no attorney in the county spends more time painting each painful detail than she does. The rest of us, though, should just get on with it. Every word we utter is a waste of the court's time.

"The point is, Your Honor, it's no surprise that Mrs. Rawlings's prints are on the fixture. Just as it would be no surprise to find my prints on the fixtures in my home, your prints on the fixtures in yours."

"That's not the point at all," Geraldine interrupts. She moves past me, closer to the bench.

"The *point* is that Mrs. Rawlings's prints share space with skin fragments, hair, blood—all from her bludgeoned husband. *Those* aren't things we'd expect to find on the fixtures in *your* home, Judge." She turns and faces me again, her scowl saying she's not about to comment on what she might find in mine.

"The exhibit proves the deceased was attacked with that fixture, Your Honor. Nothing more."

"Nothing more?" Geraldine moves closer to me and her green eyes grow wide. "My Sister Counsel is mistaken," she says to the judge. "The exhibit proves a good deal more than that."

Geraldine "Sister Counsels" me every chance she gets. It's one of those archaic traditions the Massachusetts Bar Association seems unable to part with—lawyers calling one another siblings. I find it utterly irritating. And Geraldine finds that irresistible.

She turns and points first at Louisa, then up at her captured swan on the bench. "The exhibit *does* prove the victim was attacked with it," she says. "It also proves the defendant wielded the murder weapon. And it proves she's the *only* person who did."

"It proves no such thing," I counter. "Anyone who watches *Law & Order* once in a while knows how to avoid leaving prints behind. The exhibit proves only that the murderer had access to the house, or at least to the fixture."

Geraldine looks up at the ceiling and raises both hands, as if she just scored a touchdown. "Ah," she says, her expression brightening, "my Sister Counsel brings us directly to my next point."

Her Sister Counsel didn't intend to do that, of course.

"Two people lived in that house," she continues. "And now one of them is dead. The house has a security system, Judge."

"But they didn't use it, Your Honor." I step closer to the bench. "It wasn't activated."

"Doesn't matter." Geraldine holds up one of the police reports. "There was no sign of forced entry."

She's right about that. The cops found no indication of surreptitious activity anywhere near the Easy Street estate. And Louisa noticed nothing out of the ordinary when she returned home from the club—and Lighthouse Beach—last Sunday.

"That's true," I tell the judge. "But like so many of us on the Cape, Mr. and Mrs. Rawlings weren't big on locking their doors. And plenty of people had access, anyhow. Deliverymen, construction workers, landscapers . . ."

Geraldine lets out a small laugh and shakes her head. "We all know what happened here, Judge." She stares up at the bench and points back at Louisa. "We may not know the details, but we've got the big picture. This woman knocked her husband out with a single blow. Maybe she was enraged, maybe not. Maybe she did it for the money, maybe not. Maybe she *intended* to render him unconscious, maybe not."

Geraldine turns and locks eyes with Louisa. "But render him unconscious she did. And when she realized what she'd done, she decided to finish the job. She—"

"You have no business saying any of those things, Miss Geraldine." Louisa's voice isn't trembling anymore; it's steady and strong. She's on her feet, leaning over our table, her dark eyes like lit coals. She's mad. She stares up at the judge as everyone else's eyes fix on her. "Surely this woman isn't permitted to say such terrible things about me, Your Honor. There's not a shred of truth in what she's saying. I'm going to ask you to stop her."

So much for my "let me do the talking" admonition.

Judge Long tucks his chin in and peers down over his half-glasses, the slightest hint of a smile tugging at the corners of his mouth. "Oh, but she is, Mrs. Rawlings. She is allowed to say such things about you. It's part of her job. And frankly, it'd be easier to stop a freight train."

"But the woman doesn't even know me," Louisa protests. "Her story is ridiculous."

"Your Honor." I glare at Louisa as I address the court, silently telling her to put a lid on it. "The bottom line is that the Commonwealth has nothing more than the accused's fingerprints on an item where we'd *expect* to find them." I pause and walk back toward our table, to stand beside Louisa. "Mrs. Rawlings is an attorney, Your Honor, a graduate of Yale Law School."

Judge Long is obviously surprised by this revelation. He looks out at Louisa with heightened interest. Even Geraldine seems mildly intrigued. I pause a moment, to let them assess her demeanor, before I continue. "I guarantee you, Your Honor, if she'd used that fixture to attack her husband, her prints would not be on it."

Geraldine throws her hands in the air and claims center stage again. "A defendant who's smart enough to know better," she says, "too smart to do something so stupid. Now there's something we don't see more than ten times a day."

I stay focused on Judge Long, ignoring Geraldine's sarcasm. "There's not enough here, Your Honor. Her prints in her own home. It's not enough to bind over."

He raises his hands, palms out, to silence me. "Brief it," he says to both of us. "I'll hear argument in the morning. First thing."

I turn to catch the Kydd's eye and he's waiting for me. He leans back in his chair and sighs, nodding repeatedly. He gets it, he's telling me. We have a long night ahead.

The poker-faced matron returns to our table with the cuffs and directs Louisa to put her hands behind her back. Flashbulbs begin popping again as Louisa complies. She looks up at me as the cuffs clang shut, her tears flowing freely now, her eyes panicked. She has a long night ahead too. And she knows it.

CHAPTER 21

Tuesday, October 17

Nothing packs the Barnstable County Superior Courthouse like a case that gets top billing on the late-night news. The Kydd and I were in the office until well after midnight, but at eleven we flipped the conference room TV on to see if the coverage of Louisa Rawlings would be as inflammatory as we expected. It was worse.

The parking lot is full when I arrive. It takes ten minutes and more than a little creativity to find a spot. When I approach the back doors of the Superior Courthouse, a small circle of the nicotine-dependent moves aside without changing shape. Little white clouds rise up from the center of the ring. Smoke signals.

The courthouse hallway is jammed. I push my way through, doing my best to avoid reporters and photographers, but they're everywhere. Their lights blind me and their boisterous, never-ending questions are indecipherable. Woody Timmons isn't among them, though. I spot him as I climb the stairs to the second floor. He's in an alcove talking with Officer Holt, their heads close together as if they might be keeping their voices low. They're the only people in the building who've entertained that idea.

It's a few minutes before eight when I reach the main courtroom's side door and I'm relieved to be here. This entry is reserved for attorneys, parties, and select witnesses. It's protected from the press on this particular morning by a burly guard with a shaved head. He looks altogether forbidding even before the fluorescent light catches the shiny metal on his hip. He nods as I pass, never taking his eyes from the crowd.

Every seat in the gallery is already filled. Two court officers are stationed at the double doors in back, directing those spectators just arriving to line up single file against the side walls. They call out reminders to those forgetful souls who double up. The officers are trying to keep a small portion of the side aisles clear, but they're losing the battle.

The space reserved for the press corps has tripled. Three front benches to the right of the center aisle are roped off now and most of the faces there are familiar: local guys from the small, town-based papers, even a reporter I recognize from the *Nantucket Mirror*. He looks a bit bedraggled; his suit coat is wrinkled and he could use a shave. He must have crossed the big pond on a Cape Air red-eye into Hyannis.

The city boys showed up too. All the major players from the off-Cape presses are here, *The Boston Herald*'s Lou McCabe front and center. He occupies far more than his share of space on the front bench, his physique not unlike Jabba the Hutt's, his papers and supplies strewn around him in piles. I'm always a little uneasy when Lou shows up to cover a case I'm handling. He nurtures a flair for the melodramatic.

The first row on the left of the middle aisle is also filled with faces I recognize. Steven Collier is on the closest end. Anastasia Rawlings is next to him, dressed either in Sunday's costume or a duplicate. The boyfriend Lance is just about sitting in her lap and I wonder if the beast Lucifer is underneath his coat. Taylor Peterson and one of his crewmen have ended up next to Lance somehow, and Glen Powers is on the far end of the bench, keeping his distance from the others.

Woody Timmons comes through the back doors, but he doesn't take advantage of the press's reserved seating. He goes off on his own, leaning against a side wall amid the general public. I've noticed this about Woody before. He keeps his distance when his out-of-town colleagues pay us a visit. This is his turf. He understands the rules of the local game better than any of them. And he plays his cards close to the vest.

The Kydd is already here. He's on his feet in front of the prosecutors' table, trading paperwork with Clarence Wexler, who's standing behind it. The Kydd isn't paying much attention to Clarence, though. He's listening intently to Geraldine, his expression somber. Geraldine looks downright happy, comfortable and relaxed in her tall leather chair.

The Kydd turns toward me as I drop my briefcase on the defense table. He puts a hand up to stop Geraldine's recitation and signals for me to join them. His worried blue eyes tell me to do it now, not later.

The Kydd's mouth has been open since I walked in, his lower jaw slack. He loosens his tie, as if he's desperate for air, as I approach. He looks dazed, peaked. I know that look; I've seen it on his face before, more than once. Something is wrong.

Geraldine's ready smile is my second clue. Things for Louisa Rawlings almost certainly have taken a turn for the worse. She beams up at me as I reach her table, her green eyes aglow. "Oh, good," she says, looking genuinely pleased. "The gang's all here."

"What's up, Geraldine?" I had been hoping to sound nonchalant. I'm pretty sure it didn't come off that way, but I pretend it did.

Her smile expands. "More lab results," she says,

pointing to the stack of new documents in the Kydd's hands. She rolls her high-backed chair out from the table and crosses her lean legs. She continues smiling up at me, her hands steepled beneath her chin. Whatever she's got is gloat-worthy.

"And?"

"And it seems the little missus has done quite a bit of housework," she says.

I doubt Louisa Rawlings has done a day of housework in her half century of life, but I don't say so. Instead, I fold my arms and wait. I know Geraldine. If she's hell-bent on dragging this out, a five-alarm fire in the next room wouldn't change her mind.

"The master bath," she says, shaking her blond head, "it must have been a bloody mess."

"The master bath?"

The Kydd hands me a new report from the crime lab. The *Received* stamp from Geraldine's office says it came in an hour ago. The specimen is identified by number only. The Kydd offers me the inventory sheet, the same one we reviewed yesterday, so I can match the number with the typewritten list. The specimen came from the floor in the master bathroom, Louisa's Queen's Spa, a ten-by-ten cutout from the pale oak floorboards near the hot tub. The undersides of the boards contain blood. A lot of blood. Herb's.

"She did a commendable job cleaning up," Geraldine says. She stands, leans over the table toward me, and feigns a pout. "But it wasn't quite good enough."

I'm pretty sure the Kydd is no longer the only sickly looking person in the courtroom. I glance over at him, then back at Geraldine. Words fail me. And I don't think I've taken a breath for a while, either.

If Herb Rawlings was attacked in the Queen's Spa—and he was, blood evidence doesn't lie—then Taylor Peterson's theory is all wrong. Herb *wasn't* at the helm when the *Carolina Girl* left the dock on Sunday. Someone else was. Someone who knew how to negotiate the cut. But someone who didn't know a pop-up when he saw one.

"Oh, look," Geraldine says, her downturned mouth doing a flip. "You can break the news to her now."

The noise in the gallery escalates dramatically as the side door opens and Louisa Rawlings appears. The matron had the common decency to remove Louisa's cuffs before she entered the camera-packed courtroom, a courtesy not often afforded to high-profile prisoners. It seems Louisa has added at least one member of the prison staff to the long list of mortals she's charmed.

She holds her head high as she walks to our table, not looking directly at the cameras, but not shying away from them either. She's wearing the standard prison-issue orange jumpsuit, a far cry from her usual sartorial elegance. Her auburn hair is pulled back into a loose ponytail and her face looks scrubbed; no makeup. When she reaches our table I realize her eyes are bloodshot; she probably didn't sleep much last night. And still, Louisa Rawlings is stunning.

"You!"

The Kydd and I twist in our seats. Geraldine and Clarence do too. It's a voice from the gallery, a deep one, and I recognize it from just that syllable.

"You *murdered* my father!" Anastasia is on her feet and all cameras in the room turn in her direction now.

"*Murdered* him!" She thrusts her fists at Louisa amid a hailstorm of flashbulbs.

The crowd's moderate roar rises a few decibels. Still, Anastasia is louder. "*Murdered* him!"

Two court officers rush down the center aisle, direct Steven Collier out of his seat, and then yank Anastasia from hers. Each of them takes one of her arms and together they drag her toward the exit. She shouts nonstop but she's sobbing now too. "Jesus," the Kydd mutters, "if those are real tears, there's going to be a hell of a huge black puddle on the floor."

Steven Collier and Lance Phillips hustle down the center aisle behind Anastasia and her escorts. So does half the press corps. "*Murdered* him!" Anastasia shrieks again, the loudest one yet, just as the heavy double doors slam shut behind the entourage.

The Kydd and I face front again but Louisa's

gaze remains on the back doors a moment longer. "Some college students major in history," she says calmly. "Anastasia chose histrionics."

"We have a problem," I whisper as she sits.

"Tell me about it," she replies.

"A big one."

She laughs a little and leans toward me. "Did you think I hadn't noticed, darlin'?"

"A *new* big one," I add.

She turns to face me. She's not laughing anymore.

Joey Kelsey has been the bailiff in this courtroom for the better part of a year now. He races through his morning *Oyez! Oyez!* litany and the crowd quiets. We get to our feet along with everyone else in the room, Louisa's worried eyes glued to mine. I can't explain anything to her now, though. Judge Long is already halfway to the bench and I need to address him at once, before he signals for Wanda Morgan to call the case. And before Geraldine Schilling starts talking.

"Your Honor." I'm on my feet before he has any chance to sit. "We need a sidebar." I leave our table and head toward the bench before he says a word. I don't intend to take no for an answer on this one.

A murmur swells in the gallery and Judge Long bangs his gavel. He's still standing.

"That won't be necessary, Judge." Geraldine is on my heels. "Everything we have to say this morning can be said on the record."

What she really means, of course, is that she'd like to begin trying this case today—to the public and the press. This crowd will devour what she has to say. And the reporters will distribute it to the masses in vivid detail. Such a pity to waste it all on a sidebar.

Judge Long apparently has abandoned all hope of taking his seat. He hesitates for a moment, gavel still in hand, his eyes darting from me to Geraldine and back again. He moves to the side of his bench and faces away from the spectators. "Counsel," he says, "approach."

We're already there.

"More surprise evidence," I tell him.

"For Christ's sake," Geraldine snaps, "we got it an *hour* ago."

"I'm not disputing that, Your Honor. I'm just asking for a little time to deal with it—the morning. We're entitled to that much." I point back at the noisy gallery and the judge's eyes follow. "Especially with the feeding frenzy going on out there," I add.

And frenzy it is. Sidebars almost always escalate the noise in the courtroom and this one is no exception. The crowd doesn't like being left out. The judge bangs his gavel yet again.

"Give us the morning, Your Honor," I repeat. "We'll be ready by noon."

"Nothing's going to change between now and noon," Geraldine insists.

The gavel worked. The room falls quiet all at

205

once; the onlookers still. The glass-encased pendulum clock behind the jury box says it's eight thirty-five. It's been a hell of a long day and it's barely begun. The judge looks out at the spectators again, then back at me. "It's important," I whisper.

He removes his half-glasses and rubs the bridge of his nose. Judge Leon Long is the ultimate reasonable man, but he likes to get things done. Delays, he always reminds us, are not what the citizens pay him for. "Counsel," he says quietly to both of us, "in my chambers. Now."

"What can the pampered princess possibly tell us?" As usual, Geraldine is on her feet, pacing around the room. "Is she going to say some homicidal maniac sauntered into the palace, undetected even by the security system, clobbered the prince, and then suddenly remembered Miss Marple's Rules of Manners and cleaned up the mess?"

Judge Long swivels his chair around and stares at me across the expanse of his mahogany desk. He glances up at Geraldine and then raises his graying eyebrows. The basic question buried in her dark little fairy tale is valid, he's telling me. And he's right. It is.

"I don't know, Your Honor. I don't know what Mrs. Rawlings can tell us. But we deserve an opportunity to talk with her, to think it through, to try and make sense of it."

"Make sense of it?" Geraldine stops pacing,

tosses her head back, and lets out a half-laugh. "*I'll* make sense of it for you."

I ignore her. "Look, Your Honor, the brass swan didn't add up at first either."

Geraldine throws her hands in the air. She's going to say something about apples and oranges, I think, but Judge Long speaks first.

"Ms. Schilling, I did read the Medical Examiner's report, but refresh my aging memory, please. How large a man was the deceased?"

Geraldine resumes pacing. "Large," she says. "Six-one, two-ten."

The judge rests his elbows on his orderly desk, cradles his chin in one hand. "Now I'll grant you, the accused isn't a frail little thing . . ."

So Judge Long has noticed Louisa's physique. What a surprise.

". . . but do you really think she's capable of dragging two hundred and ten pounds of unconscious weight from her house, loading it onto a vessel, and then lifting it again to dump it overboard?"

The judge's words are the sanest ones I've heard so far today. For a split second, I breathe a little easier. But Geraldine laughs again, a real one this time, and I brace. Real laughter from Geraldine rarely means anything good.

"No," she says to him, standing still now. "I don't."

The judge stares up at her, still cradling his chin, and I stare at him. We're both silent.

"I think she had help," Geraldine adds.

Judge Long studies his hands while we both absorb this information, then he sighs and looks up at Geraldine again. "And your theory is?"

Geraldine walks over and half sits on the edge of his desk, arms folded across her dark gray suit jacket, the pointed toe of one high heel pressing into the plush carpeting. "That the accused incapacitated her husband—and frankly, I don't give a damn whether she meant to or not—and then panicked," she tells the judge. "Decided she had to finish the job and get rid of him. Realized she couldn't do that without help. And then got some."

She shifts a little and turns her attention to me. "Beyond that," she says, "I don't have a theory. Unless the winsome widow decides to give me one."

I return her gaze, but not her smile. "And why would she decide to do that?"

Geraldine stands again, turns her back to the judge, and takes a few small steps toward my chair. "Oh, I don't know," she says. "Maybe because I'd ask nicely. I'd even say pretty please."

She pauses, apparently expecting a reaction to her stab at humor. I don't give her one.

"Or maybe because she knows the cause of death was drowning, not head trauma."

Now I see where she's going with this. One look at Judge Long tells me he does too.

"Or maybe because as things stand at the moment," Geraldine continues, "your Mrs. Rawlings is looking at life. Her only transportation out of Framingham is a pine box."

MCI Framingham takes maximum security to a new high—or a new low, if you happen to live there. It's the Commonwealth's warehouse for the worst of its female violent offenders. Faced with a choice between Framingham and a pine box, Louisa Rawlings might just opt for the latter. She might climb in and close the lid herself.

"What are you offering?" I ask.

Geraldine smiles the way she does when she knows I'm sweating. "Not a damned thing," she says. "At least not at the moment." She moves back to her perch on the corner of the judge's desk and crosses her legs. "Find out if your client is interested," she adds. "And then we'll talk."

I hold one hand up to Geraldine, then rest my forehead in it, looking down at my lap. I need a few seconds to think. Something is wrong with this discussion. Technically, it doesn't work. And Geraldine Schilling is nothing if not technically accurate. She never proffers a deal that isn't. Never.

Louisa Rawlings can't finger a third party, even if she's willing, without damning herself in the process. To provide specifics—and Geraldine won't barter with any defendant for generalities—Louisa will have to admit enough to cement her own conviction as well. As an accessory, at best. More likely as a co-conspirator.

Geraldine is still smiling at me when I look up

from my lap. She knows what I'm thinking, but she sure as hell isn't going to say it for me. "She'll need immunity," I tell her.

She nods, her eyes asking what in God's name took me so long. "Qualified," she says.

No surprise there. Qualified immunity is the best any prosecutor would offer under these circumstances, even one less rabid than Geraldine. Absolute immunity is almost unheard of. And at the moment, Louisa is lucky to be offered anything. She's not exactly sitting in the catbird seat.

"She pleads to aggravated assault with intent regardless," Geraldine adds. "And she does time, Martha, real time. But if she fingers the muscle in the operation, we can probably get her out before she needs a nursing home."

Judge Long clears his throat. He's got a packed courtroom waiting, he's reminding us. There are other cases on his list.

"Give us until noon," I urge him again.

He looks at his watch. "Eleven-thirty. And it might turn out to be the old hurry-up-and-wait routine. I've got a full docket this morning. But we're going to get this thing on track—one way or the other—before we break for lunch."

With that, Judge Long buzzes Wanda and tells her to send in the court reporter. Seconds later, Old String Tie joins us, a stenographer whose moniker stems from his self-imposed work uniform. He's labored here, in the Superior Courthouse, for about a century. I've never seen him crack a smile.

String Tie perches on the end of an empty chair and purses his lips at the armrests. He's annoyed. Court reporters sit on stools; chairs with armrests inhibit their elbows. Nonetheless, he sets up his narrow machine between his scrawny legs without complaint. He looks up at the judge, waiting.

Judge Long reads the docket number and case name from the paperwork on his desk, then dictates a short memo reflecting his decision to recess for the morning. The delay is necessary, he opines, so defense counsel can consult with her client regarding newly disclosed evidence. String Tie dutifully taps it all into his machine, then looks up at the judge again, fingers poised to continue. "That's it," Judge Long tells him. "That's all for now."

String Tie nods, packs up as silently and efficiently as he set up, and then leaves us without a word.

I stand to leave too.

"Attorney Nickerson," the judge says, and I turn back to face him. He looks up at Geraldine, who's still perched on the edge of his desk. She's looking at me, smug.

Judge Long turns his attention back to me and lays a hand on the pile of documents in front of him. "Officially we've adjourned so you and your client can discuss the newest lab report."

I nod.

"And you should do that," he continues. "But, like it or not, I'm going to offer a word of advice here."

A word of advice from Leon Long is fine with me. He's probably the most fair-minded human being I know. And what's the worst that could happen? Geraldine might think he's in her camp, might think she has a leg up on us? I muster a small smile to encourage him to continue.

Once again, he glances at Geraldine and then back at me. "Regarding the Commonwealth's proposal," he says, "be sure to discuss that, too. Explain it to your client. Tell her to think about it. Tell her to think long and hard."

CHAPTER 22

The Kydd and Louisa were leaning forward over the defense table when I emerged from chambers, their heads bent low, almost touching. They were engrossed in discussion, oblivious to the chaos in the room behind them. I realized as I approached the table, though, that they were actually immersed in a monologue. The Kydd was doing all the talking, Louisa not uttering a word. She sat stone-still at first. But when I got closer, she began shaking her ponytailed head, over and over.

She looked up at me when I joined them, dark brown eyes brimming, and the unbridled alarm on her face told me two things at once. The Kydd had already explained the significance of Herb's blood in the Queen's Spa. And Louisa had no idea how it could've gotten there. That was more than two hours ago. She still doesn't.

We're in lockup, in a windowless space the county passes off as a meeting room. It's about the size of a broom closet and it reeks of disinfectant. Louisa sits upright, posture perfect, at a small stainless steel table, the kind you might find laden with detergent in an industrial laundry. The Kydd slouches in his chair across from her. I'm between them, facing a cracked concrete wall painted government-issue green, and I'm just about talked out.

Louisa's mantra has been constant since we got here. She couldn't cut a deal with Geraldine even if she wanted to. And, for the record, she does not. She can't finger a muscleman because she doesn't know such a person. She had nothing to do with the attack on Herb. And she knows of no one who would want him dead.

It's ten past eleven; our time is evaporating. I want to review the evidence with Louisa once more, and I'll have to do it quickly. Every once in a while it's possible to look back on a case and see the precise juncture in the road where it took an irreversible turn toward disaster. I'm afraid we're at that intersection now. I'm afraid Louisa will look back in a year's time and wish she'd cooperated with the Commonwealth, wish she'd ransomed her golden years. I'm afraid I'll look back too, and wonder why I wasn't able to convince her.

My old wooden chair creaks and the sound seems exaggerated in the stillness of the compact room. I press my hands into the armrests and stretch, ready to delve into my "save your own skin if you can" speech again, but Louisa beats me to the punch. She stands and paces the short distance to the far wall, staring at the concrete floor. "I have a question," she says, not looking at us. "And I want an honest answer."

Fair enough. We're all entitled to that much. "Ask it," I tell her.

She's quiet a moment, takes a deep breath, and then looks up. "Do you two believe me?" She looks first at the Kydd, and then at me, as if there were someone else in the room who might field her query.

When I first moved to the defense bar, I was surprised by the number of clients who did *not* ask this question. It's one *I* would ask, I've always thought, if the tables were turned. Now that I'm faced with a client who wants to know, though, I'd rather not answer. "Louisa," I tell her, "what we think doesn't matter."

She steps backward abruptly, as if I've slapped her. "Yes, it does," she says, her voice down to a whisper. "It matters to me."

"*I* believe you," the Kydd volunteers. And he means it. There's not a trace of hesitation in his voice, not a glimmer of doubt on his face.

215

It occurs to me that the Kydd's certainty might be ever so slightly influenced by matters outside the evidence, but I don't say so.

Louisa nods at him, then turns back to me. She wants my answer too. "It doesn't matter" isn't good enough. She presses a hand against her throat, tapered fingers flat under the collar of her orange jumpsuit, and waits.

For a moment, no one says anything. And in the sea of silence that engulfs us, I realize I have to give her two answers. I *do* believe her. But I shouldn't.

"I don't think you're lying to us." I'm careful to meet her gaze while I respond. "My gut says you're telling us the truth."

She nods, only partially satisfied. She senses there's more.

"But the evidence points in the other direction," I continue. "All of it."

She reexamines the floor.

"We'd be doing you a disservice if we didn't tell you the truth."

When she looks up, her eyes are brimming again. "Then tell me," she says, almost laughing as her tears spill over. "By all means, darlin', do tell me the truth."

I decide to leave my chair first. She's too tall for me to stand eye to eye with her, but I get as close as I can. "If you are convicted of murder one, Louisa, you will waste away in the women's penitentiary until you've drawn your last breath. The Barnstable

County House of Correction will become a distant, and *fond*, memory."

Her eyes stay locked with mine. She doesn't flinch.

"And twelve jurors faced with this evidence won't have a choice, Louisa. They will convict you. *That* is the truth."

CHAPTER 23

This morning's crowd has thinned by the time the Kydd and I return to the main courtroom, a testament to the fact that at least a fraction of today's early birds hold down day jobs. The front benches are still crowded, but there are a few seats unoccupied in the back. No one's standing in the aisles anymore except the photographers, who are there by choice. And the chairs at the bar, where attorneys wait for their cases to be called, are empty. The Kydd moves Harry's old schoolbag to one of them so we can set up at the defense table.

Mrs. DeMateo's arraignment has just ended. She's here alone today, sans the mister, and she doesn't seem to miss him much. She's beaming at Harry, who's still at the bench. Harry doesn't notice, though. He's busy beaming at Geraldine. He must've persuaded Judge Long to set a reasonable bail.

Geraldine gives Harry her best "it ain't over 'til the Fat Lady sings" look, but he keeps beaming at her anyway. In this business, he always tells the Kydd and me, we have to savor the minor victories. Most days, that's all we get.

Judge Long tells Mrs. DeMateo she's done for today and she dutifully heads toward the courtroom's side door. Halfway there, she turns and waves to Harry, calling out an effusive thank-you. Her not-quite-ready-for-Hollywood smile grows enormous when he waves back, and she keeps her eyes on him until the door slams shut between them. She seems to have gotten over her initial dissatisfaction with her court-selected lawyer.

"Ain't she a peach?" Harry asks as he approaches our table. He doesn't realize Geraldine is inches behind him. She stops in front of us just as he does and they face each other for a moment. Geraldine scowls. Harry grins. "Well," he says to her, "ain't she?"

Geraldine doesn't deign to respond. Instead, she turns away from him and looks down at me. Harry is dismissed, though he doesn't seem to realize it. Geraldine folds her thin arms, silently awaiting word on Louisa Rawlings's willingness to sing.

"She's wrongly accused, you know," Harry interjects. It takes a moment for me to realize he's still arguing the DeMateo case. "It's that no-good scoundrel husband of hers who's dealing. Not his blushing bride."

Geraldine makes no effort to hide how annoyed she is. She's done with the mom-and-pop shop for now. And she's sure as hell done with Harry. She pivots slightly and points an index finger at him, her tapered nail not quite poking his lapel. "Mr. Madigan," she says, "do the county a significant favor. Get lost."

Harry looks genuinely wounded. "Now you've done it," he mumbles pitifully. "You've gone and hurt my feelings."

Geraldine reverses her pivot, flicking both hands to shoo Harry away, and then looks down at me again. Harry doesn't go anywhere; he looks at me too.

"No deal," I tell Geraldine.

She tosses her head back and laughs out loud.

I feel a little bit sick.

"And people wonder why I stay in this line of work," she says, wiping her eyes as if her laughter had induced tears. "No federal judge has more job security than I do."

Geraldine must be referring to people I haven't met. No one I know has any doubt about why Geraldine Schilling stays in this line of work. She prosecutes criminals for the same reasons spotted leopards eat raw meat: it sustains her.

I consider offering the explanation for Louisa's refusal to talk, but when I look up, it's obvious Geraldine is distracted. Her attention is focused on something over my shoulder, in the gallery. Harry stares in the same direction, his eyes as wide as they get. "Sweet Jesus," he whispers. "Morticia on steroids."

The Kydd swivels his chair around and then does his best to swallow his reaction. He leans toward me, hiding his lips from the spectators with one hand, and mouths, "Anastasia."

I force myself to sit still. We don't all need to gape at the deceased's daughter. She's agitated enough already. And besides, my mental picture of Anastasia Rawlings is alive and well. As usual, Harry hit the proverbial nail on the head.

"Daddy's little girl?" Harry asks.

"Right as always, Kimosabe," the Kydd answers.

An abrupt barrage of flashes tells me Louisa has arrived. Geraldine turns and abandons our table without another word. She'll be on in a few minutes, after all. She needs to polish her script.

Once again, Louisa stands tall, dignified, as she crosses the courtroom. Bursting flashbulbs dog her as she approaches, but her somber expression brightens as she nears our table. By the time she reaches us, she looks downright delighted.

"Harold," she says, extending her hand.

Harold?

Harry laughs, takes Louisa's hand in both of his, and drinks her in.

"You look marvelous," she says finally.

He laughs again, still clasping her hand, as if she might leave the room otherwise. "So do you," he says, "considering."

She giggles.

I've watched at least a half dozen men fawn over Louisa Rawlings in the past few days. Not one of them earned a giggle. Harry managed with four words.

"All rise," Joey Kelsey intones. Joey always does his best to sound as if he'd sing bass if he were in a church choir. He should give it up. He's a natural tenor and his efforts to prove otherwise make him sound like he's thirteen.

Harry seems unwilling to release Louisa's hand. She has to forcibly extract it from his grasp so she can take her place at the table. She blushes in the process, something I suspect Louisa Rawlings doesn't do often. Harry walks backward to a seat at the bar, his hazel eyes melded with Louisa. All of her.

None of it is lost on the Kydd. He watches their slow-motion separation, then focuses on Louisa's pink cheeks as she takes her place between us. When she turns toward him, he hangs his head and stares down at the table.

It hits me so hard I can't breathe for a moment. A truth so obvious it's almost tangible. And it was here all along, right out in the open, begging to be recognized and called by its proper name. But I ignored it, pretended it didn't exist, until now.

I steal a glance back at Harry, whose eyes haven't wavered, and then look over at the Kydd. He's studying the table as if he's never seen one before. And then the truth gels, crystallizes. Technically, the Kydd is the only lawyer in the room who has run afoul of the Canons of Professional Conduct. But in point of fact, when it comes to Louisa Coleman Powers Rawlings, we all have a conflict. All three of us.

CHAPTER 24

Geraldine was positioned in front of the bench, chomping at the bit to begin, well before Judge Long took his seat and called the noisy courtroom to order. He didn't acknowledge her at first, though, didn't give her an opening. Instead, he donned his half-glasses and peered over them to the defense table, at me. He didn't utter a word, didn't need to. His question couldn't have been clearer if he'd shouted through a bullhorn.

"Your Honor," I said, getting to my feet but remaining at our table, "the defense is prepared to go forward."

The shake of his head was barely perceptible.

And it was not intended to be unkind. Leon Long is the last member of the judiciary who would question a citizen's inalienable right to be judged by a panel of her peers. He deemed it foolhardy, though, for Louisa Rawlings to go forward under the circumstances. And I don't disagree.

Geraldine is adding the final touches to her presentation now and I suspect she'll be nominated for an Academy Award before the day is out. Under the guise of getting the substance of her case against Louisa Rawlings on the record—a legitimate end—she managed to spoon-feed every delicious morsel of this sordid saga to the salivating members of the media. More than a few reporters ran for the double doors to phone their press rooms after she showcased the brass swan. They stopped short, though, huddling in the back like an indoor football team, when she brought the bloodstained portion of the oak floorboards to center stage.

She's just about finished, I think, talked out at last, and the press benches are empty. Only the photographers remain, roaming the aisles in search of one last opportunity to bag a front-page shot. And Woody Timmons is still here too, scribbling in his notepad. He's off on his own again, this time seated on the end of the back bench.

"And so, Your Honor," Geraldine concludes, "the Commonwealth respectfully prays that the defendant be held over without bail, as she poses a clear and immediate danger to the community."

I'm on my feet. Geraldine is out of line, even by her own standards. Bail isn't an issue here; murder is a nonbailable offense. Never mind the "clear and immediate danger to the community" nonsense.

Judge Long is way ahead of me. He bangs his gavel even before I voice my objection. "Attorney Schilling," he says, "that's enough."

I sit again, certain the judge's admonition will rein her in.

"She's a cold, calculating murderer," Geraldine adds, facing our table. As fate would have it, she's facing the cameras, too.

So much for the judge's admonition. "Your Honor!" I'm up again, but I doubt my words can even be heard over the explosion of commentary from the spectators.

Judge Long is on his feet now too, pounding his gavel with abandon. "Enough, Ms. Schilling," he repeats.

Geraldine fires the slightest of smiles at our table.

"Murder*ess*," Louisa hisses.

Maybe I imagined it.

Geraldine's green eyes smolder. "*What* did you say?"

Maybe I didn't imagine it.

Louisa stands beside me and I grab her shoulder—hard—to tell her to shut up. She's not taking my advice today, though. None of it.

"Murder*ess*," she repeats calmly.

"Pardon me?" Geraldine's eyes ignite now. She seems to think Louisa is accusing *her* of murder. Even I know that's not the case, though I understand precious little else about this scene.

"What did you say?" Geraldine demands again.

"If you're going to accuse me of such dreadful acts," Louisa says, her voice low and steady, "do it right. If I had done the things you say I've done—which, for your information, I most certainly did not—I would *not* be a murderer. I'd be a murder-*ess*."

I don't think I've ever seen Geraldine Schilling speechless before. And I'm fairly certain no one else in this courtroom has either.

"Now here's a new wrinkle," Harry mutters from his chair behind us. "Just when you think you've seen it all."

Louisa wrests her shoulder from my grasp. "If you call me a murder*er* once more—" she says.

"Your Honor!" The Kydd shouts and jumps out of his chair. He grabs Louisa's elbow so hard he jolts her into silence. "Mrs. Rawlings isn't feeling well." He's still shouting, though there's no need. The rest of us couldn't be any quieter. "With the court's permission, she'd like to leave the proceedings at this time."

The Kydd moves Louisa away from our table and propels her toward the side door, motioning frantically for the startled matron to come take her off his hands. She does. And they exit before the equally surprised judge utters a word. "Permission granted," he says as the door slams shut.

The Kydd returns to our table, winded and flushed, and I give him a grateful nod. That was quick thinking on his part and I'm fairly certain it averted disaster. Louisa's defense is already on life-support. Threatening any prosecutor would be a mistake. Threatening Geraldine would be fatal.

"I've heard enough," Judge Long says, taking his seat again. He looks out at Geraldine and shakes his head. "No, I misspoke," he says. "Let me amend that. I've heard *more* than enough."

Geraldine is still standing. She looks up at the bench and gives him her best angelic face, as if she has no idea what he's talking about.

The judge turns to Old String Tie, who's been dutifully tapping away for the past hour, to issue his ruling. "The defendant will be bound over," he says. "Louisa Coleman Rawlings is hereby remanded to the custody of the Barnstable County House of Correction to await trial." The judge bangs his gavel again, just once. "We're adjourned."

We stand as he leaves the bench. He reaches the door to his chambers and turns to face us again. "I want a scheduling conference in the morning," he says, "so we can keep this thing moving. Be here at eight. And bring your three Cs."

Geraldine looks at the judge and frowns before she returns to the prosecutors' table. Judge Leon Long always tells attorneys to bring their three Cs to scheduling conferences. And Geraldine Schilling always frowns when he does.

All important dates for a case are pinned down during the scheduling conference. The discovery cutoff, the pretrial-motions deadline, and the start of trial itself are among them. Trials run more efficiently—and presumably more effectively—when both sides have enough time to do what needs doing. That's why Judge Long asks each attorney to show up with three Cs: common sense, a calendar, and a conscience.

CHAPTER 25

Wednesday, October 18

Harry slaps this morning's *Boston Herald* on our table. Even before I look down at it, I know the news isn't good. There it is. Lou McCabe's front-page headline. Over the top, even for Lou.

Goody Hallett Dances Again!

A low moan seeps into the room. I pause, thinking it sounds familiar, and then realize it's coming from my throat. I feel a sudden need to go home to pull the blankets over my head, but the pendulum clock behind the jury box says it's just five minutes before eight—A.M. I plant my elbows on the table and bury my face in my hands.

The Kydd wheels his chair closer to mine and leans on my armrest so he can read Lou McCabe's venomous version of journalism. "Who the hell is Goody Hallett?" he asks.

I sit up straight again and face him. "She's the little old woman of Nauset Sea."

"A witch," Harry adds.

"A *what*?" The Kydd starts to laugh, certain we're joking, and then stops. We're not.

"Goody Hallett is a local legend," Harry tells him. "Cape Codders believe she lived here during the eighteenth century—all hundred years of it. She made her home along the shoals, dancing all night—every night—across the beaches and over the sand dunes."

"In scarlet shoes," I pitch in.

"Scarlet shoes?" The Kydd still looks like he's sure this is a joke.

"That part doesn't really matter," Harry says.

"Yes, it does," I correct him.

"Well, okay, it matters to Marty. She's something of a clotheshorse. Anyhow, legend has it that old Goody had a penchant for conjuring up nor'easters. And an appetite for the souls of doomed sailors."

"The souls of doomed sailors," the Kydd repeats. He looks like he's starting to worry about us.

"Right," Harry answers. "Goody would whip up the weather whenever she got the whim and the ships near Cape Cod's shoals would find themselves in serious trouble."

The Kydd knits his brow, apparently having a

little trouble of his own. Harry doesn't notice. "And then old Goody would hang a lantern from a whale's tail," he continues.

"A whale's tail." The Kydd checks in with me to see if he heard correctly. I nod. He did.

"That's right," Harry says. "And to the men on the vessels struggling at sea, it looked like a lighthouse. Goody lured them to certain destruction and then gambled with the Devil for their souls."

"The Devil." The Kydd checks in again, and I take over.

"Word is that Goody outgambled the Devil and, eventually, he got sick of losing. He strangled Goody and, the following year, a pair of scarlet shoes turned up in a dead whale's belly."

"The Devil," the Kydd repeats.

"That's why the shoes are important," I tell Harry.

He nods, giving up the point, and then turns back to the Kydd. "Old-timers take Goody out and dust her off any time they sit around a campfire with their grandchildren," he says.

"To ensure the folklore lives on," I explain.

"But mostly to terrify the little tykes," Harry adds.

"The Devil," the Kydd says yet again. He takes a deep breath, folds the newspaper in half, and hands it back to Harry. "Get it out of here," the Kydd says. "Louisa is low enough. She doesn't need witch talk."

He's right, of course. She doesn't. And in spite of the inappropriateness of it all, I'm touched by his genuine concern for her. He's a good sort, the Kydd. His heart's in the right place, even if his pants sometimes aren't.

Harry tucks the folded paper under his arm and moves to a chair at the bar, behind our table. As soon as he leaves, Judge Long and Louisa enter the courtroom simultaneously, the judge from chambers, Louisa from lockup. A flustered matron rushes to deliver Louisa to us and an equally ruffled Joey Kelsey tells us to rise after everyone in the room is on their feet. I'm not the only one who's a beat behind this morning.

Louisa looks somewhat refreshed, markedly better than she did yesterday. She smiles at the Kydd and me as she joins us and I realize her eyes aren't bloodshot anymore. I'm reminded of the Rule of Alternates, a principle Harry shared with me years ago. People newly imprisoned—most notably first-timers—tend to sleep on alternate nights. It's impossible to fall asleep the first night in the joint; impossible not to the second. For some, the pattern persists throughout their entire stay in county facilities.

Judge Long tells us to sit and everyone except Wanda Morgan does. She stays on her feet instead and walks to the bench with a file that apparently needs the judge's attention. I lean closer to Louisa so I can whisper and the Kydd leans toward her too, so he can listen. "About the trial date," I ask her, "what's your preference, sooner or later?"

Left to its own devices, the machinery of the Commonwealth will deliver a case like this one to trial in about a year. But if there aren't an excessive number of discovery disputes or pretrial motions, that time can be shortened, sometimes by as much as a few months. For defendants who have a decent shot at acquittal, it's a no-brainer. They want to get to trial as fast as possible. This particular defendant, though, isn't one of them.

"That depends," Louisa answers, looking at the Kydd and then back at me, "on how long the two of you need—"

I shake my head. "That's not an issue."

She shakes her head too. "—to find the murderer."

Now *that's* an issue. "What?"

"My head is clear this morning," she says, "for the first time since this nightmare began. And now it's obvious."

"What's obvious?" The Kydd's starting to squirm.

"I didn't kill Herb," she says. "And I didn't attack him. But the only way I'm going to convince *these* people of that"—she nods toward Geraldine and Clarence—"is to prove who did."

The Kydd stares at me and loosens his tie a little.

"I'll work every minute of every hour," Louisa continues. "I'll make notes. I'll give you every detail that might be remotely connected to Herb's death. I'll do everything I can to figure out who killed him."

She pauses and looks at both of us again. "But I'm stuck in this dreadful place," she says, "so you two will have to go get him." She faces front and folds her hands on the table, as if it's all settled now.

The judge and Wanda are still poring over their file and after a moment, Louisa twists around in her chair. "Good morning, Harold," she says.

Harold leans forward and squeezes her shoulder.

She points to the newspaper in his lap. "Is that the *Herald*?"

He nods.

Her eyes move from Harry to the Kydd and then to me. "Have you read it?" she asks us.

We all nod. The look on Louisa's face tells us she's read it too.

"It's preposterous," she says, facing front again and folding her arms.

She's right, of course. *Preposterous* is Lou McCabe's middle name.

Louisa turns away from the Kydd and leans over the arm of my chair, as if what she has to say next is just between us girls. "Honestly," she whispers, "what in the world was that man thinking?"

I shrug. Louis P. McCabe *doesn't* think, as far as I can tell.

"A woman with my coloring," she continues, leaning into me and pursing her perfect lips, "wouldn't be caught *dead* in scarlet shoes."

CHAPTER 26

Geraldine leaves her table and strolls back to the bar—and Harry—as soon as Judge Long goes into his chambers. The Kydd and I are busy packing up. Clarence is too. And all of our yellow legal pads are peppered with multiple dates, the most important one either circled or underlined a few times. Louisa Rawlings's murder trial is scheduled to begin on September 18, eleven months from today.

"Splendid," Geraldine says to Harry, her face deadpan, her voice flat. "You're here."

Harry jumps to his feet and his chest puffs up a little. That might be the nicest thing our District Attorney has ever said to him. "I didn't know you felt that way," he says. He leans into her, as if he doesn't want the rest of us to hear, and uses his best bedroom voice. "One of us is going to have to break it to Marty." He shakes his head sadly. "I guess we all should have seen this coming."

"Puh-leeze." Geraldine closes her eyes and tosses a few printed pages at him. "Spare me."

Harry groans. He knows an arrest report when he sees one. "Who?" he asks.

Geraldine laughs and taps her temple, as if trying to recall. "Rhymes with *stinky*," she sings.

"Oh, for crying out loud." Harry falls back into his chair, checking the report to see if Geraldine is serious. His frown answers the question. She is.

He reads silently for a moment and then runs both hands through his thick hair before looking up at her again. "So when do we tango?" he asks. He sighs and slouches in his seat, stretching his legs out toward our table, not looking like much of a dancer at the moment.

She laughs again. "This afternoon," she tells him. "You're on my dance card." She checks her list and glances over at the pendulum clock. It's ten forty-five.

"The Rawlings matter is scheduled for one," she continues. "If you're back here by twelve-thirty, the judge might squeeze you in first. Otherwise," she shrugs and starts walking back to her table, "we'll see you and the King of the Road at open session."

I laugh and snap my briefcase shut. "You're slipping in your middle age, Geraldine. We just finished the Rawlings matter."

She frowns across the room at me, the "Get a brain, Martha" look she perfected when we worked together. "Not *that* Rawlings matter," she says. "The other one."

The *other* one? I stand and step over Harry's feet so I can walk toward her. "What other one?"

"The daughter filed a petition," she says, turning her back to me. "It doesn't concern you."

My client is charged with capital murder. Everything concerns me. "A petition for what?"

She takes a short stack of documents from Clarence, perches on the edge of her table, and begins reading. She waves me off without looking up.

"Geraldine, if anyone even remotely connected to Louisa Rawlings is going to be in a courtroom with the judge and the prosecutor on her case, I want to know about it."

She looks up at me, annoyed as usual, and then lowers her reading material to her lap and sighs. I can almost see her brain decide that answering my question is probably the quickest way to get rid of me. "The daughter," she says, "Anna-something."

"Anastasia," I tell her.

"That's it. She wants us to release the body."

I nod. It's not an unusual request.

"And the house," Geraldine adds.

"The house? What house?"

"Her father's. She's having some sort of service

for him tomorrow morning. Wants to invite the mourners back to the house for a mercy meal."

Anastasia was true to her word. She made arrangements. And she wasted no time.

"She also wants to stay there while she's on the Cape," Geraldine continues. "She can't do either of those things as long as the house is a designated crime scene, so she filed a motion asking the court to release it."

"Are you opposing the motion?" The thought of Geraldine and Anastasia in combat is frightening.

She shakes her head. "No. There's no need. The post is done. And she's entitled to her father's remains, for Christ's sake."

"What about the house?"

Geraldine hugs the stack of documents to her chest and smiles the way she always does when she knows she's holding the reins. "Anna-whoever-the-hell-she-is can have the damned house," she says. "After all, we're done with it. We have everything we need."

CHAPTER 27

In the Barnstable County House of Correction, no reasonable request goes unrefused. The powers that be rejected ours on the spot. The Kydd and I were on our best behavior when we met with Louisa Rawlings in the jail's smallest conference room. We were patient, uncomplaining, as we waited in the hallway for more than half an hour to see the matron in charge of Louisa's ward. We were as polite as Eagle Scouts when we explained the situation and asked that Louisa be brought back to the main courtroom at one o'clock. The answer was no.

"It's not on the schedule," the gum-chewing matron told us. She closed her ledger then. And she closed our discussion with it.

"We know it's not on the schedule," I reminded her. "That's why we're here."

As far as she was concerned, though, our meeting had already ended. She took off her thick glasses and used them to direct us to the door.

The schedule is of paramount importance in our county facilities, particularly on the female violent offenders' ward. This has always struck me as somewhat peculiar. Like every other woman who resides there at the moment, Louisa Rawlings has precisely nothing to do. Yet her *schedule* is not to be disrupted. She might miss a call from the Pentagon, it seems. Or the Joint Chiefs of Staff.

It took a written order from Judge Leon Long to override the mulish matron. And by the time that was accomplished, it was almost twelve-thirty. The Kydd ran out to grab a quick bite at the Piccadilly Deli, but I came back to the courthouse instead. I don't have much of an appetite today.

Anastasia Rawlings is here early for the one o'clock hearing on her petition. She's already in the hallway, outside the main courtroom, her ensemble either the same one she's been wearing all week or a reasonable facsimile. She's engrossed in what appears to be a heated discussion with Steven Collier and he's not getting to say much. Lance Phillips is seated on a nearby bench. Apparently he's not interested in their tiff; he's staring into his lap, not even looking at them. Maybe he's plotting his next murder mystery best seller.

Collier spots me first and he alerts Anastasia to my arrival with a silent dip of his jet-black head. She wheels around, dropping whatever her beef is with him, and storms down the long hallway in my direction, her hair trailing behind like the train of an evening gown gone wrong. "You," she bellows, her deep voice echoing in the almost empty corridor. "How do you sleep at night?"

I've been asked this question a number of times since I joined the defense bar a year ago. Never by anyone concerned about my well-being. "You'll get used to it," Harry promised after the first time a pompous reporter shouted it at me on the courthouse steps. I haven't.

"I want an answer," Anastasia barks, blocking my path with her substantial black-clad form, her hair shroud settling around it.

"Then ask a question that deserves one." I stand still, toe to toe with her clodhopper boots, and meet her ridiculously outlined eyes.

"Anastasia!" Steven Collier hustles down the hallway as if he's been appointed the courthouse bouncer. "Stop it. The woman is only doing her job."

This is a comment I've heard before too. I don't like it any better than the sleep inquiry. "Not so," I tell him. "I'm doing more than that. Much more."

He looks down at me and knits his inky eyebrows, apparently unable to fathom what I might mean. I walk around both of them and pass Lance Phillips, who's still examining his lap. I glance back at Anastasia and Collier again—they're planted where I left them—and then enter the courtroom through its rear double doors.

Harry is the only person in here. He's seated at the defense table looking a little bit like the Maytag repairman. His chair is pushed back, away from the table, his legs stretched out in front of him. He swivels the chair around when the heavy doors slam shut behind me and he laughs. As is often the case with Harry, I can't imagine what he finds amusing. "Marty," he says. "Here we are. Alone at last."

As if she heard him, Wanda Morgan opens the side door and pokes her head into the courtroom. "You ready, Mr. Madigan?"

"You betcha," he says, thrusting a fist in the air. "Ready, set, Rinky."

Wanda shakes her head at him and then looks at me and laughs. I take a seat at the bar as she steps inside the courtroom, allowing Rinky and a couple of guards to enter after her. Rinky must be rambunctious today; it took two uniforms to get him in here. One removes his cuffs and the other delivers him to the defense table.

"*There* you are," Rinky says to Harry as he approaches. "I've been looking for you."

The side door opens and Geraldine rushes in, Clarence on her heels carrying two briefcases.

Rinky's shoulders droop when he looks over at the prosecutors and he drops his head sadly. "Oh, *man*," he says. "*Her* again."

Harry laughs out loud and slaps him on the back, sending skinny Rinky stumbling forward a few steps. Joey Kelsey tells us to stand.

Judge Long emerges from chambers, takes the file from Wanda as he passes her, and slaps it down on the bench. He sits, signals with both hands for the rest of us to do likewise, and retrieves his half-glasses from the pocket of his robe. "Mr. Snow," he says, donning his spectacles and then peering over them, "you're back."

Rinky gives the judge a little wave. "Here I am again," he says.

Judge Long sighs and skims the police report, then looks back up, his eyes wide under raised eyebrows. "*Another* tourist?" he asks Geraldine.

"Indeed," she says, "I told you so" written plainly on her face. "Another one. A Mr. Palmer. A businessman from Pittsburgh."

"Mr. Snow," the judge says, "the members of our Chamber of Commerce work extremely hard to attract visitors to this peninsula during the shoulder seasons. You are single-handedly thwarting their efforts."

Rinky hangs his head and assumes an "aw, shucks" look, as if he's a little embarrassed by the judge's flattery.

A firm grip on my shoulder makes me look up.

It's Steven Collier. "I need to see Louisa," he says in an authoritative tone.

"Then make an appointment," I tell him, maneuvering my shoulder out of his grasp. I toss my head in the general direction of the jail. "The women's ward has set visiting hours. Call and get your name on the list."

He frowns and bends down, bringing his face too close to mine. "Today," he says. "I need to speak with her while she's here in the courtroom."

"Can't happen," I tell him. "Louisa isn't allowed to have contact with anyone in this room except her lawyers. If you want to communicate with her today, you'll have to do it through one of us."

He stares at the floor and shakes his head emphatically. It seems my response is unsatisfactory. Again. He walks away and takes a seat on the front bench next to Anastasia and Lance. He fires an icy stare my way and then fixes his gaze on the judge. He's through with me.

Harry has joined Geraldine in front of the bench. "The guy came at him from behind," he says.

"Nobody *came at* him," Geraldine replies. "Mr. Palmer *tapped* him on the shoulder to ask for directions."

Rinky Snow would fare much better, it seems, if people would just stop asking him for directions. "No knives," he calls out from his chair. The judge looks up and Rinky wags a finger at him. "No knives," he repeats, as if he's been having a hell of a time keeping this judge in line.

"Rinky didn't know that," Harry says. "All he knew was that Palmer came at him from behind."

Judge Long's eyes move from Rinky to Harry, his expression unchanged. "So he belted the guy," the judge says.

"One punch," Harry answers, shrugging, as if we're all entitled to dole out that much in the course of a day. "In self-defense."

"No knives," Rinky announces again, his finger still wagging.

"Oh, please." Geraldine looks at Harry as if he's loonier than his client. "It was *not* self-defense."

"Knocked him out cold," Judge Long notes, reading from the report again.

"For a minute or two." Harry waves one hand in the air to emphasize the insignificance of it all. "The guy was awake and oriented by the time the rescue squad got there."

Judge Long looks like he isn't buying Harry's argument this time. He leans on his elbows, folds his hands together, and rests his chin on top of them. "Mr. Madigan," he says after taking a deep breath, "I'm sorry. I appreciate what you're trying to do here. And I realize there are extenuating circumstances. But I think we need to spell the people of Chatham, take Mr. Snow off their hands for a little while." He looks down at the police report again and sighs. "Particularly the tourists," he adds, "if any are still standing."

"But, Judge," Harry tries again, "it was nothing more than an honest mistake. You or I might have made the same mistake if someone came at one of us from behind."

The judge removes his glasses and closes his eyes. He almost smiles when he opens them again and looks at Harry. "I don't think so, Mr. Madigan."

Harry doesn't think so either, of course. Too often in this business we have to swallow our pride and advocate the absurd.

"Mr. Snow," the judge says, turning his attention back to Rinky.

"No knives," Rinky, standing up, warns the judge yet again with a wagging finger.

"I can't let you go with a slap on the wrist this time, sir. No knives is right. But no fists either. You're going to spend a little time up on the hill"— Judge Long nods in the direction of the House of Correction—"so you can think about it." He faces Geraldine and Harry again and sighs. "Come back tomorrow," he says, looking at each of them in turn, "and tell me you've worked this out."

Geraldine exhales loudly, her expression suggesting she'd rather work out a business plan with the mob. Harry smiles and winks at her, as if he's reveling in their earlier intimacy.

"We have the necessary paperwork, Your

Honor." Clarence Wexler pops up from his table and scurries to the bench, delivering photocopies to Harry, the originals to the judge.

"Hey, who's the whippersnapper?" Rinky puts his question to the room at large. "Where'd that little fella come from?" It seems Rinky hadn't noticed Clarence until now.

Judge Long all but swallows his lips in his attempt to avoid laughing, but his eyes give him away. He reads through Clarence's documents, fills in a few blanks, and signs off. He's still struggling for composure when he looks back up at Harry. "If it makes you feel any better," the judge says, "the forecast calls for a cold snap."

The matron delivers Louisa to the defense table and I join her, though technically we don't belong here. We're not parties to this particular proceeding. Geraldine was right: the issues raised in the petition are between Anastasia Rawlings and the Commonwealth. We have no standing to address them. But we do want to be heard on a related matter.

The gallery is noisy again, the benches full. Anyone who checked the schedule probably assumed that the Rawlings case docketed for one o'clock is Louisa's. And apparently the press thinks so too. They're back in force, hurling scores of questions at Louisa in anything-but-subdued voices. She doesn't answer, but she does smile and flashbulbs bombard her.

Harry and Geraldine are at one side of the bench, finishing up Rinky Snow's paperwork. Rinky's prison escorts lean against the wall by the side door, their charge centered between them. The Kydd is in a seat at the bar, so there's a chair available at the table for Anastasia Rawlings if she wants it. She doesn't.

She marches past, shielding her profile with a stiff, flattened hand, a dramatic blinder against the sight of her father's widow. Steven Collier follows and pauses to give Louisa a solemn nod before he passes. Anastasia steps to the side when they reach the bench and Collier plants himself squarely in front of the judge. He intends to do the talking, it seems. I might enjoy this.

Judge Long checks in with Harry and Geraldine and then nods at the uniforms, telling them it's time to escort Rinky to his all-too-familiar digs. Rinky's not quite ready to leave the courtroom, though. He does a double-take in Anastasia's direction and then elbows the guard nearest the door. "Would ya lookit that?" Rinky says. "Ever seen anything like that before?"

Anastasia tosses her hair over her shoulder and snarls at him. The guards look somewhat alarmed by her performance, but Rinky doesn't. He seems delighted. He encircles his eyes with his hands as if he's holding binoculars, then bounces up and down and starts to walk toward her, as if he's spotted a rare bird and wants a better view.

The uniforms have a different plan in mind, of course. Each of them takes one of Rinky's elbows and they move him toward the side door. Both guards stare at the floor—eyes averted from Anastasia—as they move out of the courtroom. Rinky doesn't. He walks backward, smiling and still bouncing a little. And he gives Anastasia raccoon eyes until the heavy door slams shut between them.

Judge Long massages his temples as he watches them leave, then sighs and closes his eyes. When he opens them, he seems a bit startled to find Steven Collier smack-dab in front of him. "I'm sorry," the judge says, looking down at the mountain of paperwork on the bench, "but I'm afraid I don't know who you are, sir."

"I'm Steven Collier." He gives the judge a slight bow and an indulgent smile, as if that says it all.

Judge Long looks confused, rifling through his papers now. "Are you an attorney?"

Collier's laugh is inordinately hearty. He slaps his thigh and shakes his head; that Judge Long is a real kidder. "Oh no, Your Honor. Me? No, I'm not an attorney."

The judge checks the paperwork again. "You're not a party to this proceeding, are you?"

"No, Judge. No. I'm not a party."

"Well, then who *are* you?" the judge asks.

"I'm Mrs. Rawlings's financial advisor," Collier says, sweeping one arm back toward Louisa. He looks over his shoulder and then leans toward the judge, as if he's about to share government-classified information. "And I'm an extremely close friend of the *entire* family."

Judge Long rests one forearm on top of the other, tucking his hands inside the wide sleeves of his robe. "That's all well and good, Mr. Collier," he says, peering over the rims of his half-glasses, "but why are you standing in front of my bench?"

"Oh, *that*." Collier laughs again, and again it's too hearty. He gets it now. Or he thinks he does. He lets out a small, embarrassed cough, as if he's hosting this event and momentarily forgot his manners. "This," he says, "is Anastasia Rawlings." He rests a hand on her forearm.

Judge Long takes a deep breath. He's losing patience. "I'm aware of that," he says.

"She is the daughter of the deceased," Collier whispers, as if Anastasia might not already know this.

"I'm aware of that, too," the judge says.

Collier releases Anastasia's arm and points to himself. "And I am here to speak on her behalf."

Judge Long shakes his head before Collier finishes his sentence. "I can't let you do that, sir."

"You can't? What do you mean, you can't?" Collier's posture changes, stiffens. He seems to take umbrage at the judge's words and I wonder for a moment if he'll say: *You're a judge, aren't you?*

Judge Long sees the body language too. "It's nothing personal," he says. "But if you're neither a party to these proceedings nor a licensed attorney representing a party, then you don't speak on behalf of anyone. Not in this courtroom. Not in any courtroom. You may have a seat in the gallery." The judge points.

Collier turns and stares out at the benches as if he hadn't realized they were here until now. "But, Judge," he says, "hear me out, please." Collier clutches Anastasia's arm as if she's a toddler who might wander into traffic. "Miss Rawlings isn't up to this. She's had an awfully rough go of it. She's rather fragile."

The Kydd tries to disguise his outburst of laughter as a coughing fit, but Judge Long isn't fooled. He looks out at the Kydd, who's bent in half in his chair at the bar, and then at Harry, who's sitting next to him. Harry shrugs. "He does this sometimes," he says.

Finally the judge looks at Louisa and me. We're laughing too—a little louder than we should. "Fragile," Louisa repeats. "Oh my, that's rich."

Judge Long looks back at Collier, who hasn't budged. "Miss Rawlings will be just fine," the judge says, pointing again to the gallery. "You are excused now, sir."

Collier pivots and retreats, clearly unhappy to be denied his moment in the history of American jurisprudence. I smile as he passes. He doesn't.

Geraldine leaves her table, saunters up front, and joins Anastasia near the bench. "Your Honor," she says, "perhaps I can help move this matter along."

The judge must have a headache; he's massaging his temples again. "And for that, Ms. Schilling," he sighs, "the court would be most grateful."

"Miss Rawlings has made two requests, Your Honor. First, she'd like her father's remains released for cremation."

"And your position is?"

"The Commonwealth has no objection, Your Honor. The post was done on Monday. Evidence collection is complete."

The judge peers down at his papers on the bench and scribbles hurriedly, his signature, no doubt. He passes the form to Wanda and then looks at Anastasia and smiles. "Consider it done, Miss Rawlings."

"She'd also like her father's house released from crime scene status," Geraldine says. "She'd like to use it while she's on-Cape."

"And?"

"And we have no objection, Judge. Again, evidence collection is complete."

The judge scribbles a second time and then arches his eyebrows at Anastasia. "This must be your lucky day, Miss Rawlings," he stage-whispers, as if he doesn't want Geraldine to hear. "Attorney Schilling is usually much more difficult to get along with."

"Your Honor." I leave the table and approach

the bench. If Geraldine is feeling agreeable, I want in. "Mrs. Rawlings would like to be heard on a related matter."

"Yes," he says, looking down at his file. "I have a note to that effect."

The thunder of a small stampede makes me pause and turn. Four court officers are running, two coming toward us from the back of the room, two passing by us from the front. They're headed toward the defense table, all of them. And they're shouting now, calling out "Move it!" and "Get back!" One look at the table tells me why.

In the time it took for me to walk to the bench, Steven Collier made his way to Louisa. He stands up straight now, backs away from the chair at the bar he'd been leaning over, and smoothes his suit coat. "I'm sorry," he says to the judge, raising his hands in surrender. "My mistake. I didn't know it would be a problem."

Two of the uniforms escort him out, Collier talking nonstop as they go. I wonder if his nose is growing.

When I look back at Judge Long, he's massaging his temples yet again. "You wanted to be heard, Ms. Nickerson," he reminds me, "on a related matter."

"Yes, Your Honor. Mrs. Rawlings would like the court's permission to attend her husband's memorial service tomorrow morning."

Anastasia wheels around, her thickly outlined

eyes boring holes into the woman she couldn't bear to look at fifteen minutes ago. "No-oo," she bellows. It's a two-syllable word.

Judge Long leans forward on the bench and looks down at Anastasia, his half-glasses on the edge of his nose. "Attorney Nickerson isn't asking for *your* permission, Miss Rawlings," he says.

"Your Honor, we can't do that." Geraldine peers up at the judge with the back of one hand to her forehead, looking like her next comment might be "woe is me."

"We've done it before," he says.

"And it's a security nightmare," she answers. "Every time."

Judge Long looks out at Louisa and then back at me. After a moment, he shakes his head at Geraldine. "I don't get the impression Mrs. Rawlings is a flight risk," he says. "And I certainly don't think she's a danger to anyone."

"We don't have the staff, Judge," Geraldine says.

"That, Ms. Schilling, is a matter you'll have to take up with the legislature."

"I can't believe you're discussing this." Anastasia's baritone is much louder than the judge's. "That woman," she says, pointing like a veteran prosecutor, "murdered my father. She's not welcome at his memorial service."

Judge Long is silent for a moment. His gaze rests on Louisa and then shifts to Anastasia. "That woman," he says quietly, taking his glasses off, "is innocent as she sits here today. And she will remain innocent unless a jury of her peers decides otherwise."

Anastasia folds her arms beneath her heaving bosom and bristles. She's ready to fight to the finish. "She is *not* innocent. She killed him and everyone knows it."

The press is loving this a little too much. The judge pounds his gavel, glares at them until they settle down, and then turns his attention back to Anastasia. "Miss Rawlings," he says, pointing the gavel at Louisa, "this woman has been convicted of nothing. She's been tried for nothing. Now, I can't order you to welcome her, or anyone else for that matter, to your father's service. But I *can* tell her she's free to go." He looks down at the bench and scribbles again. "And I just did."

He passes the signed order down to me and I return to our table with it. Louisa takes my arm as soon as I sit. "Thank you," she says. "It would have been terribly wrong for me to miss Herb's service. And I confess I won't mind a little fresh air on the way, either."

I nod at her. "What the hell did Steven Collier want from you? He's lucky he didn't get himself tossed into a cell."

She smiles, apparently amused by the thought. "Steven was just the carrier pigeon," she says. "The message was from Anastasia."

Anastasia's still standing in front of the bench, as if the judge might change his mind if she hangs around long enough. I point at her. "The fragile one?"

Louisa lets out a small laugh. "One and the same," she says. "The dear girl wants me to spring for tomorrow's luncheon. Says she's broke."

"Broke?"

Louisa laughs again. "She doesn't know the meaning of the word. But no matter. I'm happy to pay for it. It's my responsibility in the first place."

She's right, of course. It is. Still, something about the request rankles me. Maybe it's the timing.

"Your Honor." Geraldine had gone back to her table when I came back to mine, but now she's at the bench again, her copy of the signed order in hand. "Will you at least make the court's permission contingent upon the availability of prison personnel?"

The judge sets his gavel on the bench and smiles. For a moment, he says nothing. His eyes move from Geraldine to Anastasia and back again. "The county coffers might have to cough up a little overtime," he says at last, "because the answer is no, Attorney Schilling. I won't."

CHAPTER 28

Thursday, October 19

A steady stream of expensive cars winds down Fox Hill Road. Most sport Connecticut plates and every one of them turns left into the driveway that leads uphill to the imposing Eastward Edge Clubhouse. Herb Rawlings's memorial service is scheduled to begin at eleven. The mourners seem to have decided en masse to show up ten minutes beforehand. And somehow, though we're almost never early for anything, Harry, the Kydd, and I arrive in the midst of them.

Behind us is a dark blue Mercedes-Benz, its polished three-pointed star glinting on the hood in the morning sunshine. Ahead, a Bentley follows a BMW—an X5, the Kydd tells us authoritatively from the backseat. The BMW follows a Jaguar—an XK8, according to our resident auto enthusiast. All three cars come to a stop in the circular driveway and we idle behind them in Harry's Jeep.

A uniformed valet attends to each of the vehicles ahead of us, opening and closing doors for the occupants and then whisking the car away. There seems to be a small army of young men in double-breasted maroon suit coats sporting the colorful Eastward Edge logo. They wear visored hats, leather gloves, and somber expressions befitting the occasion.

"Hot damn," the Kydd says as he takes in our surroundings. "I need a raise."

Harry laughs, but I don't. I twist in the passenger seat and stare, silently reminding the Kydd of his recent ethical transgressions. Many a lawyer's license has been suspended for less. He's in a precarious professional position at the moment, not one that gives him a lot of bargaining power. "Surely you jest," I tell him.

"Just kidding," he mumbles through clenched teeth.

"You'd better be."

Harry laughs again. He has no idea.

A valet is at the driver's-side door. He's older than the others and he seems to be the guy in charge. He bends down and leans in when Harry opens the window. "Sir," he says, tipping his hat, "we ask pickup trucks and, uh"—his eyes travel the length of Harry's worn-out Jeep—"*recreational* vehicles to park in the lower lot." He clears his throat, then stands up straight and points downhill, as if the matter is settled.

Harry opens his door abruptly and the man in uniform jumps back. "Nope," Harry says as he leaves the Jeep. The Kydd and I get out too. We've seen this routine—in different settings—before.

"But, sir," the valet tries.

"You asked," Harry interrupts. "I answered."

"But, sir," the valet repeats. This time, though, he holds one hand out, palm open, as he tries to explain. Harry drops the key in it. "Take good care of her," he says with a wink. "She's an heirloom."

Chief Car Parker looks like he intends to argue, but he falters, momentarily distracted by something in the line behind us. Louisa Rawlings and her prison escorts have arrived. They're in a gray van, branded *Barnstable County Sheriff's Department* in bold black letters on both sides. It's sandwiched between a shiny red Maserati and a gleaming black Lincoln Continental.

Harry shakes his head in disapproval when the bewildered valet turns back to us. "You'd better lock it," Harry says, walking away from him. "You know, this *used* to be a decent neighborhood."

We're almost inside when the Kydd stops in his tracks on the top step. "You go ahead," he says to Harry and me. "I'm going to wait. Louisa shouldn't have to walk in there with no one but prison staff around her."

Harry punches the Kydd in the arm. "That's thoughtful of you, Kydd, damned thoughtful. You're a decent son of a gun."

I give the Kydd a pointed glare, the extent of his thoughtfulness for Louisa Rawlings unspoken between us.

Draping an arm around the Kydd's shoulder, Harry turns to me and dabs at the corner of his eye, as if brushing a tear away. "We raised him right," he says.

The Kydd gives me a grave nod, confirming Harry's sentiment.

I'd like to bang their heads together.

The van's side door opens and a prison matron steps out to the cobblestone walkway. Louisa emerges next, in the same beige trench coat and wide-brimmed hat she wore on Monday's trip from her house to lockup. No doubt her butter yellow coat dress is beneath. It's unlikely that the prison-guard van driver swung by Easy Street to let her select a mourning ensemble. It's even more unlikely that Anastasia would have let her in the door if he had.

I'm relieved to see that Louisa isn't cuffed. In situations like this one, prison escorts have broad discretion regarding the use of restraints. The decision to forgo them here doesn't involve much in the way of risk; both matrons have bulging holsters strapped around their hips, after all. Still, it was decent of them. A little scrap of Louisa Rawlings's dignity can attend the service with her.

Harry and I head inside first. Louisa follows, flanked by her escorts, the Kydd trailing a few steps behind. A slight, fussy sort of man greets us, his mustache so straight it looks like someone painted it above his lip. He directs us down a short hallway to double doors at the end.

We walk through the open doors into a good-size room facing the water. White wooden folding chairs—about a hundred of them—are set up in rows, five on each side of the room, creating a wide aisle in the center. Most of the seats are already filled, even the two rows in front, which are roped off with red velvet.

Harry points to three vacant chairs on the end of row four. He goes in first and takes a seat next to Louisa's ex, Glen Powers. I follow, the Kydd right behind me. Glen looks up and nods a silent greeting to all of us. I wonder how long it's been since he and Harry have seen each other.

Harry leans over to whisper to me, "Have you two met?" He points a thumb toward Glen Powers.

"Yes," I answer. "I met him on Sunday."

"Well, that's just ducky," Harry says, feigning a huff.

"What does that mean?"

"Oh, nothing," he answers. "But the last time Powers met a woman I was seeing, he married her."

I frown at him.

Louisa and her bookends continue down the aisle, until yet another slight, fussy sort of man stops them. "I'm sorry," he says, pointing backward at the roped-off rows. "These are reserved for family."

"She *is* family," one of the matrons snaps.

The fussy man seems taken aback.

"It's all right," Louisa says, pointing backward to three empty chairs directly in front of ours. "I'll be fine right there."

"You sure?" The other escort is ready to take on the fussy little man too. It occurs to me that the matrons act as if they're Louisa's big sisters. They might bully her at will, but they're sure as hell not going to let an outsider get away with it.

"I think it's best," Louisa says. And she's right, of course. It is. Nothing good will come of her sitting anywhere near the wicked stepdaughter.

In the front of the room, the windows frame lush green hills rolling down to open ocean. Against that backdrop stands an oak podium, complete with microphone and stainless steel water pitcher. Next to it is a small table draped in smooth white linen. It holds a fragrant but gaudy flower arrangement—gold and russet mums trimmed with black crepe bows. Anastasia's selection, no doubt.

On one side of the vase stands an eight-by-ten framed photograph of the deceased wearing a tuxedo. On the other, a dull brass urn a few inches taller than the frame looks like it might have been salvaged from the set of *I Dream of Jeannie*. The Kydd points to it and his eyes grow wide as he shifts in his chair to face me. "Is Mr. Rawlings *in* that?" he whispers.

I nod.

In front of us, Louisa's shoulders shake gently, but her laughter doesn't make a sound. "Mawkish," she whispers back to us. "Wouldn't you say?"

She's facing front, so she can't see us, but we all nod anyway. It is.

Keening. From the back of the room comes a howl that can only belong to one person, and Louisa's shoulders shake slightly again. And again, she doesn't make a sound.

All heads in the room turn and the wailing ratchets up a notch, in pitch as well as volume. Anastasia is flanked by Lance Phillips and Steven Collier, each of them holding the entire length of one of her forearms, elbow to wrist. She's dressed in her usual getup, but she's added a sheer black veil for today's events. It covers her face entirely, falling below her collar in front, slightly longer in back.

"Now *that's* a damned good idea." Harry's whisper is a little too loud and Glen Powers covers his mouth with his hand. "She's a vision, don't you think?" Harry asks this question of anyone who'll listen. Glen Powers nods again.

Anastasia begins what promises to be a lengthy, slow-motion trek down the center aisle. Steven Collier almost lifts her from the floor by her forearm, Lance Phillips not quite managing the same on his side. Her wails roll out in waves now, beginning as guttural blubbering, cresting as eardrum-shattering yowls. Her head rolls in steady rhythm with the waves, face and hair shroud downward as each one begins, head thrown back and veiled face skyward as each one peaks. Her pattern changes, though, as she approaches us, and I realize this grim scene is about to take a turn toward the macabre.

The clodhoppers stop short when she reaches Louisa's row, forcing Collier to an abrupt halt and making Lance trip over his own feet. For a split second there's not a sound in the room. Anastasia's liberally linered eyes glare through the veil at Louisa and I'm relieved to see that Louisa isn't looking back at her. She sits calmly between her escorts, facing the front of the room, as if she's entirely unaware of Anastasia's presence.

Into the silence Anastasia unleashes the worst shriek of the day. More than a few of the mourners actually press their hands to their ears. The matron in the aisle seat gets to her feet, faces Anastasia, and points, telling her and her ushers to move on. I'm grateful—and more than a little surprised—when Anastasia obeys. I'm reminded once again of the unparalleled power of an unconcealed weapon.

With no small amount of coaxing from Collier, Anastasia makes it to the front row and collapses with great fanfare into the second chair from the aisle. Elizabeth Taylor could learn a thing or two from Anastasia Rawlings. I'm happy to see Lance dutifully fetch a glass of water from the pitcher at the podium. He can't deliver it fast enough, as far as I'm concerned. And I'm fairly certain everyone else in the room is thinking the same thing. Anastasia will have to shut up, at least for a few seconds, to swallow.

The two men take their seats at the same time, Lance on the aisle, Collier on the other side of the bereft only child. The water seems to help the situation. She's actually quiet for a minute, and then her wailing resumes at a more bearable decibel. Apparently satisfied that she's settled, Collier gets to his feet, checks his watch, and then walks to the podium with a few sheets of paper in hand. A mechanical screech fills the room as he tests the mike and adjusts it. At least it's a change from the human sounds we've been enduring.

"Good morning," he says, and those assembled wish him the same. "I'd like to welcome all of you to Eastward Edge. We're here, of course, to honor the life of this great man." He points to the framed photo. "Herbert Andrew Rawlings."

Anastasia keens again, her head rolling onto Lance's shoulder, and Collier waits. When the noise subsides, he continues. "The family has asked me to say a few words about Herb at this time, and I feel privileged to do so."

At long last, Steven Collier has found a spot in the limelight.

"After that," he says, "we'll hear from Paul Bagley." Collier points to the front-row aisle seat opposite Lance's and nods a greeting. "Paul was Herb's business partner for more than thirty years. He'll tell us about Herb's long and distinguished career in the practice of law, his service on more than a few prestigious committees of the bar association, and his tireless, lifelong devotion to his many corporate clients, large and small."

Collier stops, pours a glass of water for himself, and sips, turning a page in his notes. "And finally," he says, pointing to the chair next to Mr. Bagley, "the Reverend Burrows will read from Scripture and lead us in prayer." Collier sets his glass down and lowers his head, as if we're praying already.

After a moment of silence, he takes a deep breath and squares his shoulders, apparently gearing up to deliver the meat of his eulogy. "Herb Rawlings," he says, "was first and foremost a family man. He was devoted to his wife of more than twenty years . . ."

Collier pauses and looks out at the crowd, his eyes settling on Louisa. He's a hard act, Collier, but I have to give him credit at the moment. His sympathy seems sincere. She nods back at him.

". . . and to his daughter, Anastasia."

At the mention of her name, Anastasia wails again and keels over onto Lance. He manages to keep her upright in her chair for a few seconds, but then she topples forward onto the floor, pulling him along. He jumps to his feet a second later and struggles to get Anastasia to do the same. He can't, though. He can't get her to move a muscle. She's out cold.

CHAPTER 29

Steven Collier actually asked if there was a doctor in the house. There were three. It took less than a minute for the white-haired cardiologist to revive Anastasia Rawlings. And then it took more than twenty for the plastic surgeon and the gastroenterologist to talk her up from the floor.

The Kydd and I worked on Louisa's file while we waited. He began drafting our first round of discovery requests; we should serve them before the week is out. I made a couple of lists: one of the pretrial motions we're likely to file and another of those we can expect from Geraldine. Harry folded his arms and promptly fell asleep, tilting toward

Glen Powers every few minutes until Glen pushed him upright again.

When at last Anastasia was vertical, she keened intermittently as Steven Collier delivered a long-winded account of her father's magnanimous life, stopping just short of nominating him for canonization. Paul Bagley's tribute to Herb's seemingly stellar career was shorter, but it was still too long. In contrast, the Reverend Burrows's Scripture reading and prayer session were both mercifully brief. The crowd heaved a collective sigh of relief when the whole ordeal was over and then an audible groan when Collier approached the microphone yet again. Our fears were unfounded, though. He didn't foist a second sermon on us. He just invited us all back to the house for lunch.

It's almost one o'clock. We're outside again, by the circular driveway, waiting for the less-than-happy valet to retrieve Harry's Jeep. Louisa and her uniformed companions are waiting here too. Their driver must have taken a coffee break; the county van is nowhere in sight. The six of us seem to be the last of the stragglers.

Louisa watched in silence as the luxury cars departed, most of them probably destined for the mercy meal at her Easy Street antique. Glen Powers promised her he'd visit before he leaves the Cape and an elderly gentleman waved to her before climbing into a vintage gold Cadillac with a flying silver lady on its hood. A '38, the Kydd informed us. Those two were the exceptions. The other guests said nothing at all to her; walked past as if she were invisible. More than once I saw Louisa's eyes light up at the sight of a familiar face, only to dim again when the familiar face turned the other way.

Steven Collier, Anastasia, and Lance emerge from the club as a stretch limousine pulls up. I'm surprised; I had assumed they'd left ahead of the others. The driver opens the back door and stands at attention as Steven and Anastasia descend the steps and breeze past us without so much as a backward glance. Lance looks over his shoulder at us as he climbs in, though, his nonchalant expression suggesting he travels by limo all the time. He has a sizable lump on one side of his forehead, undoubtedly the result of his front-row fall. It's the same color as his girlfriend's fingernails.

Anastasia starts to follow him, but then hesitates. She turns, fixes her still-veiled gaze on Louisa, and marches back toward all of us. "Anastasia," Collier says, reaching for her arm, "don't."

She pays him no mind, steamrolls in our direction, her veil fluttering in the breeze and her fists clenched. One of the matrons takes Louisa by the elbow and pulls her back a step. The other one moves forward, to the edge of the curb. "Hold it right there," she says.

Anastasia stops and glares through her sheer black mantle, her nostrils flaring. "You people," she says, "are *not* invited to the luncheon."

"Damn," Harry mutters, clutching the lapels of his suit coat. "Story of my life. All dressed up and no place to go."

Louisa smiles at him and then turns to me. "I'm going," she says matter-of-factly. "Aren't you?"

She's not, of course. Even Judge Long wouldn't authorize a luncheon. His order allowed her to attend the service only.

"Wouldn't miss it," I tell her.

"Me neither," the Kydd adds, rubbing his hands together. "I'm starving."

The matron at the curb turns, almost smiles at the Kydd, and then faces Anastasia again. "Sure we're invited," she says. "That's why I signed up for this duty. Warden promised there'd be a good hot meal."

"You're not welcome in my father's house," Anastasia says. "None of you. If you show up, I swear I'll call the po-lice." She pronounces the word as if she's a brother from the 'hood.

The matron folds her arms and laughs. "In certain circles, missy, we *are* the po-lice."

"Never deal dialect with a prison guard," Harry says.

"It's time to go now." Collier cups Anastasia's elbow, the way he cupped mine in Louisa's kitchen, but it doesn't have the same impact. She doesn't budge. "You have guests waiting," he tries.

Guests or no guests, Anastasia stays put. It seems she plans to spend the rest of the week glaring at us.

Louisa stares back, unblinking. Her face is drawn and her dark eyes reveal the enormous toll the last four days have taken on her. The set of her jaw, though, tells me she doesn't intend to fall apart now. She won't give Anastasia that satisfaction.

The county van pulls up behind the limo, Harry's Jeep following. "Oh, look," Louisa says, sounding genuinely pleased. "It's my ride."

Harry, the Kydd, and I head for the Jeep. The matrons start for the van's side door, Louisa between them. She turns and waves to all of us—even Anastasia—before she gets in. "I'm afraid I have to go now," she says. "But I'll see y'all at lunch."

CHAPTER 30

It's seven o'clock when I pull up to the cottage and discover I've got good news and bad news. The good news is Luke's truck is parked in the driveway. It's not in the shop. The bad news is Luke's truck is parked in the driveway. He's not at school.

The two-day job at the garage turned out to take more than three. Luke has been having a great time all week. Turns out he really is a grease monkey. He thought they'd finish today, though, in time for him to make his afternoon classes. Looks like he thought wrong.

Harry's Jeep is here too. He and Luke are back on either side of the coffee table when I reach the living room. They're at it again. And again, Luke is exasperated. Harry sits frozen on the living room floor, no more animated than Rodin's *Thinker*.

"Would you *look* at this guy?" Luke says when I join them. "He's been sitting there like that for an hour."

Harry tears his eyes from the chessboard and blinks at both of us, looking like he's surprised to find us here in his chess studio. "I have? Well, then, I should take a bathroom break."

"Good," Luke answers. "I'll rearrange the board a little while you're gone."

"No, you won't," Harry says as he gets to his feet. "I'd never expect it from a person of your caliber, Luke. So that would be cheating."

"Oh, great." Luke grabs the hair on top of his head with both hands as if he's going to yank out clumps of it. "Just what we need. *Another* Harry-ism."

Harry heads down the hallway, whistling, and Luke flops sideways onto the couch. I squeeze in to sit on the end, near his size-thirteen sneakers. Danny Boy joins us, always on the lookout for a group hug. His wet nose nudges my cheek and he paws my lap, as if he might have buried something there, while his tail thumps against Luke's legs. I thump Luke's legs too—hard. "Are you *ever* going back to school, my son?"

He laughs. "Tomorrow," he says, "I swear. We didn't finish with the truck until late today and I don't have class tomorrow until ten. I'll go up in the morning."

"And back in the afternoon," I tell him.

He props himself up a little and looks at me, baffled. He's his mother's son. "Tomorrow is Friday," I remind him.

He sits up straighter and counts—days, I presume—on his fingertips. "Cool," he says when he finishes, a surprised look on his face. "It's the weekend."

Maybe his father is right after all.

Harry returns and settles on the floor again. Without hesitating, he moves a rook and then smiles at Luke.

Luke jumps up from the couch and gapes at the board. "I don't believe it," he says.

Harry's smile widens. "Inspiration. You just never know when it's going to hit."

Luke sinks to the floor to plot his next move.

"Speaking of inspiration," Harry says, looking up at me, "that was quite a performance we saw today, huh?" His upper body stiffens and he falls over sideways, a half-baked imitation of Anastasia's collapse.

"*That* part wasn't a performance," I tell him, "but the keening sure was."

"The fainting was too," he says, falling over again. "Trust me. She's up for an Oscar."

"How could anyone fake a faint? She'd have instinctively reached out to break her fall."

"The skinny guy with the ponytail broke her fall," Harry says. "He's the only one who got hurt. Well, besides me."

"You?"

"Well, yeah," he says, looking forlorn. "That mean lady with the eyes said I couldn't come to her party. She hurt my feelings."

"I wonder how the mean lady's luncheon went. I'm guessing Anastasia doesn't shine in the hostess department."

"I wondered too," he says, "so I drove by there about an hour and a half after we got back to the office."

"You drove *by* there?" No one drives *by* Easy Street. It's not on the way to anywhere.

He shrugs. "I was curious. Anyhow, all the guests had already left by the time I got there. Just one car in the driveway, a jalopy. Aside from that heap, the place looks like a magazine cover. No more cops. No more yellow tape. It looks like the goddamned Cleavers live there."

"Right now Anastasia Rawlings and Lance Phillips live there," I tell him. "A far cry from the Cleavers."

"The Addams Family?" he tries.

"Now you're talking. And now that Morticia and company have set up camp in there, I'm wondering if Louisa will ever be able to get them out."

Harry looks up at me and shrugs. "It might not matter in the long run."

"What does that mean?"

"Your move," Luke announces.

"If Louisa goes to prison," Harry says, focusing on the chessboard again, "the house will pass to Morticia anyhow. Along with everything else her father owned."

He looks up at me again and I shake my head. "Why do you say that? Anastasia is specifically excluded from Herb Rawlings's will."

"Doesn't matter." Harry leans back against the overstuffed chair behind him and Luke groans.

"If Louisa is the sole beneficiary of Herb's will," Harry continues, "and she's convicted of his murder, the will is automatically null and void. It's as if he died without one, intestate. And if he *had* died intestate, Anastasia would have inherited the whole kit and caboodle—aside from the government's take, anyhow—because she's his only child."

I knew that, of course. But I hadn't given it a thought until now. And I'm astounded that Harry knows it. It's not the kind of information that normally interests him. "Now who's the nerd?" I ask. "Don't tell me you actually attended your trusts and estates classes?"

"Hell, no." The look on Harry's face suggests I accused him of showing up for ballet lessons—in a pink tutu. "That's one of the many legal principles I learned when I got *out* of law school," he says, "about ten years out, as a matter of fact. I was assigned to a guy who couldn't wait to get his mitts on his wife's family money. She'd left him everything in her will, but dammit, she just wouldn't die fast enough. So he fed her a lethal overdose of barbiturates with her nightly highballs. Then he realized he couldn't move the body."

"Speaking of moving," Luke interjects, "why don't you?"

"I don't remember anymore," Harry continues, "but I guess she must've been a full-figured gal."

Luke groans again.

"'Course, my guy wasn't exactly Atlas," Harry adds.

"Bet he could've lifted one of those pawns," Luke mumbles.

Their banter continues, but I'm not listening anymore. I'm registering that feeling again: my stomach running laps around my brain. I force myself to ask the question a second time. I have to be certain about this. "So because the guy was convicted of his wife's murder, her will leaving everything to him was *automatically* null and void. It was as if she'd died intestate."

I had been talking to myself, really, but Harry nods anyway. "That's why her schmo of a husband ended up in the Public Defender's Office." He looks over at Luke and arches his eyebrows. "The guy wasn't playing with a full deck."

"At least he was playing," Luke answers.

I move Danny Boy's head from my lap and leave the couch. I hurry into my bedroom, change into jeans and a turtleneck, leather jacket, and hat—all black—then check to make sure the Lady Smith is fully loaded. It is. I tuck it into my inside jacket pocket and head for the kitchen door. "I forgot something," I tell Harry and Luke. "I'll be back in a little while."

"Don't worry," Luke says, "take your time. We'll be here. Right here. Right in this very spot."

Harry looks like he's full of questions, but I'm not hanging around to answer them.

The Herb Rawlings jigsaw puzzle isn't finished yet, but the border pieces are starting to connect. Whoever used a TFR to secure Herb to his watery grave knew exactly what he was doing. He knew the pop-up would let go. He knew Herb Rawlings's body—whatever was left of it, anyhow—would float away from the weight that held it on the ocean floor.

Taylor Peterson's words come back to me as I start the Thunderbird and back out in the moonlight. He was wrong about Herb Rawlings being at the helm when the *Carolina Girl* left the dock. But he was right about a few other things. Whoever dumped Herb's body in the Great South Channel knew how to negotiate the cut. He also knew a pop-up when he saw one. And, as Taylor put it, the dead guy surfaced on schedule.

CHAPTER 31

The full moon bathes Easy Street in a pale yellow glow and scores of stars light the sky. I don't give a damn about the scenery at the moment, but I am glad to be able to leave my flashlight behind in the glove compartment. Free hands seem like a good idea—I might need them to strangle Lucifer. I pat the small weight of the Lady Smith in my inside jacket pocket, cut the engine, and get out of the car.

I'm parked at number two, the saltbox, behind a row of hydrangeas on the side. My tires aren't doing anything good for the manicured grass, but I can't worry about landscaping right now. It occurs to me as I hurry down the hill toward number one that Louisa might have to foot the bill for her part-time neighbor's lawn repair. And if my hunch is even close to accurate, she'll have plenty of cash to cover it.

The forecast Judge Long mentioned was on target. It's cold. For the first time this fall, I can see my breath. And as I get closer to the water, the wind picks up, making it feel even colder. I zip my jacket to the top and pull my hat down over my ears.

The jalopy Harry talked about isn't in Louisa's driveway. I'm hoping Lance took the little lady—and her mini-poodle—out to dinner after their difficult day. But it's possible only one of the humans is out, the other inside, so I take a quick spin around the perimeter of the house, slipping behind bushes to look in the windows. A lamp is on in the living room—as is the light over the kitchen sink—but no one is here, at least not on the first floor.

I head for the front door out of habit—Louisa's got me trained—and, as usual, it's unlocked. I let myself in and walk quickly through the foyer to the living room, then check the kitchen and sunroom. Everything's in order; the place is tidy. And the rooms are unoccupied, the house still. No one's home, not even the beast.

With the exception of the unmade bed, the master bedroom is tidy too. It's lit only by moonlight streaming through the veranda's double doors. They're closed and locked, but I check out there anyway. Empty.

The Queen's Spa is dimmer than the bedroom, the moonbeams muted by the block glass behind the hot tub. I don't turn a light on, though. I don't need one.

The crunch of oyster shells in the driveway paralyzes me. But it isn't a car pulling in. It's not loud enough, and it's not the crushing sound made by tires.

Footsteps. They move from the shell driveway to the wooden deck. And it isn't one of the neighborhood foxes passing through, either. I have company. Human company. And whoever it is didn't drive here.

I force myself to leave the Queen's Spa and move to a window in the bedroom, where I'll be able to see anyone who approaches the front door. The footsteps don't travel in that direction, though. They head toward the side of the house. And they stop. There's no sound at all. Anywhere.

Now there is. There's a new noise—a rustling—and it's in the kitchen. Someone is opening the kitchen door. Whoever is here lives on Cape Cod, enters houses the way the locals do. And now the Cape Codder is inside. Walking in this direction.

The only real exit from this room is the veranda. Its double doors have two locks, though. The Kydd opened them easily when we were here with Louisa on Sunday, but I didn't pay attention to the mechanics. I won't be able to do it that fast. I could climb out a window, but I wouldn't make it in time. The footsteps are too close.

I move back into the Queen's Spa. Maybe my visitor will stop in the foyer, or the bedroom. But maybe not. The steam room would buy me thirty seconds or so. The glass is frosted, but it is glass. I'd be spotted pretty quickly. And I'd be cornered. Now I'm battling panic. Deep breaths, I remind myself. Silent ones.

The Kydd's words come back to me as my eyes find the other door. *A completely separate room for the throne.* That's my only option—the throne room. If the caller decides to use the facilities, I'm trapped, of course. But at this point, that's a risk I have to take.

I move inside and pull the door almost closed, but not completely. I can see only the far wall from in here—the tub and the block glass behind it—and I realize that means I probably won't see much of anything. It's unlikely the visitor came here to take a hot bath. But still, I leave the door open a crack, just in case I can steal a peek at the intruder.

I can. I breathe a silent sigh of relief when the gentleman caller comes into view. He doesn't turn a light on either. He's facing the hot tub, his back toward me, but I know who he is; I'd recognize that lanky silhouette anywhere. He's staring down into the tub and for a second I wonder if he *did* come here to take a bath.

I'm about to push the throne-room door open, to chastise the Kydd for shaving a solid year off my life, but something makes me pause. The Kydd is dressed exactly as I am—completely in black, head to toe. And he parked somewhere else too, just as I did. He didn't want to drive his pickup into the Rawlings's oyster-shell driveway. He stands perfectly still, staring downward.

I can't see his face but I'm nonetheless certain he's not looking into the hot tub. He doesn't give a damn about the tub right now; he's interested in the mother swan. He has the same question I have. And he came here—just as I did—to get the answer. My gut tells me to stay put while he does.

He reaches down toward one of the brass handles and hesitates. Then he takes a deep breath and turns it hard, as far as it will go. Water rockets from the swan's beak and pelts the marble tub below, filling the entire room with gushing noise. The Kydd stares for a few seconds, standing perfectly still again.

He leans down after a moment, the water still pounding, and clutches the rim of the tub with both hands as if he needs more than just his legs to support himself. As he moves, I get a glimpse of what he's already seen. It explains his weak knees. A leak.

A small stream trickles from the base of Mother Swan's neck and meanders down the outer casing of the hot tub to the pale oak below. It pools first in the ten-by-ten cutout, where portions of the planks were excised by the guys from the state crime lab, and then it spills over to the rest of the floor. The Kydd has his answer now. And so do I.

But that's not all we have. We also have a problem. Gushing water isn't the only sound I hear anymore. There's a new one—a higher-pitched noise—and I'm pretty sure I know what it is. The Kydd shuts off the water and erases all doubt.

Yip-yip-wail.

"Mr. Kydd." I can't see her—she's on the other side of my door—but there's no mistaking Anastasia's baritone. "You shouldn't have come here," she says. "I told you earlier. You're not welcome."

"Why don't you call the po-lice?" he answers, turning to face her.

Bad brother-from-the-'hood talk sounds even worse in Southern-speak. It's a fine idea the Kydd has, though; Tommy Fitzpatrick and a few of his officers would be a welcome sight right about now. But Anastasia won't call the po-lice, of course. Not now and not later. Cops are the last people on the planet she wants to see.

"No time for that," she tells him. "After all, a woman who arrives home to find an intruder in the house needs to defend herself. I'll have to get rid of you right away. For my own protection."

The Kydd actually laughs out loud. I wish he wouldn't. Geraldine was right about one thing. If Louisa had attacked her husband here in the Queen's Spa, she wouldn't have been able to dump his body by herself. Anastasia couldn't have either. She had help. And the most likely helper—Lance

Phillips—is undoubtedly around here somewhere.

My certainty about this has nothing to do with Anastasia's physical strength. For all I know, she's entirely capable of lifting her father's weight. Even if she is, though, she couldn't have dumped him in the Great South Channel alone. No one person could have. Because, somehow, that person had to get back to shore. The *Carolina Girl* never made it. Another vessel did.

The Kydd has stopped laughing, but he still looks a little more amused than he should. "What are you going to do," he asks, "sic Lucifer on me?"

Upon hearing its name, the beast emits another *yip-yip-wail*.

Anastasia doesn't utter a word, but the Kydd's demeanor does a one-eighty. It's in his eyes. Suddenly I'm panicked. His hands fly up in a "don't do it" gesture and then he dives to the floor. A gunshot blast shatters the silence along with a single block of glass behind the tub.

I release the safety on the Lady Smith. God only knows how it got from my pocket to my hand.

When I can hear again, I realize Anastasia is laughing. "Very impressive," she says. "Encore."

At first I think she's speaking to the Kydd. But now I hear another laugh—one that's not Anastasia's—and I realize she's not the shooter. She's talking to the person who is.

"Okay," he says, and he repeats his performance. The Kydd lunges toward the side wall and takes cover beside the marble vanity of the sink in front of my door. A second glass block takes a bullet.

Again, momentary deafness. When it lifts I hear clapping, applause. "And I thought we were just going to watch TV tonight," Anastasia gushes. "This is *way* better."

It's not Anastasia's voice that interests me at the moment, though. It's the other one—the man's. I heard only a short laugh and a single *okay*, but I know who's shooting. And it's not Lance Phillips.

The Kydd lifts his head above the vanity, high enough so he can see, and it's all I can do not to scream at him to get the hell back down. The shooter fires again but this time it's just for effect. The moon-snail tile takes a hit; it's nowhere near the Kydd's vanity fort. His eyes clear it once more.

And then I get it. He knows I'm here. The tilt of his head in my direction is barely perceptible, but it's there. Somehow, through the minute crack in the door, he caught a glimpse of me. He has a plan; it's plain on his face. And my gut says he aims to elicit a confession.

"All right," he says to the duo on the other side of the door. "My number's up. So get it over with already." He stays crouched behind the vanity but points toward the Mother Swan. "I guess you'll want that," he says. "It worked well for you the last time—or its twin did, anyhow."

They both laugh now—hers low-pitched and

menacing, his too loud and forced. Anastasia Rawlings and Steven Collier. Strange bedfellows indeed.

Louisa's words during our Monday-afternoon
meeting in the jury room come back to me and one
more piece of the puzzle locks into place. Anastasia
Rawlings spent her entire childhood around boats,
thanks to her father. And Steven Collier owns a vessel of his own.

"That won't be necessary," Collier replies now.
"You're breaking and entering in the nighttime,
after all, Mr. Kydd. I'm entitled to use reasonable
force to protect the home's occupants. Every court
in the Commonwealth of Massachusetts would
agree."

This man is hell-bent on practicing law.

"And just look around the room," Collier continues. "We've had quite a struggle in here."

"Why not get rid of Herb that way?" the Kydd
asks. "Why use a goddamned plumbing fixture if
you're packing a piece?"

The Kydd's plan has one thing going for it: Collier loves to hear himself talk. It's not Collier who
answers this time, though. "You fool," Anastasia
spits. "My father wasn't supposed to die."

"He was only supposed to sign a couple of documents," Collier adds. "It could have been so simple." He sounds almost wistful.

"What documents?" the Kydd asks.

This dialogue can't go on much longer. Collier
has a loaded revolver trained on the Kydd, after all.

"A new will," Anastasia says calmly.

I wonder if Attorney Collier drafted it.

"And a new beneficiary designation form," he adds, "from New England Patriot."

The life insurance. Collier would have known all about the double-indemnity clause. He'd have known about the three-year proviso for suicide, too. He's a money guy.

"My father agreed," Anastasia volunteers. "He said he would sign them. He promised." I can picture her stomping a clodhopper.

"But then he reneged," Collier complains. "Changed his mind for some reason."

"*Some* reason?" Anastasia snaps. "Please. We all know the reason."

Something tells me the reason has auburn hair and a French manicure.

"Did you confront him together?" the Kydd asks.

I'm sweltering in here. Zipping up my jacket was a mistake. I don't dare touch the zipper now, though.

"We didn't *confront* him," Anastasia says. "We tried to talk sense into him. It wasn't right, what he was doing. I'm his flesh and blood."

Collier takes a couple of steps toward the Kydd. I can see him now. "We came on Sunday morning," he says, "knowing Louisa would be at the club. We thought he'd be more reasonable without her influence. He was in the steam room when we arrived."

Collier takes another step and leans on the vanity, obstructing my view of the Kydd. "So we waited right here."

"But he wouldn't sign?" The Kydd's calm is extraordinary. It's also insane.

"He refused." Collier actually laughs. "But that's not all. He became combative. Took a swing at me. So I pushed him away."

"You shouldn't have done that," Anastasia says. She sounds close to tears all of a sudden. "That was the mistake. That's why all of this happened."

"Dear girl," Collier answers, "we've been through this a hundred times. The man left me no choice."

"He slipped," Anastasia says. "My father slipped and fell backward. No one hit him."

And there it is. Mother Swan didn't attack Herb Rawlings. Herb Rawlings walloped her.

Collier stands up straight, away from the sink, and I can see the top of the Kydd's head above the vanity.

"What's in it for you?" the Kydd asks. He points toward Anastasia. "She gets the money. But what do you get?"

I can see Collier in full profile, revolver still in hand. He has the Kydd in point-blank range now. "Twenty Questions is over," he says.

And he's right. It is.

The blast knocks me backward for a second and then I'm through the throne-room door. Collier writhes on the floor, clutching his shoulder, a pool of blood collecting on the floorboards beneath him. His weapon is nowhere to be seen. Anastasia backs up against the steam-room door and wails. It's even worse than the funeral keening—she's scared now. The beast scampers around the room in circles. *Yip-yip-wail. Yip-yip-wail.*

No Kydd.

My Lady Smith zeros in on Anastasia—Collier's not going anywhere at the moment—and I flip on the tulip-shaped lights above the sink. And then the Kydd's head pops up, as if he'd been attached to a TFR. He's in the hot tub. "Look what I found," he says, showing me Collier's revolver. His tone suggests he found a shiny new penny, head's up.

"Get out of the damned tub," I tell him.

I'm going to strangle him yet.

CHAPTER 32

Friday, October 20

The Barnstable County Sheriff's Department kept Steven Collier company at Cape Cod Hospital and then transported him to the Superior Courthouse for his arraignment. They arrived at four A.M. By then, Geraldine had completed the paperwork necessary to secure Louisa Rawlings's release. The night clerk called Leon Long at home and the judge agreed to come in as soon as all the major players were assembled. And now, at four-thirty, almost all of us are here.

Harry listened without interruption as the Kydd and I recounted the evening's events. "Sweet Jesus," he says to us now, his hazel eyes wide. "You two are dangerous."

The Kydd and I both laugh, cavalier now that we're out of harm's way. "You speak truth, Kimosabe," the Kydd intones, his expression grave.

"Think about it," I tell them. "Herb Rawlings fell backward and hit himself on that brass swan. What if Herb had landed somewhere else? A few inches to either side and none of this would have happened."

Harry lowers his chin and his eyebrows knit.

I shrug. I realize that *what ifs* don't matter in our world. This is the kind of rumination a *real* defense lawyer wouldn't indulge in. But I've certainly never laid claim to that title.

"A few inches to either side," Harry says, "and Lincoln would've gone to the cast party."

He's right, of course. Now there's a *what if*.

Steven Collier comes through the side door, flanked by county sheriffs, one arm in a sling, the other cuffed to one of his escorts. He sits at the far end of the jury box as directed, his cuff-mate standing beside him. Collier's cold eyes meet mine and I can't resist. I give him a little wave—à la Rinky Snow—and punctuate it with a satisfied smile. He deserves every last miserable day that lies ahead. Not only because he murdered Herb Rawlings, but also because he damn near succeeded in forcing Louisa to pay the price for his cowardly crime.

Anastasia enters next, between two less-than-happy-looking matrons, and it's somewhat startling to see her dressed in orange. She's not only cuffed;

she's shackled at the ankles as well. She must have gotten belligerent with her keepers. She shuffles across the courtroom without looking at her partner in crime and thuds into a chair on the end of the jury box closest to us. She glares at us, her teeth and fists clenched, and this time I figure it's the Kydd's turn to wave. He does. And he grins for her too—his signature grin.

"This is all for the best," Harry whispers from his chair behind us.

Leave it to Harry to find a silver lining. I can't fathom what it might be. The Kydd and I both turn to face him and he's staring ahead at the two prisoners. "They would have had ugly children," he says.

"Don't even go there," I tell him.

Harry starts whistling softly when the Kydd and I face front again. It takes a few seconds for me to recognize the tune. Harry's heartwarming rendition of "Daddy's Little Girl" sends the Kydd into a laughing fit beside me. And I lose it too—I can't help it. We're all punchy again. We need to go home.

Bert Saunders hustles down the center aisle and takes a seat next to Harry at the bar, nodding a silent greeting to all of us as he opens his briefcase. He's winded. He must have just been appointed to represent one of the newly accused. I don't envy him.

Harry doesn't either, apparently. He interrupts

his tender melody and leans over to Bert, looking truly sympathetic. "Makes *DeMateo* look like a walk in the park, huh?" he whispers.

Bert closes his eyes and shakes his head. "Mother of God," he mutters, "help us all."

Woody Timmons is in the still-dark gallery, on the aisle end of the front bench nearest us, his notepad and pen in hand, a small tape recorder on the bench beside him. The night clerk must be on his list of courthouse cohorts. And I suspect the clerk will be wined and dined quite nicely this afternoon at the Jailhouse. Woody's got an exclusive on this one.

Lance Phillips is the only other person out there in the darkness, in the aisle seat opposite Woody's. Lance, as it turns out, was upstairs, napping in one of the guest bedrooms, throughout our ordeal in the Queen's Spa. He showed up in the doorway when it was over, just before the Chatham police arrived, asking what all the commotion was about. He must have been in a near-coma is all I can figure. The service must have worn him out. Or maybe it was his tumble to the floor. Or maybe it was just Anastasia.

Louisa enters the courtroom next and, as Geraldine would say, the gang's all here. Louisa comes through the side door, looking exhausted, in her butter yellow coat dress and heels, beige trench coat and hat in hand. She crosses the room without a single glance at her stepdaughter or her former financial advisor and joins us at the defense table.

Once again, the Kydd holds a chair out for her. He really is gallant—a modern-day Rhett Butler at heart. "Thank you, Kevin," she says, brushing his hand. And just like that, he's pink again.

Collier and Anastasia should be sitting at this table, of course—not us. They're the accused now. But technically, they can't be arraigned until the charges against Louisa Rawlings are formally dropped. And Geraldine Schilling is nothing if not technically accurate.

The night clerk tells us to rise—Joey Kelsey's not here at this hour—and Judge Long emerges from chambers. He's in his robe, looking far more chipper than the hour justifies. We all take our seats and the judge looks around the room slowly at each of us, silent. His final gaze falls on Louisa.

"Mrs. Rawlings," he says at last, "this court owes you an apology."

Louisa turns to me, uncertain. This is a first. "Go ahead," I tell her. "No need to stop now."

She gets to her feet and looks up at Judge Long. "This court," she says in her soft Southern lilt, "treated me fairly. There's no need for an apology, Your Honor. I have no complaint."

She sits and the judge falls quiet again, his eyes not moving from her. "Attorney Schilling," he says at last, "I trust you have the necessary paperwork."

She does. She leaves her table and crosses the courtroom, hands a short stack of photocopies to me, and then carries the originals up to the bench.

The Kydd reaches across our table for the documents and I start to pass them to him, but then I think better of it. "You're off duty," I tell him. "As of this minute, you're off for the weekend. And yes," I add, "that would be Friday, Saturday, Sunday."

He beams at me. Louisa does too. "I love this job," he says to her.

Judge Long finishes signing off on Geraldine's forms, hands them back to her, and then looks over at Louisa again. "You're excused, Mrs. Rawlings," he says, removing his glasses. "You're free to go now. And you take with you the sincere apologies of this court."

Louisa turns to me. "Thank you, darlin'," she says.

I wish she'd stop calling me that.

We all head for the center aisle but Geraldine stops us. "I hope you meant that," she says to Louisa, "about being treated fairly."

Louisa takes a moment to answer. She looks Geraldine in the eyes when she does. "The *court* treated me fairly," she says. "You did your job. And I understand that. But I found you decidedly unpleasant."

Geraldine laughs. She's been called worse. "Fair enough," she says, and extends her hand. Louisa accepts it.

"I know you've never practiced," Geraldine says as we start to leave again. "But do you have any interest in giving it a shot?"

"Giving it a shot?" Louisa looks at Geraldine as if she just propositioned her.

Geraldine tosses her blond head toward Judge Long on the bench. "Well," she says, "you seem to have a way with the judges."

"Are you offering me a *job*?" Louisa lowers her voice as if the word is vulgar.

Geraldine shrugs. "I guess I am."

Harry leans over to whisper. "Shoot me now," he says, "so I can live in hell instead of Barnstable County."

He's right, of course. Geraldine and Louisa in the same office—worse than hell; hell on heels. And think of poor Clarence.

Louisa spreads her arms out toward the near-empty, cavernous gallery and laughs out loud. Dawn is making an appearance now, soft, early-morning sunlight filtering through the floor-to-ceiling windows, reflecting off the tin codfish suspended in the center of the room. I've always loved spending time in this old courtroom, but it's pretty clear Louisa Rawlings doesn't share my sentiment. "You're offering me an opportunity to spend my days *here*?" she asks Geraldine.

Geraldine laughs again. "I promise to call you a lawyer*ess*," she tries.

Louisa takes the Kydd's arm and they head for the center aisle. "You'd have to promise more than that, Miss Geraldine," she says over her shoulder. "Much, much more."

Harry stares, his mouth wide open, as Louisa and the Kydd depart arm in arm. At long last, now that the two of them have hit him over the head with it, he gets it. "That *dawg*," he says. He sounds frighteningly Southern.

We watch in silence until they're almost out of the courtroom and then Harry turns to me, smiling. "You see?" he says. "I told you so. You *do* like her."

"I was pretty damned sure she didn't murder anybody," I tell him. "But don't start planning double dates."

He's correct, of course. Louisa Rawlings is all right in my book. Even her drawl is beginning to grow on me. And at this particular moment, all's right in the world, too. Well, in Barnstable County, anyhow.

Anastasia Rawlings is on a fast track—with a one-way ticket—to Framingham. Steven Collier— the brains behind the operation to the extent there were any—won't see the light of day during this lifetime either. He's headed to Walpole, the maximum security facility for the Commonwealth's gentlemen guests.

Woody Timmons is still on the front bench, waiting for the second half of his scoop to begin. Lance Phillips is here too. He'll have sole custody of Lucifer now, I suppose. And if he can't go home and pen a best seller after this, he'd better start searching for a day job.

Judge Long is on the bench, bound and determined to dispense justice in a system that sometimes makes it difficult to do so. Geraldine is at her table, equally intent on imposing the harshest possible sentence on her new targets, even if justice be damned.

Luke, I hope, is at least *thinking* about heading back to Boston College.

Louisa Rawlings is sashaying into the sunrise, Tonto at her side. I can't help wondering how long it will last.

Me—well, I'm headed home. And Harry is beside me—right where I want him.

SCRIBNER
PROUDLY PRESENTS

FALSE TESTIMONY

Rose Connors

Available in hardcover
from Scribner in July 2005

Please turn the page for a preview of
False Testimony

CHAPTER 1

Monday, December 13

A person of interest. That's what local authorities dubbed Charles Kendrick, the senior United States Senator from the Commonwealth of Massachusetts. He wasn't a target of the investigation, they told him. He was merely an individual believed to have information relevant to the search.

And he did. Twenty-five-year-old Michelle Forrester was a member of his D.C. staff. He hired her more than three years ago, just after she graduated from the University of Virginia with dual degrees in government science and drama. An ambitious and disarmingly attractive young woman with obvious political aspirations of her own, she quickly became Senator Kendrick's preferred spokesperson. For the past year—while rumors ran rampant about his planned bid for the Democratic nomination— Michelle Forrester alone fielded questions at his frequent public appearances. She enabled the Senator to say his piece at each event and then make a dignified—perhaps even presidential—exit.

This past Thursday, Michelle handled the members of the media after the Senator addressed a standing-room-only crowd at Cape Cod Community College in Hyannis. The evening news featured a poised and charming Michelle entertaining endless inquiries from local reporters, joking and laughing with them easily and often. She stayed until their voracious journalists' appetites were satisfied, until the last of their detailed and often repetitive questions was answered. She extended Senator Kendrick's sincere thanks to all of them, for their attendance and their attention, before she left the auditorium.

And then Michelle Forrester vanished.

She was due at her parents' home in Stamford, Connecticut, the next day to help with preparations for a cocktail party to be held that evening in honor of her father's sixtieth birthday. She didn't show up—not for the preparations and not for the party. She was expected back at work in D.C. first thing this morning, her office calendar jammed with appointments from eight o'clock on. She didn't show there, either. And though her worried parents had been calling both Massachusetts and Connecticut authorities all weekend, it wasn't until her no-show at work that the search began in earnest.

Postpone it. That's what I advised when Senator Kendrick called my office at ten A.M. He'd stayed on the Cape after Thursday's speech, intending to work by phone and fax through the holidays from his vacation home in North Chatham. The Barnstable County District Attorney's Office called his D.C. number first thing this morning and his executive secretary phoned him right away with the message. It was from Geraldine Schilling—the District Attorney herself—wanting to set up a time when she might ask him a few questions. Today, if at all possible.

Senator Kendrick made it clear to me from the outset that he wasn't seeking formal representation. He simply wanted to know if one of the lawyers in our office would be available by telephone later in the morning in case he needed a word of advice during his interview. He didn't anticipate a problem, he assured me more than once. He was calling only out of an abundance of caution.

Twenty-four hours, I told him. Of course you'll cooperate with the investigation, and of course you'll do it promptly; time is paramount in these matters. But you shouldn't speak to the DA—or to any other representative of the Commonwealth, for that matter—without an attorney at your side. He was quick to inform me that he is an attorney—Harvard-trained, he added—whereupon I recited my personal version of the old adage: Never mind the fool; the lawyer who represents himself has a certifiable moron for a client.

Answer questions tomorrow, I urged. Spend this afternoon in my office, preparing, and we'll go to the District Attorney together in the morning. That way, if her questioning takes a direction it shouldn't, I'll be the one to hit the brakes. You'll remain the willing witness, reluctantly accepting advice from your overly protective attorney.

Senator Kendrick's laughter took me by surprise. I wasn't trying to be funny. After a good chuckle, he thanked me for my time. And before I could answer, I was listening to a dial tone.

CHAPTER 2

"Good of you to join us, Martha." Geraldine Schilling is the only person on the planet who calls me Martha. And she knows damned well I'm not here to join anybody. Charles Kendrick called me a second time—ten minutes ago, at one-thirty—because he's worried. And he should be.

"Party's over, Geraldine. No more questions."

"Attorney Nickerson can be a bit rude." Geraldine presses an index finger to her cheek and directs her observation exclusively to Senator Kendrick, as though I'm not in the room. "I should have trained her better," she adds. She sounds almost apologetic.

Geraldine "trained" me for a solid decade, when I was an ADA and she was the First Assistant. If she'd done the job as she intended, I'd be a hell of a lot worse than rude. I'd also still be a prosecutor, not a member of the defense bar. I lift her black winter coat from the back of an upholstered wing chair in the corner and hold it out, letting it dangle from two fingers. "Adios," I tell her. "You're done here."

She accepts the heavy coat but doesn't put it on. Instead, she takes a pack of Virginia Slims from its inside pocket and then drapes it over her arm. She tamps a beige cigarette from the pack, shakes her long blond bangs at me, then turns to the Senator and arches her pale eyebrows. She seems to think he might override my decision. She's mistaken, though; she trained me better than that.

"You're done," I repeat. "Senator Kendrick spoke with you voluntarily this morning but he's not doing that anymore. Not at the moment, anyway. He called his attorney. That's me. This is his home. And I've asked you to leave."

"Marty, is that really necessary?" Senator Kendrick is seated on his living room couch, a deep-maroon, soft leather sectional. Behind him, through the floor-to-ceiling windows, is a heart-stopping view of the winter Atlantic. His long legs are crossed—in perfectly creased blue jeans—and his starched, white dress shirt is open at the collar, sleeves rolled up to the middle of his forearms. His gray-blue eyes mirror the choppy surf, yet he seems far more relaxed than he should be under the circumstances.

"Take a look outside," I tell him, pointing to a pair of mullioned windows that face the driveway. "And then you tell me if it's necessary."

He stands, sighing and looking taxed by the effort, and crosses the antique Oriental carpet to the dark, polished hardwood at the perimeter of the vast room. I follow and stop just a few steps behind him, eyeing his chiseled profile as he parts the curtains and leans on the sill. He's silent for a moment as he gets a gander of the scene that greeted me when I arrived. "Standard procedure?" he asks at last.

"Not even close," I tell him.

Four vehicles occupy the crushed-shell driveway, all facing the closed doors of the dormered, three-car garage. The shiny Buick is Geraldine's; she gets a new one every two years without fail, always dark blue. The ancient Thunderbird in desperate need of a trip to the car wash is mine. The enormous gray Humvee, I can only presume, is the Senator's. And the patrol car belongs to the Town of Chatham. Two uniforms stand in front of it, leaning against its hood and talking, their breath making small white clouds in the cold December air.

The Kendrick estate sits on a point, a narrow

spit of land that juts out into the Atlantic. It has a solitary neighbor, a small bungalow, to the north. Otherwise, the Kendricks enjoy exclusive use of this strip, the front and sides of their spacious house bordered by nothing but open ocean. The cops are in the driveway for a reason, not passing through on their way to someplace else. The Kendrick estate isn't on the way to anyplace else.

"The one closest to us is the Chief," I tell the Senator. "Ten bucks says he'll shoot the lock off your front door if your friend the DA here presses the right button on her pager."

Senator Kendrick pulls the curtains back together and turns away from the windows to face Geraldine.

"Senator," she snaps, her tone altogether different than it was just moments ago. "We've barely begun to check out your story and already parts of it don't fly."

He takes a step toward me but still I don't look at him. Since I'm the only person in this room who hasn't heard his story, there's not a hell of a lot I can offer.

"That can't be," he says.

"Shut up, Senator." The utter shock of my command renders him compliant—for the moment, at least. Still, I keep my eyes fixed on our District Attorney. She carries little more than a hundred pounds on her five-foot-two-inch frame, but there's not a tougher DA in the Commonwealth. Geraldine Schilling is no lightweight.

I take my cell phone from my jacket pocket and flip it open as I walk toward the kitchen—and Geraldine. "At this point," I tell her, "you're nothing more than a common trespasser."

She laughs.

"And I've got the Chief on speed-dial too."

She laughs again, louder this time, but she moves toward the kitchen door.

"Mark my words," she says to both of us. "I'll be back."

CHAPTER 3

"How's Chuck?" Harry stares at the snowy road ahead as he asks, a small smile tugging at the corners of his lips. He apparently finds it amusing that the Commonwealth's senior senator is proving to be a less-than-model client.

"Chuck is the same as he was this morning," I tell him. "Difficult." I flip the heater in Harry's old Jeep up another couple of notches and shift in the passenger seat to face him. He's driving with one gloved hand, clutching a cardboard cup of steaming coffee with the other.

"Makes sense," he says. "The guy's usually the one calling the shots; he isn't used to taking orders."

"I'm not issuing orders, Harry. I'm offering advice."

He smiles at me and then swallows a mouthful of coffee. "And you're just the drill sergeant for the job." He laughs.

Now there's a sentiment every forty-something woman hopes to hear from the man in her life.

It's three o'clock and we're pulling into the Barnstable County Complex, headed up the hill to the House of Correction. We'll spend the next couple of hours with Derrick Holliston, a twenty-two-year-old creep who's accused of murdering a popular parish priest last Christmas Eve. Harry is Holliston's court-appointed defender and—according to Harry—neither of them is happy about it. Holliston thinks Harry's efforts are less than zealous. And Harry calls Holliston a lowlife bottom-feeder.

Like it or not, Harry and I will spend the rest of the afternoon walking Holliston through his direct testimony. His first-degree-murder trial starts Wednesday morning, and unless Harry can convince him otherwise in the next forty-eight hours, Holliston intends to take the stand. He plans to tell the judge and jury that he acted in self-defense; that fifty-seven-year-old Father Frank McMahon made aggressive sexual advances toward him on the evening in question; that when Holliston resisted, the older man became violent. If Harry's instincts are on target—and I've never known them to be otherwise—Holliston's story is just that. Fiction.

Harry pulls into a snow-clogged spot and parks near the steps leading up to the foreboding House of Correction. He leaves the engine running, though, and shifts in his seat to lean against the driver's side door. It seems he intends to finish his coffee before we go inside. "The guy's a liar," he says.

"You don't know that, Harry. You think he's lying, but you don't know it." Harry and I have had this discussion a hundred times over the course of the past year, but he can't let it go. It's eating at him.

"Trust me," he says. "I know."

"No, you don't. Not the way the Rules of Professional Conduct require. There were two people in St. Veronica's Chapel when it happened. One of them is dead. Holliston is the only living person who was there. No one can prove he's lying."

Harry shakes his head and stares into his coffee cup. He's struggling with the ugly issue that confronts every criminal defense lawyer sooner or later: what to do when you believe—but can't prove—your client's story is fabricated. If he could prove it—before Holliston testifies—he could move for permission to withdraw from the case completely. As it stands, with nothing but his gut telling him his client's a liar, he's stuck. And once Holliston testifies, Harry will be stuck for good. At that point, even if he were to discover slam-dunk evidence of perjury, he'd be obligated to keep it to himself. The Massachusetts Canons of Professional Ethics say so.

Harry stares through the now foggy windshield and his eyes settle on the chain-link fence surrounding the House of Correction. The fence is twenty feet high—twenty-two if you count the electrified barbed wire coiled at the top—but Harry doesn't seem to see an inch of it.

"I can prove Holliston's lying," he says, still staring uphill. "Give me fifteen minutes alone with him—in a dark alley."

"Listen to yourself, Harry. If you ever got wind of a cop saying something like that, you'd call him a miscreant. You'd raise the courthouse roof to suppress his testimony. And then you'd go after his badge."

Harry nods, conceding all points, and drains the last of his coffee. "Come on," he says, dropping the empty cup into a plastic bag dangling from the cigarette lighter. "Let's get this over with."

We emerge into the late-day mist and climb the hill toward the prison through shin-high snow.

"So what did you tell old Chuck?" he asks, glancing sideways at me. "What are his marching orders?"

"I didn't give him marching orders, Harry."

"Oh, right." He removes his free hand from his pocket and taps his temple. "Advice," he says, feigning the utmost seriousness. "You gave him lawyerly advice. What was it?"

At six feet, 210, Harry has a good half foot and ninety pounds on me. But I'd like to clock him upside the head anyway. "Simple," I say. "I told our senior senator to keep his mouth shut."

Harry laughs out loud, sending a cloud of white vapor into the cold air ahead of us. "Simple? Are you serious, Marty? The guy's been a politician his entire adult life. You think it's going to be simple for him to keep his mouth shut?"

I walk ahead of Harry as the guard at the front booth presses a button that opens the prison's enormous double doors, two slabs of black steel in the center of a redbrick mountain. "It better be," I answer over my shoulder. "The guy's front and center in a high-profile missing person case. And the young woman's been gone four days now. He damn well better keep his mouth shut."

The front desk is manned by two guards who would look ominous even without their shiny weapons. After we go through the laborious process of clearing security a third guard leads us to a meeting room. As Harry and I enter, the guard assumes a sentinel's pose in the hallway and gives me a gentlemanly nod.

Our client is already here. Derrick Holliston is seated at a small, banged-up card table and I'm initially surprised to see he's free of restraints. I shouldn't be, though. This eight-by-ten room is windowless—the air in it long past stale—and its solitary door locks automatically. The accused isn't going anywhere.

Harry drops the heavy file onto the table and roots through his jacket pockets until he comes up with his glasses. "This is Marty Nickerson," he says to Holliston as he puts them on. "She'll sit second-chair at trial."

Holliston stares at me for a moment, then turns his attention back to Harry. "Good," the less-than-satisfied client says. "You need help."

Harry looks over his glasses at Holliston and smirks, but otherwise lets the remark pass. He sits and starts unpacking the file without a word. I retrieve my own glasses from my jacket pocket and then claim the only remaining seat.

"First of all," Harry says, opening a manila folder in the middle of the table, "let's go over the Commonwealth's offer again."

"Let's not," Holliston says, mimicking Harry's cadence. "Let's tell the Commonwealth to stick its lousy offer where the sun don't shine. I told you—I ain't doin' time. Not for this one."

On the surface, Harry appears entirely unaffected by his client's comments. But I know better. He'd like to deck this smart-ass.

Holliston stands, folds his arms against the chest of his orange jumpsuit, and presses his back against the wall. He's a wiry man, five-ten or so, with a sketchy mustache and greasy brown hair that hangs below his collar. "I told you a hundred times," he says, "no deal. What're you, deaf?"

"What's the offer?" I ask them both.

"Murder two," Harry says. "Eligible for parole in fifteen. And he'll get it if he keeps his hands clean and his mouth zipped."

"You can't not consider it," I tell Holliston.

He turns toward me, his eyes wild, apparently infuriated by my audacity. "You don't know a goddamn thing about it," he says.

"You're wrong there," I tell him, meeting his angry eyes. "I know you're looking at life if you get bagged for murder one, for instance. I know life means life, as in, until you draw your last breath behind bars. And I know this deal gets you out in your late thirties—still young enough to build a decent future. Only a complete fool would reject it out of hand."

Holliston snorts and spreads his arms wide. "What's with you people?" he asks. "First I get this guy"—he tosses his head toward Harry—"wantin' to sell me down the river. And now you come in here tellin' me I don't need to have a life till fifteen years from now. What the hell kind of sorry lawyers are you? Ever hear of stickin' up for your client, for Chrissake? I ain't takin' your advice. And I'm the boss here. So give it a rest. Get to the other part of your job. Tellin' me how to tell them people what happened that night. I want it done right. And I don't want nothin' left out."

Harry's eyes move to mine. He's resigned. Holliston is correct; at this particular point in the process, he is the boss.

Harry stares at Holliston. He cups his hands behind his head, fingers laced, elbows akimbo, and takes a deep breath. "Go ahead," he says to our system-savvy client at last. "Tell us your tale."